THE MANGLE STREET MURDERS

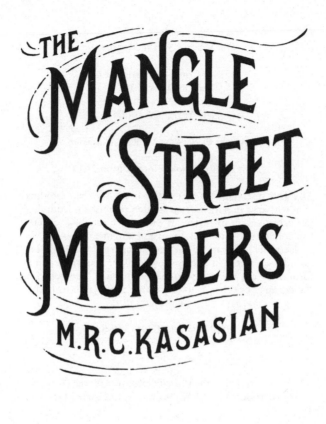

THE MANGLE STREET MURDERS

M.R.C. KASASIAN

PEGASUS CRIME

NEW YORK LONDON

F

THE MANGLE STREET MURDERS

Pegasus Crime is an Imprint of
Pegasus Books LLC
80 Broad Street, 5th Floor
New York, NY 10004

Copyright © 2014 by M. R. C. Kasasian

First Pegasus Books cloth edition 2014

ISBN: 978-1-60598-539-8

10 9 8 7 8 6 5 4 3 2 1

Printed in the United States of America
Distributed by W. W. Norton & Company, Inc.

For Tiggy, with love.

Introduction

IT IS SIXTY years since I first met Sidney Grice. He was still quite young – though he did not seem it at the time – and already well known in England. But he had yet to achieve the international fame that a series of hilariously inaccurate Hollywood films was to bring upon him.

He was a vain man and loved the limelight, but even he baulked at some of the more outrageous stories that were circulated. He never, for example, climbed the Niagara Falls in pursuit of a werewolf. He was neither as glamorous nor so athletic as that. But also he was not the sadistic monster that recent biographers have portrayed. It was only ill health that stopped him from suing E.L. Jeeveson for his scurrilous and scrappily researched book claiming that Sidney Grice had murdered his own father.

It was the fear of hurting the innocent and of legal (or illegal) action from the guilty that constrained my first accounts of Sidney Grice's investigations in the *Monthly Journal* but, with almost everybody dead now and my own life nearing its natural conclusion, I thought it time to set the record straight.

The London I first knew rose magnificently from its stench of rotting humanity. The London of today is being sacked, reduced to rubble by an enemy whose savagery is unmatched since the hordes of barbarians swept away the Roman Empire.

Whether the British Empire will be destroyed also, as so many predict, remains to be seen but I know that Sidney Grice would not have fled its capital city – for all his faults he was never a coward – and neither shall I, though the lights go out and the very earth trembles as I write this here in the cold, dripping cellar of 125 Gower Street.

M.M. 3 October 1941

1

The Slurry Street Murders

Lizzie Shepherd got the chop
Right above the drinking shop.
Janie Donnell got chopped too.
Turn around. It could be you.

Victorian skipping song (from *Rhymes and Reasons*
by Jenny Smith and Alex Duncan MacDonald)

ELIZA SHEPHERD WAS murdered. Her body was discovered on her bed at eight o'clock on the morning of Monday 28 January 1882 by her sister and roommate, Maria. They had lived on the top floor of a ramshackle pile of rooms over the Red Lion Public House, Slurry Street, Whitechapel.

Two hours later the body of Jane O'Donnell was discovered in another room along the corridor.

Both women had been brutally murdered. Their faces, limbs and torsos had been slashed and hacked exactly forty times each. There were no signs of robbery and, though there may have been a sexual motive, neither was a known prostitute. Eliza Shepherd worked as a seamstress and Jane O'Donnell had recently started serving in the bar downstairs.

In both cases the doors were bolted from the inside and had to be forced to gain access. There was little doubt, however, about the murderer's means of entry. The windows had been smashed from the outside. How the murderer reached the windows was another matter. They were some thirty feet above street level with no drainpipes or other climbing aids and it would be impossible to carry, set up and remove a ladder in such a busy thoroughfare without being noticed. The roof was not easily accessible and proved so rotten and unstable that it would not even support the small boy sent up by the police to inspect it.

It was difficult to imagine who would commit such savage acts and theories of animal attacks abounded, a gorilla from a travelling fair being most frequently cited. Rumours were rampant and a slavering lion cornered one night in Knackers' Yard turned out to be a tethered and elderly Shetland pony patiently awaiting its fate.

Stories of Springheel Jack, the legendary demon, were revived with numerous sightings of him leaping across the rooftops. In years gone by many a respectable girl had reported him jumping in front of her, shredding her clothes with his clawed hands and crushing his deadman's lips to hers, but he had never been known to kill before.

Death was common in the East End, violence and murder not rare, but the ferocity of these killings shocked even the police and the outcry led to questions being asked in both Houses of Parliament.

There was a flurry in the production of Penny Dreadful pamphlets with lurid accounts of other crimes tenuously linked to the two murders, and the press were soon issuing sensational claims about the identity of the killer. It was said that *Rivincita*, the Italian word for *revenge*, was smeared on the walls in blood and an account of a mysterious redheaded Neapolitan man seen acting suspiciously in the area led to a spate of attacks on immigrants around the docks.

A gruesome song, 'The Slaughterhouse of Slurry Street', became briefly popular as did a melodramatic production of *Murder at the Red Lion* but, with the lack of any real suspects and the absence of any further outrages, public interest waned.

The murderer was never caught but he was to inspire more than the writers of ballads and pamphlets. He was also to inspire at least one person to follow in his footsteps.

2

The Chelsea Strangler

THIS WAS MY last day. Mr Warwick, the land agent, arrived promptly at nine, and I handed him the keys and set off in a cart without even a backward glance. My family had lived in the Grange for three hundred years and no doubt it would stand the same again without us.

George Carpenter, the old gamekeeper, drove me with his ancient donkey, Onion, struggling up Parbold Hill and skittering down the other side so hesitantly that I feared we might miss the train, but we arrived in good time and George carried my carpet bag to the platform.

'Mrs Carpenter made you this.' He held out a small package in brown wax paper tied with brown string. 'She thought you might get hungry.'

I thanked him and he shuffled his feet.

'We held the Colonel in great regard,' he told me.

I put five shillings into his broken hand, and the train whistled and jolted and pulled away. And I wondered if ever I would see him again, or Ashurst Beacon, or the shallow poisoned River Douglas, winding as a saffron thread under the straight-cut Leeds–Liverpool Canal.

I changed stations at Wigan Wallgate, waiting head bowed at the roadside for a procession of miners' families to pass behind four coffins. It was only three days since the colliery explosion and the town was still angry.

At Wigan North Western I purchased a book from W.H. Smith & Son, and was soon off again in a ladies-only compartment with no corridor. It was a non-smoker but, as it was otherwise unoccupied, I was able to enjoy all of Mrs Carpenter's game pie, three cigarettes and a small cup of gin from my father's hip flask before the train ground screechily to a stop at Rugby.

There was a great deal of shouting and slamming, but I was beginning to believe that I should be left alone when, just as the guard blew his whistle, the door swung open and a middle-aged, well-dressed lady clambered aboard and sat opposite me. She had a haughty humourless expression and for a while we were silent, but then the lady sniffed the air.

'Have you been smoking?'

'No.'

She took off her left glove, laid it with her hat on the seat beside her, and looked at me.

'What is that you are reading?' She peered over. 'The Shocking Case of the Poisoner of Primrose Hill. What utter tosh. You should try The Chelsea Strangler. It is very grisly and much more amusing.' She sniffed again. 'You have been smoking.'

'I might have been,' I said and the lady smiled. She had small white teeth and her chin was pointed like a child's.

'Then you shan't mind if I do.' She produced a silver case from her handbag. 'Would you care for a Turkish?' She struck a red safety match and lit both our cigarettes with it, sucking deep into her breast. 'Oh, that is better. I have been absolutely frantic for one all day. Charles does not approve, which is why I keep my right glove on, to prevent my fingertips being oranged. Smoking is my great secret. Do you have any great secrets? Of course you have, and you must tell me the most scandalous of them before we quit this carriage.'

A long time ago I killed a man – the finest that ever lived – but I shall never hang for it.

'Charles says it stunts the growth,' the lady was saying. 'As if I am likely to grow in any desirable direction at my age. I shall be forty-two tomorrow, not that he will remember. He can recall all Dr Grace's batting scores but struggles with his own children's names. He forces small boys to learn dead Greek. What a gruesome thing to do.'

The lady took a breath.

'Happy birthday.' I offered her my flask and she swallowed a cupful in one draught.

'Harriet Fitzpatrick,' she said. 'Call me Harriet.'

'March Middleton. March.'

'Going to London, March?'

'Yes. It is my first time.'

'The best shops and the worst people in the world.' She stubbed her cigarette out on the floor. 'You may find the most exquisite dresses but have to step over a starving child to enter the premises. Are you visiting relatives?'

'I have no relatives,' I said. 'My poor mama's heart failed with the strain of being delivered of me twenty-one years ago, and my poor dear papa was killed last July when he fell over a waterfall in Switzerland. I spent the next three months writing an account of his life, which was published just before Christmas. *Colonel Geoffrey Middleton, His Life and Times.* Perhaps you have read it.'

Harriet shook her head and asked, 'But where shall you stay?'

'With my godfather who has kindly volunteered to become my legal guardian.'

'Oh, you poor thing.'

She had a tiny nose and I was quite envious of it.

'It is probably for the best.' I dropped my cigarette on the floor and ground it out with my foot. 'Papa took a great loss on the stock exchange last year and had heavily mortgaged the house. He left me so little capital, most of which I cannot touch until I am twenty-five, and such a small income from munitions that I could not hope to continue the maintenance of our home and, since the bloom of my youth is rapidly fading, I am unlikely to ensnare a husband before I am too old.'

Harriet laughed and said, 'Forgive me. Please continue.'

'If my godfather had not turned up,' I said, 'I do not know what I should have done for I am unsuited to trade and too proud to go into service. So I was most relieved when he wrote to offer his condolences and say that my father had done him a great kindness once, and that he was anxious to repay the debt.'

Harriet looked at me thoughtfully. 'May I ask when you last saw this good-hearted gentleman?'

'Oh, but I have never met him,' I said. 'Nor indeed do I recall my father ever talking about him.'

Harriet took another drink from my flask before handing it back.

'Are you sure your inheritance is small?' She looked at me as one might an injured stray. 'I should not like you to be tricked out of your fortune by some unscrupulous scoundrel.'

'It is very small indeed,' I said, 'and I did consider such a possibility. So, before I accepted the proposal, I instructed my father's solicitor to conduct some enquiries. By all accounts Mr Sidney Grice comes from a good family and is a man of the highest reputation.'

Harriet coughed.

'Sidney Grice, the private detective?'

'You know of him?'

'I should say so,' Harriet said. 'One can hardly open a newspaper without learning something of his exploits. Why, only last week he very nearly foiled the kidnapping of the Archduke of Thuringia in Hyde Park, and it is rumoured that he has extricated the Prince of Wales from scandal on numberless occasions. Oh, you are so lucky. I wish I had such a dashing, heroic and clever man to look after me.'

We had two more cigarettes to celebrate my good fortune and finished the gin, and Harriet fell silent and I looked out of the window and watched the hills flatten and the greenery turn to brick and the bricks get higher and redder, and it seemed no time at all before we had pulled into Euston Station.

'Will you be all right?' Harriet asked, and I told her that I would.

'I come up on the same train, the first Tuesday of every month,' she said. 'If you should need a friend.'

'I am sure I shall make a great many friends,' I said, and Harriet looked at me.

'London can be such a lonely place.'

She stood and leaned forward to adjust her hat in the small mirror over my head. I got up, caught a glimpse of myself, my complexion unfashionably brown from too many long walks without a parasol and my hair dun and dull, and I thought of Edward for the hundredth time that day.

'Look out for pickpockets,' she told me, 'and foreigners. Any more gin?'

'I am afraid not.'

A porter was coming up and Harriet pulled down the blind.

'Have you ever been kissed?' she asked.

'No,' I said as she leaned towards me, fragrant with lavender.

I closed my eyes.

'You have now,' she said, and the blind snapped up and the porter opened the door and we clambered down, and Harriet winked. 'Take care.' And she hurried off into the crowd.

3

❖◦❖◦❖

The Pig and the Perfume

I FOUND MY way out easily to that monstrous arch known as the Gateway to the North, where I waited.

All around were the noise and confusion, but what struck me most forcibly were the smells. Smoke, horse excrement and unwashed bodies combined to create an overpoweringly noisome stench. Hundreds of carriages, from stately broughams to small landaus, vied with hansom cabs, omnibuses and delivery carts to make chaotic progress along the Euston Road, and countless pedestrians in finery or rags jostled between them, calling out to each other above the shouts of street sellers.

A grimy girl in a crumpled black dress stood against a pillar, looking about her expectantly.

'Are you Molly?' I asked.

'Shit off,' she said, and stumbled away.

'I shall take it that you are not,' I called after her.

I waited a few more minutes and looked about me. A pig had been tethered to a standpipe and a boy in a sailor suit was trying to ride it. The buildings were grimy and cloaked in a grey haze, for the air itself was dirty. I could feel it gritty on my skin.

A dumpy girl in a maid's uniform of black, with a pressed

white apron, came hurrying up and approached two young ladies before myself.

'Miss Middleton?'

'Yes.'

She had a mass of ginger hair tied up under a starched white hat. Her nose was bulbous and her face pink and freckled.

'I'm Molly, Mr Grice's maid. I'm very sorry to keep you waiting, but we had a dead duchess to deal with, and she was a lot more trouble dead than when she was alive. May I take your bag? Please follow me.'

There was a squeal and a scream as we stepped out of the arch and I spun round to see that the boy had fallen and the pig was standing on him.

'Don't be afraid,' Molly said. 'It's only a pig.'

We made our way across the road followed by a dozen or so ragamuffins.

'Clear off,' Molly said, but they gathered round me, begging for pennies until I had none left to give.

'Mind where you step,' Molly warned. 'You wouldn't believe a horse could turn hay into something so nasty. Do you have horses in the country?'

'Yes, of course.'

'We have a lot in London,' she said. 'They bite.'

We got across the road and Molly pushed her way through a group of cloth-capped men standing outside a public house.

'Look out for pickpockets,' she told me over her shoulder, 'purse snatchers, sailors and foreigners. Those—'

There was a shrill wail, and I turned to see a man in a sealskin coat standing over a cowering woman and striking her upheld arms with a long stick.

'Stop that at once,' I called out, and he twisted round to look at me.

'Says who?' His words sprayed rancid into my face.

'We do,' I said.

'I don't,' Molly said, taking a step back.

'Not her,' I said. 'Me and Monsieur Parquet.'

His eyes flicked about.

'I don't see no foreign geezer wiv you.' He poked the stick under my nose.

'Monsieur Parquet is the inventor of the synthetic perfume known as Fougère, which means "fern",' I said. 'You are probably unfamiliar with it.' I wiped my cheek with my hand-kerchief. 'But I always carry a little wherever I go, and if you will excuse me for a moment...' I delved into my carpet bag. 'There you are.'

The man glanced at my bottle and laughed mockingly.

'What the hell—'

'Please do not swear,' I said, and puffed two squirts into his eyes.

'What the—' The man dropped his stick to clutch his face.

The woman put down her arms and grinned bloodily. ''E smell better now.' She scrambled to her feet and hobbled away.

'I'll get you later,' he called after her, violently rubbing his eyes. 'And you,' he added as we hurried off.

'A word to the unwise,' Molly said. 'It don't do to interfere between a man and a woman.'

'Would you rather I had let him hit her?'

Molly wiggled her nose. 'Who's to say she didn't ask for it? Men are more reasonable than we are. She probably looked at him funny or something.'

We turned left on to Gower Street and the commotion, though still great, decreased as we went along it. 'Another word,' Molly said. 'I shouldn't mention this to Mr Grice when you meet him. He don't like ladies what show off.'

A water cart trundled by.

'Why are the cobbles made of wood?' I asked.

'That is to muffle the horses' hooves,' she told me, 'so the sick can get some rest and the dying go to theirs a bit more peacefully. That's the Universitaly Hospital there. Mr Grice explained it all to me. He's a very clever man and very nice and he didn't even tell me to say that.'

Number 125 was a tall, terraced Georgian house, white-fronted on the ground floor and red brick above, with an iron balcony on the first floor and separated from the pavement by a basement moat and railings. We climbed the four steps to the black-painted front door, and Molly produced a key on a string from around her neck and admitted me to a long narrow hallway.

'One moment, please,' she said, and went to the first door on the right to announce me.

'And not before time,' a man's voice said. 'I have not had a cup of tea for forty-two and a half minutes.' And with that, the creator of the voice came out of the room to offer me his hand.

4

The Listeners

SIDNEY GRICE WAS not at all what I expected. Though he stood erect, he was not much taller than my five feet and two inches, and slightly built. His hair was thick and black and swept back from a high forehead. His nose was long and thin and there was something almost effeminate about his appearance, with his bowed lips, smooth pale face and a dimple on his delicately constructed chin.

'Miss Middleton.' His greeting was civil but not effusive. His hand was small with long slender fingers, but his grip was strong. 'How unlike your dear mother.' His voice was soft but clear.

His eyes were pale blue and glassy, though his gaze was direct and his lashes were long and curled up in a way that I could only dream of.

'You knew her?'

'It was my privilege,' he said. 'The pity is that you did not. You have no luggage?'

'Only this travelling bag. My boxes are to follow.'

'We will take tea at once, Molly. Come, Miss Middleton. Let me show you around your new home.'

I followed him through the open doorway into a good-sized morning room. Straight ahead were two high-backed leather armchairs either side of a fireplace. To the right were six upright chairs round a low mahogany tea table. At the far end, behind a wooden filigree screen, tall windows opened on to the street.

'The screen is to conceal me from snipers,' he said.

'Have you ever been shot at?'

'Many times.' He touched his left shoulder. 'But only hit once. I prefer it when they miss.'

I laughed and Sidney Grice looked at me bleakly.

'That was not a joke,' he said. 'Get down!' With that he threw himself to the floor and I kneeled quickly beside him. 'Absolutely hopeless,' he said. 'You will have to be faster than that in a real emergency.'

'If you were wearing a bustle you would... Oh!' I looked up at the window in horror. 'Look out!' Sidney Grice flung himself down again as I got up. 'Annoying, isn't it?' I said. 'I do not think we shall play that game again.'

Sidney Grice brushed himself off. 'It is a game that may well save your life one day.'

'I would rather die sensibly,' I told him, and he put his hand to his right eye.

Behind us was a library with four-leafed doors folded back so that the two rooms flowed into one. The library was lined with shelves, all crammed with books and papers, and one wall backed a row of oak cabinets each with four drawers.

'These two chambers make up my study, the heart and mind of the house.'

'You have a great many files,' I said.

'I am compiling a catalogue of every crime committed in this country throughout the century,' he told me. 'A Herculean task, but I am convinced that it is time well spent. It is a proven fact that criminals repeat their own and each other's acts. So I am creating a system whereby every crime can be cross-referenced and an instant solution found as to its method and perpetrator. Is that alcohol I detect on your breath?'

He looked at me sharply.

'I felt a little faint as I disembarked,' I said. 'But a passing parson very kindly gave me a sip of brandy, from what I believe is called a hip flask, to revive me.'

'It is gin,' Sidney Grice said.

'Oh, really? I would not know the difference.'

He narrowed his eyes and we went back into the hall.

'Surely there must be *some* new crimes,' I said, but Sidney Grice huffed.

'The criminal mind is perverted and convoluted but almost invariably unimaginative,' he said as Molly came out in a fluster.

'Oh, sir.' She went pink. 'What an incomplete disaster. We are quite out of Afternoon tea. We have some Morning and mountains of Evening but there is not a mouse-dropping of Afternoon to be had.'

Sidney Grice scowled.

'Then go and get some immediately, and be sure it is weighed properly,' he said. 'Idiotic girl,' he added as she scurried out. 'That,' he pointed past the stairs, 'is the domestic world. I shudder to think what goes on down there.'

The first floor had a drawing room looking across to the university buildings. At the back was the dining room with a dumb waiter and the faint smell of cabbage.

'Whilst we are alone I shall tell you something which you will find embarrassing,' Sidney Grice told me. 'You are wearing brown shoes.'

'I know.'

He winced. 'Brown is for the country. One wears black in town.'

'But I left the country this morning,' I said. 'At what stage should I have changed them?'

Sidney Grice frowned. 'I see you have spirit – a modern but not a feminine quality. With regard to your question, I believe that Kilburn is generally regarded as the outermost reach of civilization. I never venture beyond it.' He sniffed the air. 'I smell smoke.'

I sniffed too but could only smell his coal tar soap.

'Do you mean metaphorically?'

'No, literally. I dislike metaphors.'

'And brown shoes,' I said. 'Is your house ablaze?'

'My house is never ablaze,' he said. 'It is tobacco smoke. I trust you do not indulge, Miss Middleton.'

'The train was so heavily laden that I was obliged to travel in a smoking compartment,' I said.

Sidney Grice's right eye disappeared, his eyelids collapsing into a meat-red cavity. I yelped and he caught his eye and popped it back into place.

'Damnable thing.' He pulled his upper eyelid down. 'I went all the way to Egeria in Bohemia to have it made, hand blown to Professor Goldman's precise measurements, and still it does not fit.'

'How did you lose your own?'

'I did not *lose* it.' He flicked his hair back with a proud jerk of the neck. 'That would imply a carelessness which is alien to my nature. It was plucked from its socket by a Prussian renegade when I thwarted his attempt upon the life of the Crown Prince. The world has yet to appreciate the debt it owes me for that deed. When Kaiser Wilhelm II is on the throne of the unified German states we can look forward to an era of peace across Europe that will last a hundred years.'

'The world already holds you in high esteem,' I said. 'My friends often compare you to Edgar Allen Poe's detective, Auguste Dupin.'

Sidney Grice's lips curled.

'How splendid it is to be compared to an idiotic fantasy from the scribblings of a colonial lunatic,' he said, 'especially as he has obviously read of my achievements and made a clumsy attempt to emulate them.'

He had a curious gait, I noticed, dipping to the right, though he seemed to have no trouble mounting another flight of stairs.

The second floor had two bedrooms, his at the front and the one to be mine, facing a red-brick hospital building. Between them was a small room.

'The pride of my house.' Sidney Grice stepped aside to show me the bathroom. The fittings were indeed splendid, a white-enamelled bath on clawed brass feet, a white porcelain sink on a tall fluted pedestal and a matching water closet with a high cistern. 'We have running water, cold and hot, as long as Molly keeps the stove alight.'

'What luxury.' I did not tell him how unsavoury I thought it to have a closet in the house. Little wonder one heard accounts of so much pestilence in London if all houses were so unhygienically equipped.

The top floor was an attic, he explained, which contained a box room and the servants' quarters.

'How many servants do you keep?'

'I only have Molly and a cook. The cook does not live in and keeps to her kitchen. I do not believe I have seen her since she had the impertinence to offer me seasonal greetings on

Christmas Day two years ago. The occasional scullery maid comes and goes, I am told, but they are of no interest to me.' He paused. 'Clearly Molly is not yet returned. It seems we must answer the summons of that doorbell ourselves.'

'I did not hear anything,' I said, and Sidney Grice clicked his tongue.

'Your ears are younger and probably more sensitive than mine. You hear but you do not listen. The call is obviously urgent to judge from the rapid tugging at the pull. Let us stand quietly for a moment, then tell me what you hear.'

'Should we not answer the door first?' I asked, but Sidney Grice shrugged and said, 'An urgent caller will always wait. Listen.'

We stood together in the corridor and far away I heard a bell, small and sharp, repeatedly clinking.

'I hear it now.'

'What else?'

I listened. 'Nothing.'

'Do you not hear the traffic outside, the rattle of wheels, the clop of hooves on cobbles, the cries of hawkers and mendicants in the street, the flutter of pigeons on the roof, the west wind drawing across the chimney tops?'

I listened harder. 'I hear a faint hubbub,' I said, 'and the bell is getting frantic.'

'A bell is inanimate and can no more be frantic than it could formulate an algebraic theorem.' Sidney Grice scrutinized a small ink stain on his little finger. 'But it would seem that our visitor is.'

We made our way back down the stairs.

'See to the door,' he said, and went into his study.

The lady to whom I answered the door was tall and elegant, with finely carved features white as limestone, though her cheeks were a little flushed as if by exertion. In her early forties, I estimated, she was well, though not richly, dressed in black and her hair was dark brown, neatly pinned under a simple hat with a gauze trim hanging just over her eyes.

'Is this Mr Grice's house?' She was struggling for breath.

'It is.'

'I must see your master.' She was clearly in a state of great agitation.

'I have no master,' I said, but took her through.

Sidney Grice was pretending to browse through a geological journal, but stood up from his armchair and ushered our visitor into the chair facing his across the unlit fireplace. I stood in the middle of the room, uncertain whether to stay or go.

'You cannot know how glad I am to see you.' The woman arranged herself. 'I have heard it told many a time that you are really a fictional character.'

Sidney Grice's neck reddened a little and his cheek ticked; he put his hand to his right eye.

'The blame for that lies in the luridly inaccurate reportage of my cases by cheap periodicals,' he said. 'As you can see for yourself, madam, I am here before you in flesh and blood.'

The lady put her hands over her mouth and nose. She had a ruby ring on the third finger of her right hand.

'There was so much blood,' she said.

I looked at her green eyes. They were wide with horror, and I looked at Sidney Grice and, though it was not possible, it seemed that both of his were shining.

5

Horrible Murder

'IT IS TOO horrible.' Mrs Dillinger caught her breath. 'My poor daughter.' She swallowed. 'Stabbed... stabbed to death and my son-in-law arrested for her murder. You must help me, Mr Grice.'

Sidney Grice sighed. 'I am under no such obligation, madam. But, since you are here and I am bored, what is your name and those of the people involved?'

'I am Mrs Grace Dillinger.'

'I assume you are a widow.'

'Yes, my husband died two months ago.'

'And left you with child?'

'Yes. It is expected in August.'

Sidney Grice waved his hand. 'Continue.'

'My son-in-law is William Ashby. His wife, my daughter is—'

'Was,' Sidney Grice corrected her.

'Was Sarah.'

Sidney Grice took a small brown leather-bound note-book from the table by his chair and jotted the details on the first page with a silver pencil, as Mrs Dillinger reached into her handbag and brought out a rectangular white envelope. Her nails, I noticed, were neatly clipped and she wore a heavy rose-gold wedding band twined with a fine black thread.

'William has written you a note.' She held it out and Sidney Grice took it as if it were soiled, flicked the envelope open, withdrew a twice-folded sheet of paper and let it fall into his lap with little more than a glance.

'What evidence is there against your son-in-law?' he asked.

'None at all.' Mrs Dillinger knotted her slender fingers.

'Then he has no more to fear than I,' he told her, 'for there is no evidence against me either.'

Mrs Dillinger pulled on the lapel of her coat.

'He was in the house at the time,' she said, 'but he was asleep in the next room.'

'Is he a heavy sleeper?'

'Quite the reverse. He usually wakes at the slightest noise. It was the sound of a door opening and closing that disturbed him.'

'Which door?'

'The outer door of the shop at the front of the house. It has a bell which sounds when the top of the door strikes it.'

She was lightly perfumed with Damask.

Sidney Grice toyed with his signet ring. 'Is the bell suspended on a hinge or a coiled spring?'

Mrs Dillinger touched her forehead with the fingertips of her right hand and the ruby glinted darkly.

She said, 'What? A hinge, I suppose. What does it matter?'

My guardian observed her for a moment. 'A hinged bell sounds but twice whereas a sprung bell makes a repeated clatter, on average five to seven double clangs, depending upon the force with which the door strikes it.'

Mrs Dillinger composed herself. 'I see.'

'But nothing until then?'

'No.'

'And where was your son-in-law?'

'In the back room. The kitchen.'

Her boots had been well cleaned and blacked, but were splattered with fresh drops of mud.

'And your daughter?'

'The middle room. Their sitting room.'

'And these rooms are confluent?'

'Yes.'

Her clothes were well made but old. They had been repaired in places and obviously dyed for her mourning period, as the original floral pattern was still just discernible.

'With no other access to the middle room? A window perhaps or a skylight?'

'No. None.'

Sidney Grice leaned towards her.

'So your lightly sleeping son-in-law slumbered through the brutal slaying of his wife only a few feet away?'

Mrs Dillinger stood up suddenly and caught hold of the mantlepiece.

'Really, Mr Grice,' I said and stepped towards her, but Sidney Grice signalled me to stay back.

'Was there any blood on your son-in-law's clothes?'

'He was covered in it.' Mrs Dillinger closed her eyes. 'He took her into his arms.'

Her voice was barely audible and she was breathing heavily.

'And she was already dead?'

'Yes. I think so.' Her voice rose suddenly. 'I do not know.'

Sidney Grice wrote something else in his book. He had a small scar on his right ear, I noticed.

'And nobody else was in the house at the time?'

'No. No one.'

Sidney Grice looked at her for a while.

'Where were you when all this was going on?' he asked.

'In church.'

'On a Monday night?'

'There was a meeting of the Society for the Conversion of Heathen Children in Africa.'

'There is no shortage of those in London,' Sidney Grice said. 'Was your daughter happily married?'

Mrs Dillinger broke into sobs and Sidney Grice tapped his teeth with the pencil. His teeth were clean and straight.

'How can you put her through this?' I asked.

'This is nothing compared to what the police and prosecution will ask of her and her son-in-law.'

'I thought you were supposed to be on my side,' Mrs Dillinger said.

'I do not know what misled you to that conclusion,' Sidney Grice said. 'I have not expressed any support for your cause.'

Mrs Dillinger let go of the mantlepiece and swayed, and I stood ready in case she collapsed.

'Then I must go and find somebody who will.'

Sidney Grice shrugged, but Mrs Dillinger stayed where she was.

'I repeat my question,' he said. 'Was the marriage a happy one?'

'Very... They were devoted to each other. He called my Sarah the apple...' Mrs Dillinger stopped, unable to continue.

'Would you like a glass of water?' I asked, but Mrs Dillinger whispered, 'No. Thank you.'

I took her arm and guided her back into her chair, pulling up one of the upright chairs to sit myself beside her.

Sidney Grice tapped his feet together and said, 'Did they have financial problems?'

'No more than anybody else. They made enough to live on.'

Mrs Dillinger cleared her throat.

'They?'

'Sarah worked in the shop also.'

'Are you employed?'

'I give private tuition in the pianoforte and French Conversation, and I sometimes take in children whilst their parents are unable to look after them.'

'For money?'

'Yes. I need it all the more since my dear husband died.'

'And how did he die?'

Mrs Dillinger shivered. 'He was killed by a footpad on Westminster Bridge for his father's watch which did not even work. Is this relevant?'

Sidney Grice compressed his lips. 'I do not know yet. Was your daughter's life insured?'

The front door slammed and footsteps raced along the hall.

'For a very small amount, I think, but I do not know the details.' Mrs Dillinger's face tightened. 'And I do not see what that has got to do with anything.'

'The court may find it has something to do with every-thing. How old was...' Sidney Grice consulted his notes '...Sarah?'

'Nineteen.'

'Why, she was younger than I,' I said, and Sidney Grice said, 'Please do not interject again, Miss Middleton. How old is your son-in-law, Mrs Dillinger?'

'Thirty-four.'

The mantle clock struck the quarter.

'Quite a difference.' Sidney Grice leaned back. 'Perhaps your daughter was tired of being with an older man.'

'Fifteen years is nothing,' Mrs Dillinger said. 'And I have told you... they were devoted.'

'Perhaps he caught her with another man and killed her in a rage.'

Mrs Dillinger straightened her back. 'She was a loyal and decent girl and would never have betrayed him, and my son-in-law is a gentle and kind man. He could never have been so cruel.'

'Where is he now?' Sidney Grice extruded a little more lead from his pencil.

'He is being held in Marylebone Police Station.'

'And what is the address of this incident?'

'13 Mangle Street, Whitechapel.'

'Mangle Street,' my guardian mused. 'Now there is a place with history. I know of six other murders along that road, the first being in seventeen forty as I recall, and the most recent being that of a certain Matilda Tassel and her two daughters, who were killed with an axe.'

'How tragic,' I said.

'Thank you for your shrewd forensic critique, Miss Middleton.' He scratched his cheek. 'Perhaps William killed them too.'

'Or perhaps their murderer killed Sarah.'

'I believe her husband died of consumption whilst awaiting trial,' Sidney Grice said, 'but I shall check with my records later. One last thing.' He was still writing. 'My services are very expensive and your means are obviously limited. Quite how do you propose to reimburse me?'

Mrs Dillinger took a small black-edged handkerchief from

a pocket in her coat. 'But surely your first concern is to see justice done?' And Sidney Grice smiled unpleasantly.

'It might be a novel diversion,' he said, 'but if word got about that I was prepared to lower my extravagant fees for the deserving poor, I should have every jackanapes in London sitting on my doorstep.'

'But I have no money.'

My guardian raised his left eyebrow.

'Then how do you propose to pay for this consultation?'

Mrs Dillinger looked at me and back at him blankly.

'I thought...'

'I do not want your thoughts,' Sidney Grice said. 'I want your money.'

Her eyes filled with tears.

'Have you no human feelings?' I said.

'I am neither silly nor sentimental if that is what you mean.'

Mrs Dillinger rubbed her forehead. 'I will pay whatever you ask.'

'This,' Sidney Grice held his pencil vertically, 'is a Mordan Mechanical of the very latest spring-loaded design, silver-plated and engraved with my initials. It was a gift from one of my many grateful clients and must have cost her twenty-four guineas. I doubt you have that much to your name.'

Mrs Dillinger folded her handkerchief and blotted her tears with a corner. 'William will pay you. He has a regular income.'

'Which has been put into abeyance by his arrest and will cease the moment the trapdoor opens,' Sidney Grice said, and Mrs Dillinger sat back heavily.

'You are a monster.'

'We both earn our keep protecting the innocent.' Sidney Grice twisted the lead back into his pencil. 'But in my case the stakes and therefore the remuneration are higher.'

'But I have nothing to give you.'

Sidney Grice shrugged.

'Then I have nothing to give you either, and your son-in-law will almost certainly hang.' He snapped his notebook shut. 'I bid you good day, Mrs Dillinger. Expect my bill of charges by the next post.'

Molly came, carrying a black-lacquered tea tray.

'Shall I bring another cup, sir?'

'That will not be necessary. Our visitor is about to leave.'

Mrs Dillinger stood up again as if in a dream, casting about for something she did not have. I rose to steady her.

'Show Mrs Dillinger to the door, Molly.'

For some reason Molly turned to me. I looked away.

'This way please, madam.'

A tress of Molly's hair was escaping from under the side of her cap. It dangled over her ear.

'No,' I said, and Sidney Grice glanced up sharply.

'Whatever do you mean?'

'Mrs Dillinger may not have the money,' I said, 'but I have a small portfolio of shares in my inheritance. I do not know if you follow the stock exchange.'

'I never gamble.'

'I have one thousand shares in the Blue Lake Mining Company of British Columbia, which are currently valued at two shillings and sixpence each, which makes them worth one hundred and twenty-five pounds in total. I am unaware of your usual scale of fees but you can have them all if you agree to take on this case.'

Sidney Grice's face was expressionless.

'I will think about it.' He spoke so casually that I knew this must be much more than he would demand normally.

I took a small breath. 'There is, however, one condition.'

'And that is?'

'That I accompany you.'

Even as I spoke I knew that he would tell me it was out of the question.

'I should like to see how my father's money is spent,' I said, 'and I may be of some use.'

Sidney Grice smirked.

'I cannot imagine how,' he said, 'but it might be amusing. Very well, Miss Middleton. Consider my services engaged.'

6

The Green Flag

SIDNEY GRICE SMILED thinly as Mrs Dillinger left his library.

'You will soon see your small inheritance evaporate if you take pity on every stray that comes scratching at my door.'

I struggled to keep my voice calm. 'Have you no heart? The woman's husband and her daughter have been taken from her brutally and her son-in-law faces the prospect of the gallows, and she is left with nothing but the expectation of a child which she will probably not be able to support.'

'If she wants charity she should go to the workhouse.' He tossed his notebook on to the table. 'Or the allegedly Christian church she attends. Besides, how do you know that he is not guilty?'

I sat down to face my guardian, and thought about the question but could not answer it.

'There are several precedents for this crime,' he told me, 'the most recent being that of Jonathon Carvil, the Sidmouth Stabber, as he was so colourfully styled by the popular press. The details are, at first glance, remarkably similar. He too claimed to slumber in the next room whilst his wife was butchered – quite literally in this case – her body was expertly jointed and trussed as if for the spit and her hands were never found. It transpired that he had intercepted a message from his wife to her lover that very day. I hope you are not easily shocked, Miss Middleton.'

'I do not think so,' I said, 'and please call me March.'

'Very well, March,' he said. 'I am generally known as a casual fellow but, given your position as my ward, I do not think it proper for you to address me by my Christian name.'

'I should not dream of it.' I poured us both a cup from the willow-pattern tea set.

'Stop,' my guardian cried out as I lifted the milk jug.

'Whatever is the matter?'

'I will not drink the mammary excretions of cattle,' he said. 'Even the smell is nauseating.'

'You make it sound disgusting.'

'I make it sound what it is. Especially when one remembers that the cow only has milk to spare because her calf has been dragged from her to have its throat cut. If I were not such an excellent host I would not have milk in the house. Even the word curdles on my tongue.'

I put the jug down and asked, 'What happened to Jonathon Carvil?'

'He too claimed to have been disturbed by a door closing. The jury did not believe him.'

'Were you involved in that case?'

I noticed there were no pictures on the walls or photographs on the desk.

'Carvil consulted me.' He sniffed his tea suspiciously. 'And I counselled him to flee the country, but he ignored my advice and took the drop in consequence. I never like to lose a client but it taught me one very important lesson – always to insist on being paid in advance.' He screwed his face up and tugged sharply upon the bell pull. It had an ivory skull on its end, which joggled about when he let go. 'This tea is cold and stewed.'

'And you think the Ashby case will take the same course?'

'Almost certainly.' Sidney Grice tossed me the letter. 'Take a look at that.'

On the envelope in big clumsy capitals was written in pencil:

MR GRISE DITECTIVE

The sheet of paper was similarly inscribed, the words sloping down to the right of the page:

DEAR MR GRISE
PLEASE HELP ME I AM AN INNASENT MAN
YOURS TRUELY
WILLIAM ASHBY.

Molly came in, and he said, 'Fill my bottle, Molly, and when the doorbell is rung, I shall answer it myself.'

'Yes, sir.' Molly left, and Sidney Grice asked, 'What do you make of it then?'

'It is an uneducated hand.'

'Obviously. But why was it written?'

'To ask for your help,' I answered, and Sidney Grice snorted.

'I hardly think so,' he said. 'Why send that half-illiterate scrawl with such an articulate and attractive woman to plead your case?'

I said, 'You seem to have formed a very good opinion of her,' and Sidney Grice tugged his ear.

'One of the most intelligent women I have ever come across,' he replied.

I finished my tea and asked, 'But what other reason could he have for writing it?'

Sidney Grice put his fingers to his eye.

'I do not know the answer to that yet.' He pushed the eye towards his nose. 'But I cannot help feeling that the key to the whole problem might lie in this letter.' He stood up. 'But we have wasted enough time already. I must run up the flag.'

We went into the hallway, where there was a small brass wheel with a handle on the wall, and he proceeded to turn it contra-clockwise about half a dozen revolutions.

'It raises a green flag outside,' he explained. 'The local cabbies know that I tip well enough for them to look out for it.'

Molly hurried up with a brown bottle which he took from her without a word, slid it into a scratched leather satchel on the table and lifted an Ulster coat from a rack on the opposite wall.

'Where are we going?' I asked and Sidney Grice paused, arm in sleeve.

'We?'

'Have you forgotten my condition?'

'I never forget anything,' he said, slipping his coat on, 'least of all conditions, and I shall take you to any meetings that may be conducted during this investigation. But I am going now to the mortuary, hardly a place fit for the entertainment of a young lady.'

'I have not asked to be entertained,' I told him, 'and, if you will not take me, I must tell you that our agreement is terminated.'

He chose a silver-topped ebony cane from an old oak stand. 'You would disappoint Mrs Dillinger so cruelly because you cannot have your own way?' He put on a wide-brimmed soft felt hat.

'It is not I who breaks our contract.'

The doorbell rang and he said, 'It is no place for feminine sensitivities.'

He turned the handle clockwise and put the satchel over his shoulder.

'I may be feminine,' I said, 'but nobody has ever accused me of being sensitive. You leave me with no choice but to withdraw my offer.'

Sidney Grice scowled and opened the door to a cabby.

'I shall be out directly.' He turned back to me. 'I will not be dictated to, especially by a girl.' He snatched up a pair of leather gloves. 'Besides, it is very cold in the mortuary. You will need your cloak.'

7

•═╍╍═•

The Hansom Cab

I N THE HANSOM cab Sidney Grice explained.

'Evidence deteriorates,' he said, 'but at very different
rates. For instance, the hand of man can be seen on the
pyramids of Egypt some thousands of years after they were
built, but if a butterfly were to land on that ledge, the evidence of its presence would disappear the moment a breeze
took it away.'

'Unless one managed to make a photograph of it,' I said,
and my guardian tutted.

The hansom lurched round a pile of wood and Sidney Grice
said, 'There are three main portions of evidence in this case.
The first is the victim, or rather her body, and she must be our
primary concern, for bodies and the clues which they might
give us deteriorate rapidly. The second is the scene of the
crime. The longer evidence is left, the more likely it is to be
deliberately or accidentally destroyed or removed. The third is
the suspect himself. We can leave him to the last because we
know that he is not going anywhere. It may give him time to
fine-tune his story but, in my experience, the longer a criminal
is in police custody, the more he is likely to lose his nerve and
become confused or even confess. Once we have identified and
examined those three items – victim, scene and murderer – it

is only a question of linking them, and then we can all go home for a nice cup of tea and look forward to a good hanging.'

Sidney Grice took the bottle from his satchel, uncorked it and took a swig.

'The Grice Heat Retentive Bottle,' he told me. 'It was made to my instructions in a glass-blowing factory on the island of Murano.'

We bounced over a pothole and my head hit the window. 'What does it do?'

'Why, it keeps my tea hot enough to drink with pleasure for up to three hours.' He took a swig. 'It consists of a smaller bottle inside this outer bottle, the space between them being filled with lambs' wool which, as you are aware, is a great retainer of heat. This is why we make our clothes and blankets from it.' He took another draught and reinserted the cork, tapping it firmly into place with the ball of his thumb. 'One day I shall go into the manufacture of my invention and retire to my estate in Dorset, where I shall write my memoirs, drill for oil and keep bees.'

The horse stumbled and the hansom rocked.

'I have an improvement to suggest.' I caught hold of the steady strap. 'You could design a cup to put over the end and perhaps clamp on to the bottle.'

'And what benefit would that bring?'

'Why, then you could offer your companion some refreshment as well,' I said.

Sidney Grice considered the matter before shaking his head. 'It would only add to the already considerable difficulty and cost of manufacture. Besides which I never travel with anyone to whom I should wish to offer my tea. There would be less for me and what would be the point of that?'

'Kindness,' I said, and my guardian rolled his eye.

'The poor, I am told, are kind to each other but that is because they have nothing to lose,' he said. 'The rich cannot afford to be. What did you make of Mrs Dillinger?'

He put the bottle away.

'She seemed a very nice lady,' I said.

'But what did you notice about her?'

I let go of the strap.

'She has been comfortably off and fallen on hard times, but never desperate ones.'

'And how did you come to those conclusions?'

A man on a dappled horse overtook us and blew me a kiss.

'Her dress was of good quality but she could not afford to buy new mourning clothes so she had it dyed,' I said, 'and she had done some minor repairs to it. Also she wore a ruby ring, which must have been expensive, but she has not been forced to sell it yet. What did you observe?'

'All those things,' he said, 'and the most beautiful green eyes I have ever seen. I should not be surprised if there were aristocratic blood in her veins as well.'

'As well as what?'

'As well as mine,' he said. 'Charles Le Grice was at the Conqueror's side at Hastings and would have been lord of all Northumbria if he had not fallen out with William about who shot the arrow which killed a stag in Colchester.'

'I cannot imagine a Grice falling out with anyone,' I said, and my guardian looked at me.

A street urchin ran alongside and jumped on to the running board.

'Spare a copper, guv.' But my guardian rapped the boy's knuckles with his cane and he fell away.

'How did you set out to become a private detective?' I asked as we swung round a fruit stall.

'*Personal* detective,' Sidney Grice said. 'Bedrooms are private. I am *personal*.'

'When was your first case?'

'Whilst I was still at school,' he told me. 'I was able to prove that the boy who had been awarded the Latin prize had cheated with the aid of his housemaster, with whom he had struck up what I can only describe as an inappropriate relationship.'

'That was a noble deed.'

We were making good progress up a long straight road, the clatter of hooves on cobbles reverberating from the tall buildings either side.

'And lucrative,' Sidney Grice said. 'The father of the boy who rightfully received the prize gave me two shillings for my services. It was then that I realized I could use my natural quick-wittedness, acute senses, superlative observational powers and prodigious intellect in the profitable pursuit of criminals.'

The hansom slowed.

'It must be very satisfying to see justice done,' I said, and Sidney Grice puffed.

'It is more satisfying to see people punished, but I do like to be sure they are the right people. Of course, the higher one moves up the social strata the more important this becomes. One can afford to make mistakes with the occasional prostitute, but you would have to be very sure of your facts indeed before you hanged a bishop.'

We turned down a narrow alley before coming to a halt, and there was only just enough room for us to scramble out along the side of a high wall.

'Wait for us here,' Sidney Grice called up, but the cabby shook his head.

'Not 'ere,' he croaked. 'It give me goose-flesh, it do, and it spook me 'orse, and a spooked 'orse ain't no more use than a blind beggar's dead fleas on these streets. I'll be up there at the end of the alley.'

'Mind the drain,' Sidney Grice said as we went round the front of the hansom. 'And watch out for the horse. Horses bite.'

He rapped on a plain black door. The horse was reversing reluctantly.

'Horses like to see where they are going,' Sidney Grice said.

'We do have horses in the country,' I told him.

'Quite so,' he said, 'but these are London horses.'

He let the knocker fall again and a hatch slid open in the door.

'Good afternoon, Parker.'

'Mr Grice.' The door was opened by a short man in a stained laboratory coat. 'Come in,' he said, but as we stepped forward he stopped us. 'What's this about? You know there's no ladies allowed in here.'

Sidney Grice turned to me. 'I did warn you, Miss Middleton. You had better go and wait in the cab.'

I reached into my cloak pocket and brought out a card.

'Do you know what this is?' I asked.

Parker screwed up his eyes and said, 'No.'

'It is a permit from Her Majesty's Office of Structural Examiners to enter and inspect any building in the kingdom upon demand, and you would be committing an act of treason if you were to deny me access.'

'Blimey,' Parker said and stepped aside.

We entered a square hallway with five doors leading off it. 'Which case are you on?' Parker asked. 'It can't be the poisoned vicar. Mr Cochran's already got that one. Not the Dukc Road double drowning, I hope. Getting a bit slimy, they are.'

'Mrs Sarah Ashby,' Sidney Grice said.

'Oh, the chopping. She's in Room Four.' Parker took a ring of keys from his coat pocket and rattled them one by one in the lock.

'That was a railway ticket,' Sidney Grice murmured.

'Possibly,' I agreed, as Parker found the right key, swung open the door and said, 'Are you sure you're up to this, miss? I've known experienced peelers turn funny in this room. One of them toppled over, hit his head and ended up on a table himself.'

I nodded. 'Please proceed.'

'Take my arm,' Sidney Grice said, 'and tell me the moment you feel unwell.'

I felt unwell already, but I would not have admitted it for all the opium in Bengal. The stench of death had filled my nostrils.

8

The House of Death

I HESITATED A little for I knew that smell and the horrors
that came with it.

'I shall be perfectly all right,' I said, rejecting the prof-
fered arm as we went in.

It was a large low-ceilinged room, sloppily whitewashed
and lit by flaring gas mantles on windowless walls. There
were a dozen narrow pine tables in a row in the centre of the
room, each covered with a stained white sheet, the shapes
unmistakeable beneath them and the smells all too recogniz-
able – freshly opened bodies, rotting flesh and the eye-stinging
sharpness of carbolic acid burning in my lungs.

The body of a young man lay in the far corner and the
sheet had slipped off his upper half. He had obviously been in
a fire. His skin was blistered and his hair had been burnt off.
But it was his face that shocked me. It was charred almost to
the bone. I looked about for something to steady myself but
there was nothing. I stood alone.

We stopped at a table in the middle.

'Here we are.' Parker whipped back a sheet and the tor-
tured face of a toothless old woman sprang out. 'Oh, sorry.
This is Mrs Ashton. Run over by an hearse in an hurry, she
was.' We went to the next table. 'Here we are.'

Parker clearly felt less flamboyant this time, for he lifted the cover back carefully to reveal a face. At first glance Sarah Ashby might have been slumbering. Her eyes were closed and her expression was one of peaceful repose. Her face was pale and haloed in long golden waves, her lips slightly parted as if in a contented smile. She might have been having a beautiful dream were it not for the place where she slept and the cut in her left cheek from the base of her little nose, almost to her ear, so deep and gaping that her back teeth grinned horribly through a second pair of lips in the parted muscles.

Sidney Grice stepped to her side and peeled back the rest of the sheet, leaving it below her feet at the bottom of the table. Sarah Ashby was naked, unearthly white and spattered in dark blood, and her neck and body were punctured by numerous black gashes. He whistled silently.

'Pretty thing, wasn't she?'

'Sliced up good and proper,' Parker said with relish.

'Oh, you poor thing,' I said.

'Where are her clothes?' Sidney Grice asked.

'Gone to the incinerator,' Parker said, and Sidney Grice looked at him sharply.

'What? All of them?'

'Of course. They weren't no good to anybody else, the state they were in, all ripped and soaked in gore.'

Sidney Grice closed his eyes briefly. 'The man is an imbecile,' he said, making no attempt to lower his voice.

'Now see here, Mr Grice—'

'Did you remove her clothes yourself?'

'Of course.'

'What was she wearing?'

'A grey dress with bone buttons at the back.'

'Still fastened?'

'Yes.'

'High- or low-necked?'

'High. Why?'

The floor was unevenly tiled and had been sluiced into sludgy puddles, and I saw that Parker had vulcanized galoshes on.

'Was there anything in the pockets?'

A long-legged spider ran over Sarah Ashby's arm and slid on its thread to the floor.

'Nothing valuable.'

'What then?'

'I don't know. A handkerchief. A piece of liquorice. I ate that. It was no use to her and I gave it a wipe first.'

'Have you ever heard of germs?' I asked and Parker grinned.

'Yes, and I've heard of fairies, but I never met anyone who's seen one.'

'Was she wearing any undergarments?' my guardian asked.

'Yes.'

'Upper and lower?'

Parker looked at the floor. 'Please, Mr Grice. There's a lady present.'

'You may find this difficult to believe,' I told him, 'but I am already aware that women wear undergarments.'

Sidney Grice grunted and said, 'Both?'

'Yes, both.' Parker shuffled about. 'No corsets, though.'

'And did the rips in her clothes match the wounds?'

'As far as I remember, yes, but I...' Parker's mouth stayed open but he did not finish his sentence.

'So you didn't take her clothes off and find far more wounds than you expected?'

'No. I don't think so.'

'No. You do not think,' Sidney Grice told him and, turning his attention back to Sarah Ashby, took her left hand in his. 'Such doll-like fingers,' he said, bending and straightening them all at once, then twisting each a little and wiggling them side to side.

His nails were filed neatly short. He seemed lost in thought. Her nails, I noticed, were chipped but clean, but something was wrong.

'Where is her wedding band?' I asked.

'She wasn't wearing one,' Parker said.

'But her finger has a white ring around it.'

'I cannot help that,' Parker said. 'If she was wearing any jewellery I would of handed it in as regulations require. Mr Grice knows me well enough to know that.'

'What is this?' Sidney Grice raised her right hand. 'See that?'

The nail of her right index finger was cracked and something was caught in it.

'It looks like a hair,' I said.

Sidney Grice clipped a pince-nez on his nose.

'Not a hair.' He put her hand down and rooted through his satchel for a small pair of steel tweezers and a white envelope, lifted her hand again and tugged something out. 'Look.' He held it up to the light.

'A yellow thread,' I said as he deposited it in the envelope, licked and sealed the flap, and scribbled a note on the back.

Sidney Grice crouched and lifted the hair to examine an ugly laceration in Sarah Ashby's throat. It ran all the way under her left jaw.

'This is very important, Parker,' he said. 'Has the body been washed or wiped at all?'

'No. That's not in my job and the women only wash people what are being reclaimed by relatives and the like.'

'You are sure?'

Parker nodded.

'That is quite a wound,' Sidney Grice said.

'Yes,' I said. 'But it did not kill her.'

Sidney Grice turned to me. 'Go on.'

'I have seen something similar,' I said, 'when two sentries at barracks in Bombay had an argument over a local girl. I helped my father to suture him. For a throat to be cut fatally, the thick blocks of muscles over the carotid artery or jugular vein have to be sliced through. This is not deep enough.'

'Quite so,' Sidney Grice said. 'So what did kill her?'

'I am not sure,' I said. 'She has so many wounds.'

'Forty,' Parker said. 'I've counted.'

'I am amazed that he can,' Sidney Grice muttered, and pointed to a wound below Sarah Ashby's left breast, an oval crater about two inches across. 'That is what did it. Hand me my bag, Miss Middleton.'

He took out a thin steel spatula, flattened at both ends, and he passed it gently into the hole. 'See how far it slides? That is a good six inches. The blade would have penetrated the abdominal wall and up through the diaphragm straight into the heart. She would have died instantly. It angles a little to the left as well, so we are looking for a left-handed killer. Help me turn her, Parker.' The two men twisted Sarah Ashby on to her right side. 'You are in my light, Miss Middleton.'

'I beg your pardon.' I went to stand in a greasy stain at the lower end of the table and he ran his fingers through her hair again.

'Just as I thought,' he said. 'A slight depressed fracture of the occipital skull but no injuries to her back.' They let her lie back again. 'So what do we have? One wound to the face and one to the neck and thirty-eight to the chest and stomach, one fatal. Notice anything odd about the wounds, Miss Middleton?'

I shook my head.

'They are of two distinct types.' He pointed with the spatula. 'Long slashes and smaller stabs. The stabs are unusual. Obviously, skin tends to distort and spring back again when cut, but the overall impression is that they have a wavy outline. You can see it quite clearly here where the tissues are firmer on the shoulder. Almost S-shaped.'

Sidney Grice walked down to her feet.

'That is odd.' He bent down. 'Her great toe is bruised. Was she wearing any boots, Parker?'

'No boots or stockings,' Parker said.

'You are sure?'

'Sure as eggs is not potatoes. What are you doing?'

Sidney Grice had taken hold of Sarah Ashby's knees and forced them apart. He leaned forwards and peered upwards.

'Show some respect.' Parker curled in disgust as Sidney Grice moved slightly to one side.

'No sign of any traumatic penetration,' Sidney Grice observed.

'For the love of God,' Parker said, covering his mouth with a filthy hand and taking a step sideways.

'Do you know what I think?' Sidney Grice asked, straightening his back.

'No,' I said.

'I think it is time to go.'

'I couldn't disagree less,' Parker said, wiping his dirty palms on his dirtier coat.

'To Mangle Street?' I asked.

'Home.' My guardian produced a bar of soap and a little towel from his bag. 'It will be too late by the time we get to Whitechapel and we are more likely to miss or even destroy the evidence in the dark. No, Miss Middleton, I was thinking of a nice cup of tea, and I am sure you could do with a bite to eat.' He went to a tap on the wall.

'Wouldn't mind a drink myself,' Parker said.

'Then I shall not detain you any longer,' Sidney Grice said as he dried his hands and packed his things away.

'No I meant—'

'I am fully aware of what you meant.' Sidney Grice put some coins into Parker's hand.

'Why thank you, Mr Grice.'

'And if that impostor Cochran shows his face do *not* let him anywhere near her.' Sidney Grice turned to me. 'Only last month he poached my decapitated architect and got two pages in the *Evening Standard* for a case that even you could have solved.'

'It must have been idiotically simple then,' I said.

My guardian lifted the sheet over Sarah Ashby, pausing when he reached her head.

'The face of an angel,' he said, letting the sheet fall.

'Did we pass the inspection?' Parker asked as he showed us to the door.

Outside, the light was already failing and I was glad that it was cold. My shaking could be passed off as a shiver.

9

The Same Moon

E MADE A quiet couple at either end of the dining-room table.

'Do you usually dine alone?' I asked.

'No,' he said. 'I always dine with a book. This is a particular favourite of mine – *A Brief Study of African Parasitic Worms* – beautifully illustrated with coloured drawings.'

'Does it not put you off your dinner?'

'Why should it? I am not planning to eat one.'

I sipped my soup, but I have never liked tomato. It looks like blood and smells like sweat to me.

'If I had known more about the subject three years ago,' Sidney Grice continued, 'I might have been able to prove that Lord Jennings went much further up the Ivory Coast than was believed at the time, and thus saved his companions from the charge of deserting him and being drummed out of their regiment.'

I tried some more soup. My guardian had finished his and turned a page, bringing out an ivory-encased pencil and placing it parallel to his knife.

'How did you know my father?' I asked, and Sidney Grice's eye fell out. He caught it deftly and put it into his waistcoat pocket.

'I shall not divulge any information about your father.' He produced a black patch out of his jacket, like a conjurer with bunting, and tied it over the socket. The effect was mildly comical but his expression was not. 'Except that I owe him a great debt which I am partially repaying by tolerating your presence in my house.'

'You are too kind.'

'I am not at all kind but I do honour my obligations.'

He mopped his bowl with a piece of bread.

'What was my mother like?'

'A famous beauty.' My guardian sprayed a few crumbs over the white starched tablecloth. 'And the thinly disguised heroine of a trashy novel. Her eyes, it was said, were like sapphires in the sun, and her hair was burnished gold.'

'Not mousey like mine?'

He wiped his lips with his napkin and replaced it on his lap. 'Not in the least. Nor was she scrawny.'

I put down my spoon.

'But what was she like as a person? My father never spoke of her.'

'That is not for me to say.'

'But surely—'

'Please do not ask me about them again. For reasons I cannot divulge it is not appropriate.'

'But—'

He raised his hand and turned back to his book, grunting to himself as he pencilled a note in the margin.

'Who is Mr Cochran?' I asked.

'Never mind who he is.' He pointed the blunt end of his pencil at me. 'I will tell you what he is. He is a posturing, vainglorious, publicity-seeking, self-opinionated, jumped-up, inobservant, illogical, ineffectual, grasping braggart.'

Molly came, a little breathless, to clear the plates.

'This soup was tepid,' Sidney Grice told her, not even glancing up from his book.

'Thank you, sir.'

'That is not an endorsement,' he said. 'Nothing should be tepid. Tea should be hot and drinking water cold. Do you even know what tepid is?'

'Indeed I do, sir,' Molly said. 'Cook was telling me it is how she feels about you. So it must be a good feeling.'

My guardian *tsked* as Molly brought three covered dishes from the dumb waiter and put them on the sideboard to serve us boiled potatoes, cabbage and carrots. I waited to see if my guardian would comment, but he was tucking into his food before she had even closed the door.

'Are you not hungry, March?'

'Very,' I said, 'but I was waiting for the meat.'

'Have you not seen enough meat today,' he asked, 'without wanting to put some more into your mouth?'

I picked up my knife but put it down again.

'What is it now?' he asked.

'How can you refer to the mortal remains of a young woman as *meat*?' I asked.

'Skin, muscle and bone.' He tracked the salt up and down his plate. 'Meat by any definition. Throw a leg of mutton with a leg of man into the lion's pit and see if it differentiates between them.'

He speared a piece of carrot on his fork and popped it in his mouth.

'How can you be so callous?'

'Weep for the living,' he dabbed his mouth, 'and, as for your charge of being callous, it is not I who feeds upon the dead.'

'But if you allow yourself to think like that you would never eat any meat at all.'

'I do not.'

'Not even ham?'

'Especially not ham. I have known pigs that are as wise as judges and a great deal more intelligent than juries, and certainly more fragrant.'

We had water with our meal, a small etched carafe each with a crystal glass tumbler.

'Tepid,' Sidney Grice said. 'You should bring a book to the table, March. It would relieve me of the strain of making pleasant chatter. What are you reading at present?'

'I have not a book with me yet,' I said.

'Then I shall lend you Swinburne,' he said.

'Thank you,' I said. 'I love his ode to Sappho.'

'Not that degenerate half-wit's perverted gibberish.' My guardian wiped his mouth on a cloth napkin. 'Samuel Swinburne's *Treatment of London's Sewage*. His chapters on the problems of disposing of human waste are most informative and entertaining.'

'Is there to be a sweet pudding?' I asked, still hungry.

'Sugar blackens the teeth, which is why I only partake of it once a week,' he told me and I laughed. 'How could anything so white and pure do that?' Then all the images rushed back. 'Oh, how can I be amused on such a day as this?'

'The human mind is not capable of comprehending or containing this world's agony,' Sidney Grice said, 'or we should all go mad.'

I took a drink of water. 'Whoever savaged that poor girl must surely be insane.'

'I have seen one hundred and eighty-six bodies in my professional capacity.' My guardian mashed his potatoes with his fork. 'But I have not seen any murder so coldly calculated as that we witnessed today.'

'I do not understand.'

'And I am not sure that I do either,' Sidney Grice said, 'yet.'

And so to my room.

I looked out of the window and saw the same full moon that I had watched last night hanging over Hunger Hill, but which shone tonight on the roofs of a vast metropolis which I and four million people called their home. It was difficult to believe that I had begun the same day in my own home two hundred miles away.

I performed my toilet, brushing my hair one hundred times, changed into my cotton nightdress and bedsocks, for the night air was chill, and wrote my journal at the table.

I put the journal back in my writing box and pressed the button under the inkwell to open the secret compartment.

They were still there, your twelve letters carefully bound in a black ribbon with a band of gold. I read the first one.

Always remember... you wrote, but I could not read on. I retied the ribbon and touched the gold.

And afterwards I read my Bible. Oh, death, where is thy sting?

But what of Sarah Ashby? Was the victim of such savagery now at peace? I kneeled by my bed and prayed for her and for those I had loved and lost, and for the mother I hoped to know one day, and for the first time I prayed for the soul of Sidney Grice, for surely even he had one.

10

The Scene of the Crime

MANGLE STREET RAN short and straight, connecting two busy thoroughfares, and the shop was easily found terraced between two houses, one boarded up and the other serving as stabling for a team of donkeys, two of which peered mournfully out at us as we passed.

'They do not even have room to turn round,' I said. But Sidney Grice was crouching to inspect a dead rat on the pavement.

'Poisoned,' he said, 'like Cochran's vicar.'

There was a shop of *Curious Objects* opposite.

'The only thing curious about those shops is that they exist.' My guardian stood up. 'They are nothing more than a staging post from the dustbin to the rubbish tip.'

Under a sheet metal canopy by the front door, a police constable with a drooping straw-coloured moustache sat smoking a briar on an empty beer crate, with his regulation cloak wrapped around him. He stood wearily as Sidney Grice introduced himself.

'Inspector Pound told me you'd sent a telegram.' The constable tapped his pipe out against the wall. 'He didn't say nothing about the girl, though.'

The ash blew over my dress and I shook it off.

'I am helping Mr Grice,' I said.

'In whose opinion?' Sidney Grice murmured.

The shop window was barred and had no curtains or blinds. Above it was fixed a white board on which *Ashbys Ironmongery* was painted in black.

'Lord preserve the apostrophe.' I pointed up. 'It is going the way of the dodo.'

'Horrible squiggly things.' My guardian shuddered. 'The sooner we are rid of them the better.'

'I was supposed to get my breakfast an hour ago,' the constable said, and waved us through as if we were traffic.

'Regular habits are essential to the digestion,' Sidney Grice told him. 'I would lend you a book on the subject if I supposed that you could read.'

'The way I feel I could probably eat it.' The constable plonked himself down again.

'Why are you so rude to people?' I asked.

'That is not a person. It is a policeman.' Sidney Grice twisted the door lever. 'And he can no more afford to have feelings than I can. Note the bell.'

It clanked twice when I opened the door and twice again when I closed it.

I looked up. 'Hinged, as Mrs Dillinger told us.'

We found ourselves in a short narrow shop, a wooden-topped counter with a raised flap facing us.

'Look at the floor.' Sidney Grice pointed.

'So many muddy footprints,' I said.

'Not mud.' He scraped a line with his toe. 'Blood – and this floor was well swept and washed recently.' He tapped it with his cane.

I looked about me. The walls to either side had shelves piled with boxes of nails and screws and assorted carpentry tools, some hanging on hooks on the wall behind the counter, some in baskets on the floor, hammers, axes and a rack of knives behind the counter.

'No shortage of weapons here,' Sidney Grice said as we went behind the counter and through an open door into the room behind.

It was there that we came upon the scene of the murder. The sitting room was small and windowless. It was furnished with a bed to our left, a misshapen armchair to the right, and two pine chairs facing each other at a small square wooden table before an unlit fireplace in front of us.

'Oh dear God,' I whispered.

'You will not find much sign of him here,' my guardian said.

I saw now what Mrs Dillinger had meant by *so much blood*. The walls and furniture were splattered with it, dried and blackened, and there was a coagulated puddle with dozens of bootprints all over the uncarpeted floor. The stench was unmistakeable. It was my father's surgery the day after battle. In the cold silence it reeked of the screams of the slaughtered.

'Not much room to move in here.' Sidney Grice swung his cane in an arc. 'And yet there is no other sign of a disturbance. Not a chair has been overturned; nor an ornament broken. How does that tie in with your idea of a frenzied attack? Hello,' he stepped forward to peer more closely at the wall to the left of the fireplace. 'What is this here?'

I went to look with him and saw that what I had assumed was another splash was in fact a word, written in blood, at about eye level on the wall beneath a broken gas mantle. The letters were crude and smeared and about a foot tall, fading towards the end, but their meaning was unequivocal.

'*Rivincita*,' I read out. 'It is Italian for *revenge*.'

'Oh, how disappointing,' Sidney Grice said. 'I had hoped it would say something sensible. A name might have been useful.'

'Was that word not found at the Slurry Street murder scenes?'

'Possibly.' He turned. 'There is a lot of blood on this table.' He pointed to a crusted pool, kneeled, and looked up. 'But none underneath it except what has seeped through the cracks.' He prodded the floorboards with his cane. 'This is the only space large enough for her to have fallen – here between the table and the door we came in. The rug has been saturated and a dozen oafs have trampled it everywhere. If she hit her head on this old sewing machine as she fell that would account for the fractured skull. See, there is a cake of blood and some hair on the wheel, the very match of hers.' He bent to put a few strands in an envelope, sealed and wrote upon it, and straightened up to look about again. 'What is in the fire?'

'Nothing much,' I said. 'Just ash.'

'There is no such thing as *just* ash.' He picked up an iron poker to rake it around. 'Every burnable substance on this unnecessarily large and absurdly varied planet produces its own distinctive product of combustion. This is paper ash. Now, March, why does anybody burn paper?' He tapped the wall.

'To start a fire.'

'This paper *was* the fire.' He crouched beside it. 'And why have a paper fire which gives little heat, and only for a while, when you have a scuttle of coal on the hearth? It is quite warm in here anyway. Both you and I know that paper is not cheap and it is always useful even when it has been written on

– for lighting purposes as you say, but also for wrapping, and very handy in a shop where the profit on the sale of a few nails, for example, is negligible. No, this paper has been burnt for one reason only, to hide whatever was written on it. See how finely it has been powdered.' He poked under the grate. 'Not so much as a legible scrap. What is all this stuff?' He raked the ashes and some cinder out. 'Looks like bones to me.' He picked up a charred piece the size of a forefinger. 'Rabbit thighbone, I should say. Yes, and there is a rabbit's tooth and – what have we here? – this blackened ring,' he took a handkerchief from his trouser pocket and wiped it, 'is a wedding band. To whom do you suppose it might belong?'

'Sarah Ashby,' I said.

'If I were a betting man I would wager a considerable fortune on it.' He wrinkled his brow. 'But why is it here?'

'Perhaps her murderer put it there.'

'But why? You could not hope to destroy it in such a feeble blaze, and why would you want to? Why not take it and pawn it? It is not engraved and so not traceable, and you could probably get a pound or so for it.' He put the ring into an envelope in his satchel and got to his feet again, wiping his fingers clean. 'So what are we to think? That a criminal lunatic hacked Mrs Ashby to death without waking her husband or disarranging a stick of furniture, lit a fire of manuscripts, slipped her ring off and threw it in, then pulverized the ashes, pausing only to write a cryptic foreign message on the wall in her blood?'

'What do you think happened?'

'I do not know,' Sidney Grice looked about him, 'but I *will* find out. Let us have a look through here.'

11

The Jewelled Dagger

A PLAIN-PLANKED open door led directly into the back room, a kitchen with a rust-holed woodstove, a wooden stool and an upright chair painted brown. There was an uncurtained window with four cracked panes above a stone sink and an iron hand pump on a rickety draining board. Sidney Grice tapped the floor and walls and leaned back to look at the ceiling.

The back door led into a small cobbled yard with a privy to the right. He glanced into it, then strode to a high solid-wooden gate to the rear left. The ground was littered with broken roofing slates and old nails.

'This has not been locked for a long time. The bolt is covered with rust.' He looked at his fingers. 'And blood.' He tugged the gate open. 'And some on the outside handle too. That's nice. Must be a burst drain.' He wiped his hands on the towel from his satchel and left it hanging out.

The alley we looked on to was a running sewer, awash with a stream of slow-swirling water, thick with effluent. I put my handkerchief over my mouth and nose and saw that my guardian was doing the same as he leaned out, holding on to the gatepost as he peered up and down. He pulled himself back. 'So what do we have? Let us assume the murderer came in through the gate and across the yard to the house. See those smudges? A little faint, but obviously sludgy footprints, and clear enough to distinguish toe from heel.' We followed them to the back door. 'But there are no footprints going back again or into the house. In fact the kitchen is the one room with a clean floor. Why might that be?'

'The murderer could have taken his boots off so that he did not awaken William Ashby,' I said.

'But where did he put them down?' he asked. 'I did not notice any mud in the house and it is my job to notice everything.'

'Perhaps he put them on some paper and threw the paper in the fire.'

'Perhaps he did.' Sidney Grice looked doubtful. 'In which case William Ashby slumbers peacefully in one of those two chairs while the murderer stands on the threshold three feet away unlacing his boots, with the door open wide, and Monday night was quite blustery as I recall. Then he goes into the sitting room where he comes across the unfortunate Mrs Ashby, places his boots on some paper and stabs her forty times.' We went back through, the blood gleaming dully in the light from the back door. 'Nobody could expect to hack a woman to death without even an audible gasp, therefore he must have closed the door first... If you would perform that deed please, March.'

The hinges squeaked as I pulled the cast-iron handle, but the frame was too warped to allow the door to be fully closed. It was still ajar six inches when it jammed against the lintel.

'More curious by the minute.' Sidney Grice tugged but the door would not shut. 'Then he lights a fire, throws the wedding ring in, crumbles the ashes and goes out via the shop, and then and only then, does William arise and investigate the noise.'

We went back into the shop and he opened the double glass doors of a cabinet behind the counter. Neatly hung on brass screws was everything from bone-handled penknives to a vicious-looking machete.

'Look at these.' He flicked a fly away from his face. 'You could kill an ox with that hatchet. Now this one is interesting.'

My guardian indicated a knife shaped like an oriental dagger, the handle curved and encrusted in faux jewels of red and green coloured glass. But there was something wicked about the blade: no more than six or seven inches long, the burnished steel tapered to a lethally fine point and the edge, razor-thin, was wavy.

'That cannot be the knife.'

'What better place to hide a straw than in a haystack?' He pulled out his handkerchief to lift the knife out and scrutinize it. 'If it were the weapon it has been well cleaned, but it is worth looking at further.' He wrapped up the knife and slipped it into his satchel.

'Your hearing, as you have already demonstrated, is poor. If you will go and sit in the kitchen, closing both inner doors on your way as far as you can, we shall conduct a small experiment. You must stay where you are but call out every sound you hear, no matter how irrelevant it seems. Do you think you can manage that?'

'I can try.'

I went back through the sitting room, my eyes fixed on the blood-soaked rug where Sarah Ashby must have breathed her last, and sat in the upright chair by the stove, trying not to imagine the blade penetrating her chest and bursting her heart, stabbing her body again and again, slitting her slender white throat and her pale little cheek.

'I hear traffic,' I called, 'carriage wheels and horses' hooves coming from the main street, I should think, and a dog is barking, a yappy one... A church clock... striking the quarter hour... Somebody shouting, two people, women, but I cannot hear what they are saying. The shop bell... A pigeon is cooing. Still traffic all the time, but a bit muffled now... A floorboard creaking... Rustling.'

The door from the sitting room squealed open and Sidney Grice appeared on tiptoe.

'I was able to go out of the front door silently,' he said, dropping on to his heels, 'simply by putting my hand over the bell. Why did the murderer not do the same? It is all but impossible to come in without it ringing, though. Was it easy to hear?'

'Yes, quite loud.'

'And, even though I crept through the sitting room, you heard something.'

'Yes, but if I were asleep...'

'Think of all the activity that must have been going on in there.' He knocked on the wall behind the bed.

'Why do you keep tapping everything?' I asked.

'This shop is obviously part of a larger building,' he said. 'Often these structures are divided with flimsy walls and false ceilings, but these are solid and there are no trapdoors or secret doors. So there are only two ways in or out of here and we have been through them both.' Sidney Grice puffed out his cheeks. 'Come on, March. Let us go on to the street.'

12

The Little Match Girl

THE CONSTABLE WAS already on his feet when we stepped outside.

'I told you to clear off,' he was shouting at a ragged match girl as she scurried away, scratching the ground before her with a long stick.

'Leave her be,' Sidney Grice said quietly. 'She could be our first witness.'

The constable guffawed. 'Not much of a witness. Blind as a slug, she is.'

'All the less reason to bully her,' I said.

'He is a policeman. It is his job to bully people,' Sidney Grice said. 'Excuse me,' he called as the girl stepped round the dead rat.

She stopped and turned, her eyes covered in bandages torn from old sacking, as we hurried to catch up with her.

'I ain't done nuffink wrong,' she said, and I saw that she was no more than a child, eleven or twelve years old, shoeless, with bowed legs and arms little thicker than her stick. She hardly looked strong enough to support her own body, let alone the heavy wooden tray hanging from a rope around her neck.

'That seems unlikely,' Sidney Grice said, 'but we only want to talk to you.'

'Who's *we*?'

'This is Mr Grice and I am Miss Middleton. We mean you no harm.'

At some time in the past her left cheekbone had been broken for her face had an angular depression.

'What d'you want then?'

'Just a few questions,' Sidney Grice said, 'and I shall pay for your answers.'

''Ow much?'

I noticed her upper and lower front teeth were missing and she had red spots around her lips.

'That depends how truthful your answers are.' He raised her chin with his cane handle. 'And you may be sure that I shall know.'

'Are you the law?'

'I am a gentleman.'

She put protective hands over her tray. 'My sister told me to stay clear of them.'

'Mr Grice is a respectable gentleman,' I told her.

She cocked her head. 'That's the sort she warned me off.'

Sidney Grice chuckled. 'Is this your regular place of business?'

'Might be.'

'And were you here on Monday, the day before yesterday?'

The match girl started. 'You can't stick that on me.'

'We are not accusing you of anything,' I said.

'Not yet.' My guardian leaned forwards to scrutinize her.

'I was sittink there on my patch all day. Ask anyone. Loads of geezers come by all the time. One of them was a peeler. 'E gave me a happle.'

'What colour was the apple?'

She looked blank.

'That was unkind,' I said.

'And your *patch* is usually outside the ironmonger's shop?' Sidney Grice asked, unabashed.

'Just where that peeler is now,' she nodded. 'He's sittink on my box what Mr Hashby puts out for me. 'E's a gent, Mr Hashby is. Lets me sit there all day 'cause it's sheltered from the rain and my wares don't get wet. I get beaten if they do. 'E brings me water and bits to eat sometimes. 'E gave me a cup of milk just after the eight o'clock bells.'

'How was his manner?'

'Same as ever. 'E's a quiet sort. No side to 'im. No airs. No graces. 'E's a goodun, Mr Hashby is.'

'What was Mrs Ashby like?' I asked, and Sidney Grice clicked his tongue.

The match girl sucked in her cheeks one at a time and said, 'Like a lot of fings, she was.'

'What sort of things?'

'Like a miserable dung cow mostly. Always movink me on when 'e wasn't about. 'E caught her pushink me out into the snow once. 'Ad a good old barney about that, they did. 'Ad lots of good old barneys, they did.'

'What about?'

My guardian groaned. 'This is not a ladies' sewing circle.'

The match girl picked her nose and wiped it on her shoulder.

'Everyfink and nuffink, I should fink.'

Sidney Grice walked round her.

'So how was business on Monday?' he asked from behind.

She half turned her head. 'I didn't get nuffink. In fact I got worse than nuffink. Some bleedin' bleeder pinched one of my boxes and I got a clout and no supper and 'ave to pay for it.'

'Who stole your matches?' I asked.

'I—'

'Never mind that,' my guardian broke in. 'I am hardly likely to take up the case. How was business for Mr Ashby?'

'He didn't get nuffink neeva. Not a soul came in all day or night.'

'You are sure of that?'

'As sure as catshit.'

He came back to face her. 'What time did you finish?'

''Bout midnight. Bit after.'

'But why do you work so late?' I asked.

'There's blokes comink out of the pubs bowf end of this street and there's some of 'em wants a light.'

'And you heard nothing?'

The match girl pulled the remnants of a woollen coat tighter about her chicken-bone shoulders.

''Course I 'eard somefink. I may be blind but I ain't deaf. You'd better make this worf my while, mister.' Her voice dropped. 'I pushed open the door to put the empty milk cup back inside like I always do, when I 'eard Mr Hashby scream-ink. *Oh my Gawd, Sarah. 'Elp! Murder!*'

'And then what?' Sidney Grice asked.

'Nuffink.' The match girl spat at her feet. 'I scarpered and that's it.'

Sidney Grice reached into his trouser pocket and produced two coins.

'Now,' he said, 'you may have both these coins if you can tell me what they are.'

The match girl picked something out of her hair and crushed it between her forefinger and the black broken nail of her thumb.

''Ow am I s'posed to do that then?'

'Use your eyes,' he said.

'How cruel you are,' I said.

'Just as you used them when you walked round that dead rat without even touching it with your stick.'

The match girl shook her head. 'It was there when I came up the road.'

'I had moved it several inches with my cane.'

'I smelled it.'

Sidney Grice laughed and tossed the coins high in the air, and the match girl caught them deftly.

'It is not she who is blind,' he told me. 'It is our friend in uniform over there. I think we have finished here, Miss Middleton.'

'But why play games with her?' I asked as we walked back along the passage. 'If people realize she is not blind she will lose her trade, and she is half-starved as it is.'

'I wanted to see how good a liar she is,' Sidney Grice prodded with his stick at a tramp sleeping on the roadside, 'and, unusually for a member of the crueller sex, she proved herself to be a poor one.'

We walked past one of the public houses the match girl had spoken of, the Duke of Marlborough. The fumes of beer and gin were overpoweringly delicious.

'What now?' I asked as he flicked a broken pot out of the way.

'Well, March. How about some liquid refreshment? I believe that we have earned ourselves a good strong drink today,' he said, 'of tea.'

I wish I could say it was love at first sight. You came in bleeding from a head wound, having tried to smash a champagne bottle over it for a wager. It was three o'clock in the morning and I was cross. Not only had you disturbed me, you had dragged my father out of bed when he had a long day and an early start before him. He had to stitch your scalp. I held the kerosene lamp with one hand and tried to hold you still with the other and I told you off for making a fuss, and then you vomited over your mess kit and I told you off again.

You came to apologize the next morning, very pale and sorry for yourself, more of a contrite boy than a warrior of the Empire. I could not even pretend to be cross when you presented me with a wilting white rose, stepped backwards, tripped over a box of bandages and opened up your wound again. It was the start of love at second sight and love at second sight is love eternal. You told me that so it must be true.

13

Marylebone Police Station

MARYLEBONE POLICE STATION was much quieter than I had expected, with just one ragged family sitting resentfully on a bench. The police would have already dealt with the drunks and assaults from the night before, Sidney Grice explained, and most of the policemen would be out patrolling the streets or cadging refreshments from hotel kitchens.

The desk sergeant put his pen down and gazed at us with watery eyes.

'Hotels is a valuable source of information, Mr Grice,' he said, 'and even amateurs as like yourself must see the necessariness of that.'

'If it were a crime to murder the English language you would be unpicking ochre even now,' Sidney Grice told him. 'I am here to interview one William Ashby.'

'On whom's authorityization?' He dipped his pen in an inkwell and wiped the handle clean.

'Mine.' I turned to see the speaker of that word coming into the hall. It was a tall man, in his early thirties I guessed, slim and dark-haired with a rule-straight side-parting. He had neatly trimmed moustaches and a smart charcoal suit. 'Good afternoon, Mr Grice.'

The two men shook hands.

'Inspector Pound,' my guardian said. 'May I introduce Miss Middleton, my assistant on this case?'

Inspector Pound put his thumbs into his pockets. 'Since when have you needed assistance from a girl?' His eyes were powder blue, iced with contempt.

Sidney Grice said, 'I am training her to be of help in dealing with more delicate feminine cases.'

This was news to me, but I returned that cold gaze and said, 'I am delighted to make your acquaintance, Inspector Pound, especially after following so many of your investigations in the newspapers.'

In truth I had never even heard of the inspector, but it seemed to me that the frost of his gaze melted a little as he adjusted his tie and said, 'As long as she doesn't go swooning at the first hint of bad language.'

'I won't if you don't,' I said, and the inspector sniffed.

'I shall answer for her composure.' Sidney Grice tucked his cane under his arm.

'You are in good time,' Inspector Pound said. 'We are just about to question the prisoner again.'

'Has he said anything yet?' Sidney Grice asked as we passed down a long echoing corridor.

'Just what you would expect.' The inspector had a long easy stride and I had to walk quickly to keep up with him. 'He loved his wife. He was asleep. He doesn't know anything.'

'And what do you make of him?' Sidney Grice was limping quite badly as he struggled with the pace.

'I don't know,' the inspector said over his shoulder. We stopped at an end door and I saw that he was troubled. 'The devil of it is, Mr Grice, he seems such a nice chap, very gentle and unassuming.'

'Remember Libby Jacobs.' Sidney Grice took a breath. 'As sweet a girl as ever trod this earth. She garrotted her four sisters with a cheese wire in order to have a bed to herself, though.'

'All the same,' Inspector Pound said, 'you get a nose for these things and mine tells me he is an innocent man.'

'With all due respect to your nostrils' – Sidney Grice flicked his hair back – 'I think I shall see what the man has to say for himself before I make any judgements.'

'You may mock.' The inspector put his hand to the door. 'But it is not often wrong.'

'Before we go in,' Sidney Grice reached into his satchel to bring out two pieces of white card, tied with a string bow which he tugged open. 'Have you ever seen this before?'

The inspector glanced over.

'It is the letter Ashby wrote to ask for your help.'

'Did you see him write it?'

'Yes, and I saw him put it in the envelope and write on that and hand it to his mother-in-law.'

'And how was her demeanour?'

'Very upset, sobbing, at one point she fainted.'

'How did she fall?' I asked.

'Downwards, of course.' The inspector rolled his eyes.

'No, I meant...'

'I had her down as much more self-contained than that,' Sidney Grice broke in, and Inspector Pound snorted.

'She had just lost her daughter and been told that her son-in-law was accused of the murder.'

'But she took his side. Did she not?'

'Most definitely. She told him not to worry. She would get the best help available.'

'And here I am,' Sidney Grice said as the door swung slowly open.

14

The Hounds of Hell

THE MAN WAS seated at a table, head on hand and eyes closed. He was under a tall grilled window, side on to us, in a shabby grey suit with a collarless open-necked shirt. A portly constable stood behind him.

'Hello, Ashby,' Inspector Pound said, and the man opened his eyes. 'You have a visitor.'

The prisoner looked at us and seemed to light up a little. He half stood but the constable put a hand on his shoulder and pressed him down again.

'Mr Grice,' the prisoner said. 'I recognize you from your photograph in the newspapers. You must have received my letter. Thank you so much for coming.'

'I am Miss Middleton,' I said. 'I am here to help.'

His face lit in a brief strained smile. 'I am much in need of that.'

It would have been difficult to guess his age for his face was darkened by stubble and paled by distress, but there was still something boyish about it. Perhaps it was the dark yellow mass of hair falling into a long fringe over his forehead or the eyes so big and brown, though slightly reddened now. Had I not known differently, I would have judged him to be in his late twenties.

'Fetch two chairs,' Inspector Pound told the constable.

'And a cup of tea would be welcome,' Sidney Grice called after him, and then stood surveying the prisoner for a while.

'Let him stand for a moment,' he said to the inspector. 'It is not right to shake hands with a seated man.'

William Ashby rose stiffly to his feet.

'You have a strong grip and a direct gaze,' my guardian told him, 'but I have seen many a villain with as honest a face.'

'The world knows me for a decent man.' William Ashby's voice was firm and clear. 'I don't think you will find anyone to disagree with that.'

Sidney Grice paused. 'Why did you write that letter?'

William Ashby looked puzzled. 'To ask for your help, Mr Grice.'

My guardian scoffed. 'You will have to do better than that.'

'I cannot do better than the truth.'

'What are you?' Sidney Grice surveyed him head to toe. 'Five foot six?'

'I should say so.'

'And are you left- or right-handed?'

'Left.'

'In everything?'

'Pretty well.'

'So you write with your left hand?'

'Yes.'

Somebody was whistling as they walked along the corridor.

'And you hold a knife with your left? When you are eating, I mean.'

'Yes. Always.'

The whistling got louder, then faded.

'Please be seated.'

Sidney Grice put his satchel on the floor, hung his coat carefully over the back of a chair and sat to face the prisoner, placing his notebook on the table between them.

'How old are you, Mr Ashby?'

'Thirty-five in July.'

Sidney Grice wrote something in his notebook, but crossed it out immediately.

'If you wish to celebrate that birthday you had better answer truthfully.'

'You may rely upon that, sir.' He glanced at me.

'Unfortunately for you, I cannot,' Sidney Grice said, 'for you have already told me at least one untruth. You are not a fraction over five feet and five inches.'

William Ashby looked aghast.

'But I have not measured myself for years, Mr Grice.'

'It is such a small detail,' I said.

'It is the small details that decide whether a man walks free or to the gallows,' Sidney Grice said. 'I do not suppose you told a deliberate lie, but an inaccurate fact is misleading whatever the motive behind it.'

William Ashby put his hands on the table palm down and inhaled deeply.

'I shall try to be more accurate.'

'You are not from round here originally.'

'No. I come from Lancashire.'

'Wigan,' I said, and William Ashby looked surprised. I added, 'I know the accent even though you have learned not to drop your H's. I was—'

'Thank you, Miss Middleton,' Sidney Grice broke in.

The constable returned, struggling with two chairs and kicking the door shut behind him.

75

'No tea then?' Sidney Grice asked and the constable huffed.

'I only have two hands.'

'Even without your police training I had observed that,' Sidney Grice said, 'but I also note that they are both free now.'

Inspector Pound nodded to the constable.

'Nice and hot,' Sidney Grice said as the constable lumbered off.

Inspector Pound sat at the end of the table and I between my guardian and the wall.

'And how old was your wife?'

'Sarah was just turned nineteen.'

'So young,' I said, and Sidney Grice asked, 'Did you celebrate her birthday?'

'I bought her a pair of cotton gloves.'

'What colour?'

'Brown. I do not see—'

'It is not for you to *see*.' Sidney Grice's voice flashed with anger. 'The barrister who uses all his professional cunning to try to propel you to your grave will not explain the purpose of his questioning. How long had you been married?'

William Ashby met my eyes again in a silent plea.

'I am sorry... one year in April just gone.'

'Happily?'

William Ashby cleared his throat. 'Very.'

'Never a cross word?'

'Many a cross word,' William Ashby said, 'and all of them regretted then forgotten. Have you ever been in love?'

'With my work,' Sidney Grice said, 'and I have an ivory-handled revolver which I am quite fond of. Was this your first marriage?'

The constable returned with a mug of tea.

'Yes. Though I was engaged to be married when I was twenty-three.' William Ashby hung his head for a moment. 'She died of the fever.'

'And no one could save her,' Sidney Grice mocked.

'That is a horrible thing to say,' I told him.

'And was your wife's life insured?' my guardian asked, as if I had not spoken.

'Yes. For one hundred pounds with Jonah Insurance. I took out the policy just before Christmas.'

The constable coughed to cover his amusement and Sidney Grice made another note, underlined it, and said, 'Why so much? Indeed, why any at all?'

William Ashby ran his fingers through his hair. 'I don't know. I took advice.'

'From whom?'

'Mr Jonah himself.'

The constable sniggered.

'Share the joke, man,' Inspector Pound said.

'He's a bit of a card, old Jonah.' The constable grinned. 'Sell you the spit in your mouth, he could. Insurance is his latest trick, but be sure he will never pay a penny out to anyone. He closes his businesses the moment the claims start coming in and opens another the next day.'

I watched William Ashby but his reaction to this news was one of complete indifference.

'I hope you did not do it for the money then,' Sidney Grice said and, for the first time, the prisoner flared. His face reddened and he clenched the edge of the table as if to upturn it.

'I did *not* kill her,' he said. 'Not for money. Not for rage. Not for jealousy. Not for nothing. I loved...' He put his face in his hands. 'Dear God, how I loved her.' William Ashby's shoulders shook with sobs and Sidney Grice leaned forwards to separate his fingers and peer between them.

'Real tears,' Sidney Grice said, and leaned back to jot something down.

'Have you no heart?' I asked.

'Not him,' Inspector Pound said, as Sidney Grice surveyed his tea and pulled a wry face.

'It has been contaminated by milk.'

'Everybody has milk,' the constable said.

'Twenty-five per cent of the men and twenty per cent of the people in this room do not,' my guardian said, and slid the mug across the table. 'Would you like it?'

William Ashby looked up. 'Why, thank you, Mr Grice.' He wiped his face with his sleeve and took a noisy slurp. 'I am sorry. Please continue and I shall try to contain myself.'

Sidney Grice's manner remained brusque. He put his pencil down and said, 'You have no children?'

'No. None.'

'Nor lost any?'

'Not even in stillbirth.'

My guardian pulled out his watch and flipped open the lid. 'How was your business performing?'

'Quite well. We keep busy most of the year.'

'In profit?' He clipped the lid shut.

'A pound or two a week.'

'Your wife died on Monday night.'

'About eleven thirty, yes.'

'Tell me about Sunday.'

William Ashby had a gulp of the tea. 'What would you like to know?'

'In what way did it differ from every other Sunday?'

William Ashby chewed his lower lip at the corner and

smoothed back his hair, and said at last, 'I cannot think of anything unusual, Mr Grice. We generally lie in a bit later on Sundays. The shop is closed, of course, unless anybody knocks.'

'And did anybody?'

'No.'

'You do not go to church?'

'No, but that doesn't make me a murderer.'

'That much is true,' Inspector Pound said. 'We hanged the Rector of St Bartholomew's two years ago, and you could not find a more regular churchgoer than he. Mr Grice was of great service in helping me to bring him to justice.'

My guardian waved an impatient hand and asked, 'Did you go to school?'

William Ashby looked indignant. 'Yes.'

'Where?'

'A Miss Brickett ran a class on Divers Street in Whitechapel. I went until I was twelve.'

'I thought you were brought up in Wigan.'

'Until I was seven. My father brought us down to London in search of work. He was a carpenter.'

'What about Monday?' Sidney Grice asked. 'Did anything untoward happen before, say, ten o'clock that night?'

'Nothing that I can think of.'

William Ashby finished his tea but still held the mug. His hand was trembling.

'Was it a busy day?'

'No, sir. It was a very quiet day. We had two customers in the morning and none at all after that.'

'What did they buy?'

'One bought a length of twine, the other a quarter pound of tacks.'

'Were you in the shop all day?'

'We were both in the house all day but we took it in turns to man the shop. I did the morning. Then we both did the afternoon. I tidied the shelves a bit and Sarah swept and washed the floor. Then I did the evening until about nine o'clock, then Sarah took over again.'

'You keep long hours.'

'We can't afford to lose any custom. If we are closed people will go elsewhere and may never come back.'

Sidney Grice was busy writing but I could not read his notes. He used some kind of shorthand, tiny complex symbols with occasional sweeps like musical clefs.

'No strangers loitering about? Nothing suspicious?'

'Nothing that struck me or that Sarah mentioned.' The prisoner stared into his mug. 'I wish to God we had seen something. I would not have left my wife in the shop alone if I had any concerns.'

Sidney Grice tapped his teeth with his pencil and said, 'Tell me exactly what happened from nine o'clock onwards.'

'It was only just after nine by the church clock,' William Ashby answered. 'Sarah came in and said she had left me some bread and cheese in the kitchen. I took a glass of milk out to Tilly.'

'Who is Tilly? The cat?' Inspector Pound asked.

'A match girl. I let her shelter in my doorway. She is half-starved, poor thing, and she has a cruel master – her own uncle, I believe.'

'And then?'

'I went out the back to the kitchen.'

'And your wife was still in the shop?'

'She was polishing the countertop.'

'So you ate your bread and cheese?'

'Yes.'

'Any rabbit?'

William Ashby looked bemused. 'No. We had a rabbit for our Sunday dinner, though.'

'In the kitchen?'

'No. In the sitting room by the fire.'

Sidney Grice made a note followed by a large question mark.

'And what did you burn in the fire?'

'Wood, I think. It is cheaper than coal and I had an old packing crate.'

'Not paper?'

'No, but Sarah burnt some paper on Monday afternoon. I was cross with her for I dislike the waste, but she said it was just old scraps from clearing up the shop so I let the matter drop.'

'You did not fly into a violent rage?'

William Ashby took a sharp breath and let it shudder out of him.

'I thought you were here to help me, Mr Grice.'

'Mrs Dillinger made the same mistake.' Sidney Grice smiled fleetingly. 'I am here to discover the truth. If you are innocent, I shall be all the help you need. If you are guilty, the hounds of hell shall not save you.'

William Ashby's gaze lingered in mine before he pulled away and looked my guardian in the eye.

'If you can prove the truth, that is all I ask.'

'Perhaps you accidentally stabbed her,' Sidney Grice said. 'Maybe your wife ran on to your knife or you slipped – nobody could blame you for that – or perhaps you just meant to cut her a few times to teach her a lesson. That would only count as manslaughter with a sympathetic jury.'

'I did not kill her,' William Ashby said quietly and slowly. 'I should be arranging a Christian burial for my wife and comforting her mother, not being held here like a common felon.'

Sidney Grice shrugged. 'What did you do after your supper?'

'I fell asleep.'

'When?'

'About half an hour later. I don't have a watch and the clock only strikes the hour.'

'Where?'

'In my chair by the stove.'

I heard a clinking and glanced over to see my guardian toying with two halfpennies, flipping them over in his left hand.

'Was the stove lit?' Sidney Grice asked.

'No. Sarah did her baking on Sunday.'

'Would the sitting room not have been more comfortable?'

'Certainly, but I just fell asleep in the chair.'

The constable sneezed into his hand.

'Was the back door open or closed?'

'Closed.'

'Locked?'

'No. We use it to get to the privy so we only lock it at night.'

'What about the door into the sitting room?'

'Closed as far as it goes. The frame sags in the middle.'

'And that from the sitting room to the shop?'

'Closed to cut the draughts.'

Sidney Grice winced and rubbed his left shoulder.

'And when did you awake?'

'About eleven to a quarter past, I suppose. I didn't check the time. How could I?'

'So you slept for two hours in an upright wooden chair?'

'How did you know what chair it was?'

Sidney Grice raised a finger. 'You are quick off the mark, Mr Ashby, but I have not come here for you to cross-examine me. I ask you again. Why sleep in the kitchen when you have a serviceable sitting room with an armchair and a bed?'

'Have you been in my house?'

'Answer the question, Ashby,' Inspector Pound said, and the constable shifted wearily on his legs.

William Ashby looked about himself.

'Stay seated,' the constable said.

'I don't know. I just fell asleep.'

'Can I say something?' I asked.

'Mr Grice's presence is unorthodox enough.' Inspector Pound looked at his watch. 'If word got out we had a mere girl interrogating our prisoners we would be the laughing stock of London.'

Sidney Grice handed me his pencil and I wrote on a clean page, *The chair was rickety.*

'Tell him that,' Sidney Grice said, and the inspector huffed.

'The chair was rickety and not very comfortable,' I said, and William Ashby nodded.

'I was a drummer boy in the Loyal North Lancashire Regiment when I was fourteen,' he said. 'On a forced march I could fall asleep without breaking step. Sometimes the whole platoon would do likewise. If I can sleep marching up a mountain in driving sleet, I can sleep as well in a chair as you in your feather bed, miss.'

'So you are a heavy sleeper.' Sidney Grice slipped the coins back into his pocket.

'No, sir. Very light. I wake at the slightest sound usually. When you have been on watch you learn to sleep with your ears open.'

'A drummer boy on watch?'

'I took the Queen's shilling when I was sixteen.'

'Why the Lancashires? You lived in London by then.'

'It is a family tradition – my father and grandfather and—'

'I know what family tradition means,' Sidney Grice interrupted. 'How long were you in the army?'

'Fifteen years.'

'And then?'

William Ashby's left cheek ticked for a few seconds.

'I came to London to work in my Uncle Edwin's shop and that's where I met Sarah. We fell in love and got wed and then Uncle Edwin died.'

'How convenient.' Sidney Grice scratched his ear. 'Was he stabbed to death as well?'

William Ashby shuddered and shook his head. 'He was sixty-nine with a bad heart and weak lungs, and he left everything to us – the shop immediately and the rest of his estate to be put into trust for another five years.'

Sidney Grice circled my comment and said, 'Why were you so tired? By your own account you had not had a heavy day's work.'

'I slept badly on Sunday night. Something disturbed the donkeys stabled next to the shop. The rats, I expect. We get a lot since the sewer burst. And I can assure you, Mr Grice, if you have four braying donkeys on the other side of a lath-and-plaster wall, you would have to be a very heavy sleeper indeed not to be disturbed.'

'So what woke you up on Monday night?'

'The shop bell ringing.'

'How many times?'

'Just once.'

'Then what?'

'I went to see if Sarah was all right.'

'Why would she not be?'

'I don't like her dealing with customers late at night. There is a public house either end of our – my street. We get drunks and troublemakers. Not often, but a woman by herself is fair game to a man with a belly full of ale.'

William Ashby turned the mug slowly. It had a chipped rim.

'So you woke up and went into the sitting room immediately?' Sidney Grice asked.

'Pretty well.'

'Did you do anything first?'

'No. I just didn't see any reason to hurry – would to God that I had.'

'Did you have your boots on?'

'Yes.' The tic started again.

'And laced?'

'Yes.'

'The same boots as you are wearing now?'

'Yes.'

'Stand up and show me the soles.'

William Ashby rose and turned away and lifted his feet up, one at a time like a horse at the smithy.

'Thank you.'

'Sit,' the constable said.

Somebody was shouting in the corridor – a woman – something about oysters, and a door slammed.

'What about your clothes?'

'His mother-in-law brought him a change,' Inspector Pound said. 'They were saturated in gore.'

'And where are the soiled clothes now?'

'She took them to launder,' the inspector said, and Sidney Grice's hand shot to his eye.

'And you let her walk out with them?'

'No need to get upset, Mr Grice,' Inspector Pound said. 'We searched the pockets but there was nothing in them except a stained handkerchief.'

My guardian massaged his closed lids.

'Stained from blood soaked through the pocket or from being used to wipe something?'

Inspector Pound shrugged. 'Stained.'

'And what of the bloodstains? Were they in pools or droplets? Were the knees of his trousers soaked? Was the jacket damaged – buttons torn off or loosened, or lapels misshapen? Sleeves stretched? Stitching snagged? What of his shirt? Buttons missing, handprints, rips?'

'It was just a ruined old suit,' Inspector Pound said.

'And quite possibly one of our most important witnesses,' Sidney Grice said, and the constable chuckled.

'Be quiet,' Inspector Pound told him.

'When God created fools he put the biggest of them into uniform and gave them helmets to prevent any thoughts entering their heads,' Sidney Grice said, his face almost drained with anger, as Inspector Pound turned on him.

'I will not have you address one of my officers in such a manner,' he said.

'When is washday?' I asked.

Inspector Pound stood up. 'That does it,' he said. 'I will thank you both to step outside this room.'

'I was only asking Mr Ashby when Mrs Dillinger does her laundry,' I said. 'Few women do it more than once a week.'

Sidney Grice said, 'I hardly—'

'Now,' the inspector said and flung open the door.

15

The Last Sigh

OUT IN THE corridor Inspector Pound waited for two constables and an old woman to go by.

'I am surprised at you, Mr Grice. I can just about tolerate the presence of a girl at an official interrogation, but I cannot have you insulting the force and one of my officers in front of my prisoner.'

The woman was handcuffed and struggling.

'On a point of law,' Sidney Grice said, 'William Ashby is Her Majesty's prisoner, not yours and—'

'And nothing,' the inspector broke in. 'It is completely unacceptable. And as for you, Miss Middletone—'

'Middle*ton*,' I said.

'Middle-whatever. I told you not to interview the suspect.'

'No, you did not,' I said. 'You told me you could not have a mere girl interrogating him and, whilst I may be a girl, I assure you, Inspector, there is nothing *mere* about me.'

The inspector looked at me for a while and laughed.

'Looks like I have met my match here,' he said, and Sidney Grice smiled.

'If I have caused offence, please accept my apologies.'

The woman started to growl.

'We will let it pass.' Inspector Pound straightened his tie, and one of the constables screamed. The woman had dropped to the floor and was biting his ankle. The other constable hit her three times with his truncheon and she flopped to the floor. Inspector Pound shook his head wearily. 'What do you make of Ashby then?'

'Guilty as Cain.'

'Can you prove that?'

The injured constable kicked the woman's stomach and leaped back as she snapped at him again.

'Given time,' Sidney Grice said, and we went back into the room.

William Ashby was blowing his nose and the constable came to attention.

'So when *is* washday?' the inspector asked.

'She was going to do the clothes straight away,' William Ashby said. 'They had her daughter's blood on them.'

We sat at the table again.

'So what happened after you heard the bell?' the inspector asked.

'I went into the sitting room.'

'The door opens outwards from the kitchen, does it not?' Sidney Grice asked, and William Ashby nodded. 'I went into the sitting room, expecting just to pass through, but then I saw her.'

'What part of her?' Sidney Grice said.

'Her feet and the bottom of her dress.'

'You are sure about that?'

'Yes. Why?'

Sidney Grice flicked back a page of his notebook and circled a line of shorthand.

'Her dress had not risen up her legs?'

William Ashby stopped turning the mug.

'No,' he said. 'Her dress was not disarrayed.'

He put the mug down very carefully.

'How was the room lit?'

'By the gas lamp turned low, and I suppose there would have been light coming from the door to the kitchen. Oh, and the door to the shop was open.'

'You are sure?'

'As certain as I am here.'

'And where was she lying?'

'On the floor.' William Ashby paused and coughed. 'Between the table and the wall.'

'What colour were her boots?' Sidney Grice asked, and William Ashby ran his fingers through his hair.

'I don't remember. Black, I expect. The light isn't very good and I wasn't paying attention.'

'But you saw her boots?'

William Ashby looked at me and I returned his gaze.

'Yes.' He looked away. 'I think so.'

'You *think* so?' Sidney Grice said. 'You have just told us you saw her feet. Did you see her boots?'

'I must have but I did not notice the colour. Why would I?'

'How many pairs of boots did your wife have?'

'Two. One black and one brown. Why is this so important?'

Sidney Grice was very still. He was fixed on the suspect as I have seen a python with a monkey. Very quietly, he said, 'Did anybody take your wife's boots off after she was found?'

William Ashby blinked. 'What? No. Why would they?'

'Because she had none on when she was taken away.'

William Ashby looked baffled. 'Maybe they were stolen,' he said. 'Good boots cost money.'

Sidney Grice touched his eye. 'Both pairs are still under the bed.'

William Ashby swallowed and pushed his fringe back. 'Maybe I was wrong. Maybe she had none on. It was dark and—'

Sidney Grice broke in. 'So how can you be so certain that her dress was not disarrayed?'

'I don't know.'

'Your wife would not man the shop barefooted.'

'No, I suppose not.'

'Then why was she barefooted?'

'I don't know. I can't think straight.'

Sidney Grice was scribbling furiously.

'Let us leave the matter of the boots for a moment,' Inspector Pound said. 'What happened next?'

'I went over to her.' William Ashby's voice died in his throat and he closed his eyes. 'I thought she must have fainted.'

'Was she prone to fainting?' I asked, and the inspector shot me a glance but said nothing.

'No.' He opened his eyes and whispered, 'But then she was not prone to being murdered.' He stared at us and at nothing. He sucked the air and blew it out, looked up and then down and said, 'I saw her and it was horrible. My beautiful Sarah lay there on the floor and I hardly knew her. She had become a thing, a disgusting waxwork. It oozed and stank of blood. The eyes like a dead animal and the mouth was open, stupid and revolting. She had been taken from me and some... thing flung on to the floor in her place. I ran into the shop, hoping to see her there, to scoop her in my arms and carry her to safety... But the shop was empty. No Sarah. Nothing. I must have dreamed it or somehow got it all wrong. But when I ran back into the sitting room, sweet Jesus, she was still there, and I kneeled at her side and picked her up and I thought I heard a sigh and I thought *She is still alive. She has just had some accident and fallen over. I will call Tilly to fetch a doctor.* And then I saw the opening in her throat and her open mouth full of blackness, and I knew.'

I reached out and put my hand on his, white with clutching the mug, and he looked at me, his eyes burning with pain, and he swallowed and licked his lips and said, 'God bless you, miss.' I knew then, as certainly as I have ever known anything, that William Ashby was innocent of the murder of his wife.

'Do you want to have time to compose yourself?' Inspector Pound asked gently, but William Ashby shook his head and said, 'It will not get any easier.'

'Go on.' Sidney Grice lifted my hand away and dropped it on the table.

'I laid her back.'

'Did you move her body away from where you had found it?'

'No. I just held her and laid her back.'

'She was still warm?'

A spasm of disgust welled up in William Ashby's throat. 'Yes.'

'And not stiff?'

'For heaven's sake,' Inspector Pound said.

'I've seen men die,' William Ashby said. 'She was just gone when I first went into the room. It was only that I could not let myself believe it.'

'You said she sighed,' Inspector Pound reminded him.

'I thought she did.' William Ashby plunged his hands into his hair. 'It may be I was wrong.'

'I have seen men die too,' I said, 'when I used to assist my father in surgery. They would sometimes groan as we lifted them from the table. He told me it is the air being forced from their lungs.'

'What did you do then?' Sidney Grice asked.

'I stood up and I cried out *Help! Murder! Murder!* And I went into the shop and cried it out again, and I ran into the street and I saw Tilly running round the corner and a drunk staggering after her.'

Sidney Grice leaned suddenly towards him.

'What did the drunk look like?' The words snapped out.

'I don't know.'

'Man or woman?'

'Man.'

'Well or badly dressed?'

'Badly. Very badly, I think. What does it matter?'

'Perhaps it was the murderer pretending to be drunk,' Inspector Pound said. 'Would you recognize him again?'

'No. It was dark. The nearest gas lamp is on Hopper Street. We live in its shadows... We lived... ' His voice wandered away and he looked lost.

The constable straightened his back.

'What happened next?'

'I cried out again and people came. Then a peeler, who sent a boy running to get help. Mr Brown who owns the donkeys and sleeps above them came. We have had many arguments about the noise they make, but he put a blanket over my shoulders and gave me a gin.'

William Ashby put the mug down heavily and covered his face and blew between his hands, while Sidney Grice sat back and looked at him. He might have been regarding a creature in a menagerie rather than a man so recently and so cruelly made a widower. He leafed through his notes and added a few more.

'*Rivincita*,' he said, as though to himself. William Ashby's face was blank. Sidney Grice looked at him. 'What does *Rivincita* mean, Mr Ashby?'

'I don't know.'

Sidney Grice scratched his forehead and fell silent. He was not looking at the prisoner or anyone else. He seemed to be inspecting his fingernails.

'Is that it?' Inspector Pound asked.

'Very nearly,' Sidney Grice said, 'but I should like the prisoner to look at this.'

Sidney Grice delved down and brought out the white cloth bag, tipping its content on to the table.

'Do you recognize this?' he asked, and William Ashby reached out and his hand trembled.

'Leave it,' the constable said, and the hand hovered before it fell away.

'It is very like one of the knives I had in my shop.'

'One?' Sidney Grice queried.

'I had two,' William Ashby said. 'They were made for me about three months ago by Philby's Cutlers on Midden Street. I drew the design myself from my memory of an Arab dagger I saw once in barracks. I thought they might sell well as a novelty, but I only sold one of them and that was a week ago.'

'To whom?'

'I don't know his name, but I would know him again anywhere,' William Ashby replied. 'He was a foreigner, Italian, I should say from the way he stuck A's to the end of his words.'

'Describe him,' Sidney Grice said.

'A strange man.' William Ashby blinked rapidly. 'About normal height but that was all that was normal about him. He had an enormous head and a huge shock of curly red hair and long drooping moustaches.'

'Red also?'

'Yes, and a big hooked nose, and a long flapping cloak and a canary waistcoat, and he carried a stick with an ivory top in the shape of a monkey.'

Sidney Grice perked up.

'Canary?'

'Yes. Yellow.'

My guardian tugged his earlobe and asked, 'Do you or did your wife own any yellow clothes?'

'No. None.'

I opened my mouth, but Sidney Grice put his finger to his lips and said, 'Continue.'

'He came into the shop, striding about like he was on a stage. He took a quick look about him and pointed at the knife. *Showa me that.* He had a quick look at it and said *Thata will serve me nicely.* And he paid and walked straight out of the shop with it clasped in his hand. He didn't even want it wrapped. Sarah was there too. We laughed about him.'

'Did he say anything else?'

'No.'

'Did you tell anybody else about him?'

'Mrs Dillinger,' William Ashby said, 'and a few customers, just for the joke.'

'So this is the knife you did not sell?'

'It looks like it,' William Ashby said, 'and, if you took it from my cabinet, it must be.'

'Have you ever used it?'

'No.'

'Or cut yourself with it?'

'No.'

'Have any customers touched it?'

'No.'

'You are certain of that?' Sidney Grice was rattling out the questions so fast that William Ashby hardly had time to answer.

'Yes.'

'Did your wife ever touch it – to polish it, for example?'

'No. I looked after the knife cabinet. She did not like it.'

Inspector Pound turned the knife over.

'Looks clean.'

'Do not touch the blade,' Sidney Grice said, and turned back to William Ashby. 'So you are willing to swear that this blade has never had any blood on it whilst it has been in your possession?'

William Ashby looked him straight in the eye. 'On my life, Mr Grice.' And Sidney Grice smiled coldly. 'Your life may well depend upon it, Mr Ashby.' He picked up the knife again and said to the constable, 'I shall need a clean bowl of clean water.'

The constable looked uncertain.

'Well, see to it, man.' Inspector Pound clicked his fingers and the constable hurried out. 'What is your game, Mr Grice?'

'You know my interest in science, Inspector,' my guardian said. 'Well, there is a certain professor of pharmacology at the University College by the name of Cornelius Latingate, and he has devised a chemical analysis which is specific to the presence of haemoglobin.'

'I'm sorry, Mr Grice,' William Ashby said, 'but you have lost me.'

'It is a test for blood.' Sidney Grice took his watch out but did not open it, making it spin on its chain and swing side to side. 'It can detect the presence of blood on an apparently clean surface or material for up to five days after it has been put there. Imagine finding a bloodstained garment, for example. The owner of that garment insists it is paint. This test can verify or refute his story. The older tests only detected iron, and would show positive reactions to blood *and* rust. This test detects a protein present only in blood and is so sensitive that it will demonstrate a drop so small as to be invisible to the naked eye.'

'But if I had killed my wife with that knife why would I put it back on display?' William Ashby asked.

'Who said it was on display?' Sidney Grice jumped in.

'It was in my cabinet.'

'Was it?'

'I know it was, that very day, because I took out all the knives and polished them,' William Ashby said.

'But was it in the cabinet after the murder?'

'I suppose it was. I did not check.'

'Your wife was killed with a knife with a blade shaped like this, Mr Ashby.'

William Ashby sat up and said, 'Then it must have been him.'

'Why would an Italian stranger murder your wife?'

'I have no idea.'

'Why would he behave in such an ostentatious manner? It could only be to make sure that you remembered him.' Sidney Grice stopped his watch spinning and peered at the back of it.

'I don't know.'

'*Rivincita* means *revenge*. It was written on the wall in your wife's blood.'

'No.' William Ashby swept the mug on to the floor. 'You are just saying these things to torment me.' He stood up.

'It is true,' I said, and the prisoner put his hand to his mouth.

'Sit down, Ashby.' Inspector Pound stepped towards him and William Ashby sank back on to his chair, breathing fast.

'Why would an Italian want revenge upon your wife?' Sidney Grice slipped the watch back into his waistcoat.

'I don't know, Mr Grice.'

'Did she or you have any Italian friends or enemies?'

'No.'

'Any Italian ancestry or connections of any kind?'

'Not that I know of.' William Ashby put his hands down, trying to calm himself. 'I don't know who he was or why he did what he did, but I do know one thing, Mr Grice. There is a madman on the loose and he must be found immediately before he murders some other poor woman and, when he does, will you accuse her poor husband too?'

The door opened.

'If your knife fails the test, then I shall follow your unlikely lead,' Sidney Grice said as the constable returned, carrying a white-enamelled basin and placing it very carefully on the table.

'You took your time,' Sidney Grice told him.

'Sorry, sir, but there wasn't a bowl in the station.'

Sidney Grice touched it and flinched. 'The water is near frozen.'

He produced a blue bottle with a handwritten label on it from his bag and tipped a few white crystals into the basin.

'Observe,' he said, 'how clear the solution is.'

We all stood to watch.

'Now,' Sidney Grice said, 'observe what happens if I take this knife and swirl it around the solution to wash any possible residue off it. See that? It has turned red. There is no doubt about it. This knife has been in contact with blood within the last few days.'

'But that is not possible.' William Ashby looked bewildered.

'There is no doubt about it,' Sidney Grice said, and William Ashby sat down suddenly and ran his fingers over his brow.

'I remember now,' he said. 'I nicked myself when I wiped it.'

'Show me the cut.'

'It was very small.'

'It was deep enough to bleed so it cannot have healed yet.'

William Ashby looked at us both and inhaled deeply, and said, 'I do not know how, Mr Grice, but you have put a noose round my neck.'

'How did that knife get blood on it?' Sidney Grice asked, but William Ashby lowered his head and did not reply.

'I am damned,' he said at last.

'So you are,' Sidney Grice said and snapped his notebook shut.

———— ❖ ————

16

The Red Book

'I WILL SEE you out, Mr Grice,' Inspector Pound said, and we pushed back our chairs. 'Take him back to the cell, Constable.'

William Ashby did not look at us as we left, though I looked back at him, climbing to his feet, a crumpled man.

'Come into my office.' Inspector Pound led us into an even smaller room, the desk piled high with manuscripts and red-bound volumes. 'I cannot offer you a seat.' The one chair was overflowing with more papers. 'I could take a year to sort through the paperwork that my superiors expect me to do and let a thousand murderers, housebreakers and pickpockets run free.' He leaned back on the edge of the desk. 'Well, that was a pretty experiment, Mr Grice. Are you sure it is fool-proof? Something like that will swing a case, but we will not look very clever if the defence can show that your crystals change colour with strawberry jam.'

He toed a ball of paper under the desk.

'Professor Latingate will back us all the way.' Sidney Grice leaned his shoulder against the wall. 'He is a good performer in the witness box. Juries are impressed by academic titles and he can show them enough chemical charts to convince them he knows what he is talking about. I have seen him demonstrate his test to an audience of fellow scientists who were invited to bring whatever substances they thought might change the colour of the crystals, and not one of them succeeded.'

'Funny.' Inspector Pound frowned. 'I would have bet my liver on him being innocent.'

Sidney Grice snorted and said, 'Ashby knew he had been caught out. He said as much.'

'I do not think he did,' I said. 'I think he was dumb-founded. He did not know how to counter your science.'

'Mr Grice has never been wrong yet,' Inspector Pound told me. 'Why, we had Gertrude Rayment, the Lambeth Poisoner, walking free before he was able to prove that she had reset her grandmother clock to concoct an alibi.'

'It is not only the test that shows his guilt,' Sidney Grice said. 'It is the whole gamut of inconsistencies in his version of events that condemn him.'

'How so?' I tried not to show my loathing of his smugness.

Sidney Grice gave his little smile. 'If we are to believe Ashby's account of events, a preposterous Italian man came into his shop and flamboyantly purchased the very weapon with which he intended to murder the lady of the house a couple of weeks later.'

'But why would he make that story up?' I asked.

'To send us on a wild goose chase for somebody we could never find because he never existed.' Sidney Grice measured his words for my poor brain. 'He was doubtless hoping to make us think the Slurry Street murderer was on the prowl again.'

'If that rumour was circulated there would be mass panic.' The inspector picked up a red book and stuffed it on to a shelf. 'Which is another good reason to discount it.'

Another book fell dully off the end of the shelf and he booted it under his desk.

'What about the writing in blood?' I asked. '*Rivincita*.'

Inspector Pound shrugged. 'The sewer press claimed that was smeared on the walls in Slurry Street, but I never saw it.'

'But it seems such an unlikely story to make up,' I said. 'Who would believe it?'

'If a story is unlikely, then it is unlikely to be true,' Inspector Pound said. 'Surely even a girl can see the sense of that.'

'If a story is unlikely to be made up, then it is likely to be true,' I said. 'Surely even a man can grasp that logic.'

The inspector puffed and said, 'You should hear some of the tales we get. We had a man yesterday who said that all the stolen goods in his cellar were put there by a man from the moon. An Italian is a little easier to believe than that.'

Sidney Grice waved his hand irritably and said, 'Next we are expected to believe that he sat in an uncomfortable chair fast asleep while this fellow opened his back door.'

'Why the back door?' Inspector Pound asked.

'Because there are muddy footprints in the yard to the door, which stop at the threshold, and because he claims that the shop bell only sounded once,' Sidney Grice said. 'So this fabulous Italian let a cold draught and the outside noise in, took off his boots, crept past, opened a squeaky door and murdered Sarah Ashby without Mr Ashby even stirring.'

'If he were lying, surely he would have pretended to be a heavy sleeper,' I said.

'His mother-in-law had already gainsaid him,' Sidney Grice said, 'and, though he could not have known that, he knew she would in court. Also, the match girl, who was well-disposed to Ashby and ill-disposed to his wife and so may be tempted to corroborate his story, has already told us that nobody entered or left the shop for some hours before he raised the alarm.'

'And why would his wife be in her bare feet if she were working in the shop?' Inspector Pound said.

'Precisely.' Sidney Grice jabbed the air with his forefinger. 'I have examined her feet and, although she had a bruise, they were clean and soft with no splinters in them. The shop floor is rough and unplaned.'

'But he is so gentle,' I said.

'He was a soldier,' my guardian reminded me. 'Soldiers shoot and bayonet people for a living. How gentle an occupation is that?'

'I still do not believe it.'

'There are a few loose ends,' Sidney Grice said, 'but I have no doubt that I shall be able to tie them together. Why do you think I offered the prisoner my mug of tea?'

'Because you did not like it,' I answered.

'Because I never intended to drink it,' he continued. 'I noticed that his left hand was more developed than the right, but I needed to be sure. A left-handed man will shake hands with his right. He may even have been bullied at school to hold a pen with his right and at home to eat right-handedly, but he will invariably pick up a cup or glass with his left, just as William Ashby did repeatedly. You will remember, Miss Middleton, how I observed from the fatal wound that the murderer was left-handed.'

'But why would he kill her?' I asked, and knew immediately what the answer would be.

'For the insurance,' Inspector Pound explained patiently. 'A hundred pounds is no mean sum of money. I have never had so much all at once in all my life, and I doubt he makes that much in four or five years.'

'And we already know they argued over trivial things such as the match girl taking shelter,' Sidney Grice said. 'I am sure, if we ask the neighbours, we will find they argued about more than that. He admitted himself that they quarrelled about her burning that paper. Trivial things mount up in a marriage and, when added to a huge financial incentive, it does not take much of a spark to set things off. He was not to know that the policy was worthless.'

'But he showed no emotion when he found out that he had committed the murder with no possibility of profiting from it, even if he escapes the hangman,' I said.

A pigeon struck the window and fell away.

'He's a cool one. I will grant you that.' The inspector picked an old apple core off his desk and tossed it to the bin, where it bounced off the rim on to the floor.

'And why put the murder weapon back on public display?' I asked.

'Perhaps he intended to dispose of the knife elsewhere but found his exit blocked by the sewage,' Sidney Grice said, 'which would explain the blood on the gate handle and the footprints going back to the house, and the fact that he had taken his boots off when he got to the house. You remember I asked to see them. They were quite clean. Probably he used some sheets of paper to wipe them and the knife and put the paper in the fire, but there was still hardened mud in the cleats of the soles. Besides, where better to hide a knife than in a cabinet of knives? If it had been found stuck down the back of a cupboard, it would instantly have raised suspicion.'

'I thought you said he argued with his wife about burning the paper,' I said.

'There's the cleverness of the man,' Inspector Pound said.

'He told us they had argued about that but they probably argued about something else. I, for example, am always having to scold my sister for her poor housekeeping.'

'I am still not convinced,' I told him, and Sidney Grice laughed unpleasantly and said, 'Fortunately, it is not you we have to convince, Miss Middleton.'

'I understand your reservations.' Inspector Pound kicked the apple core into a corner. 'For I had them myself until Mr Grice settled my doubts with his irrefutable arguments. But you have to understand, dear girl, that the erratic fluttering of the feminine heart is no match for the clear logic and penetrating insight of the masculine brain.'

'Thank you for explaining that,' I said, and the inspector smiled and reached out and, for one awful moment, I thought he was going to pat me on the head.

'That is all right,' he said and patted me on the head. 'Let me show you to the door.' Back in the corridor, he said, 'You are new to London, are you not, Miss Middleton?'

'Yes. I have lived in many places but never London before.'

'A word to the wise then,' he said. 'Watch out for the horses – they bite – and for foreigners.'

'What do they do?' I asked, but he shook his head and said, 'I hope you shall never find out. Good day, Miss Middleton.'

I stood on the pavement while Sidney Grice hailed a series of cabs which all seemed to be occupied, and found myself outside a butcher's window. The carcass of a piglet hung from a steel hook, skinned and flabby and thick with flies; and a string of rabbits glared glazedly through the smeared glass. Trotters stood in a neat line like second-hand shoes and a cow's tongue drooped slimily off a shelf. I remembered what my guardian had said about meat, but most of all I remembered the field station and the agonies of the mutilated, and the man made monstrous because he had no face.

Sidney Grice had fallen into an argument with a Chinaman over who had seen a hansom first, and while they quarrelled two young men jumped in and it drove off with the Chinaman running after it. I put out my hand and an empty hansom stopped.

'125 Gower Street, please.'

'Off to see Sidney Grice, are you?' the driver called over his shoulder. ''E lives there, 'e does. Queer cove by all accounts.'

With a flick of the whip we were off. On the way home we passed the New Gloucester Theatre. The doors were closed as one would expect in the afternoon, but there was a sign on the door *Rigoletto Performance Cancelled.*

'You see, March,' my guardian said and laughed. 'You can never find an Italian when you want one.' And he reached over to pat my hand.

17

The Duke's Head

THE DUKE OF Marlborough's head had been knocked off and his horse was chipped, presumably by children throwing stones.

'A word of warning,' Sidney Grice shouted over the rumble of a passing coal wagon. 'There will be men in there whose judgement has been impaired by the overconsumption of alcohol. You may well find things a little lively.'

He shooed a balding mongrel away with his cane.

'It seems peaceful enough,' I said and, indeed, the saloon was almost deserted. Two old men sat playing a game with torn cards and another stood at the bar looking into his empty beer glass.

The barman was rolling a cigarette and looked up angrily as we approached.

'Can't you read?' he asked.

'How kind of you to enquire,' Sidney Grice said, 'but, since this is not a lending library, I cannot see why my literacy is of any concern to you.'

'No women.' The barman scooped up two used tankards and put them on the shelf behind him. 'That's what it says on the door.'

'Why, I thought that was a complaint and I was trying to

rectify it.' Sidney Grice ran his finger along the brass bar-rail.

'I don't like clever jacks and I don't like women. Get out, both of you.' The barman pointed to the door.

A large wet brown fungus was growing from the side of his nose and up under his right eye, almost obscuring it. I searched through my handbag.

'Do you know what this is?' I asked and the barman snatched it from me.

'A railway ticket,' he said. 'And you'd better 'urry 'cause it's dated last week. Out.'

Sidney Grice reached into the pocket of his Ulster and asked, 'Do you know what this is?'

'Half a sov,' the barman said.

'It is indeed,' Sidney Grice said, 'and I should like to give it to you.'

'What's stopping you?' The barman divided a pile of half-smoked scrapings with a rusty knife.

'Your surly attitude.' Sidney Grice wiped his finger on a handkerchief. 'And the fact that you have not answered my questions yet.'

'The fact is you 'aven't asked any yet.' The barman twisted some orange shreds into a yellowed scrap of newspaper.

'William Ashby.'

'The Mangle Street Murderer.' The barman nodded. 'I know you now. You're posh coves in search of a thrill, the sort what slips the caretaker half a crown to nose around the scene and look at the blood and shudder and go 'ome for muffins in front of the fire. You make me sick, your sort.'

'Did you know him?' I asked.

'No,' the barman said. 'I don't believe 'e ever set foot in 'ere. I wish he 'ad, then 'arf of Fleet Street would be in 'ere wanting stories and tippling off expenses, and they can tipple for the Empire, those 'acks can. Is that it? Cough up.'

My guardian held up the coin out of the barman's reach. 'You never went to his shop?'

'No, and I've answered all your questions so cough up.'

Sidney Grice slapped the coin on the bar top and said, 'That was money ill spent. I would have got more from the dog outside.'

'Fleas and distemper for a start,' I said.

'I know him,' the old man at the bar said, and Sidney Grice turned.

Apart from his faded grey and bloodshot eyes, the old man's face was scarcely visible beneath his thickly matted tobacco-stained beard and enormous tangle of greasy grey hair.

'You do?' I asked.

'Indeed I do. Nice old boy. His name is Jasper.'

'What are you talking about?'

'The dog, of course.' The old man scratched himself inside the front of his brown corduroy trousers.

My guardian snapped, 'I am not interested in the dog.'

'Yes, you are. I heard you both talking about him.'

'The Lord did not test Job's patience as he has tested mine.' Sidney Grice turned away. 'Come along, Miss Middleton. We are wasting our time with these wretched people in this wretched place.'

''Ere,' the barman said. 'Who and where you calling wretched?'

Sidney Grice began to tell him, but I was more interested in the old man.

'I hope you do not mind me observing but you seem very well-spoken for a man in your straits,' I said.

'You may observe what you like if you buy me a pint,' he said, and I slipped him a shilling.

'That should buy you a few.'

'I was born a toff. Mine was one of the few noble families to stay true to the old faith, but they still managed to come out of the Reformation richer than they went into it. Town houses and country mansions, thousands of acres, armies of servants, the lot.' The old man slid the coin to the barman, who filled his glass with flat dark stout without pausing in telling my guardian how stuck-up he was. 'All gone now, though... gone...' His voice trailed off.

'What happened?'

'I would sooner drink from a drain,' Sidney Grice was saying.

'Went into a project for constructing a tunnel all the way from Dover to Calais.' The old man raised his glass to me. 'Just imagine being able to set foot in France only two hours after leaving our shores, no matter how the wind might blow, the thunder crack and the sea rage over your head. Put everything I had into that scheme.'

'So what went wrong?'

The old man drank deep and wiped his lips with the back of his hand.

'We had not excavated a hundred yards nor left dry land before the government got wind of it and closed our business down. They seemed to think the Frenchies would be sending their armies through it, though Boney was put under porphyry with pomp long before we had started. We lost every farthing.'

'Come along, Miss Middleton,' Sidney Grice said.

'Surely a man of your education could find some employment,' I said, but the old man shook his head and said,

'Nobody will employ a man who is their better. They feel uncomfortable. And few men are better than I.'

'Have you no friends?'

'I had a hundred,' he said, 'whilst I was prosperous.' He took another draught. 'But they were gone like seagulls in a storm as my fortune died, leaving only debts in its estate.'

'This is a madhouse,' Sidney Grice said. 'No wonder Ashby never set foot in the place.'

'I know him,' the old man said.

'Do not start that again.' Sidney Grice chopped the air with the flat of his hand. 'We are not talking about that verminous mongrel.'

'I was referring to William Ashby.' The old man drained his pint and slid the glass back to the barman. 'I know him well.'

'What is your name?'

The old man straightened and clicked his heels. 'Sir Randolph Cosmo Napier, at your service.'

'No. Your real name,' Sidney Grice said.

'Sir Randolph Cosmo Napier,' the old man said with a slight bow from the waist.

Sidney Grice peered at him closely.

'Good lord,' he said. 'I believe you knew my father.'

18

The Man in the Rabbit Skin Coat

GOING TO THE theatre seemed too trivial an occupation for my guardian but he had been sent two tickets
by the playwright, whose lost writing case he had
retrieved, and told me that an evening out might improve my
humour.

The play was a comedy, though you would not have known
it from Sidney Grice's pained expression throughout.

'I do not know who committed the greater crime,' he said
as we collected our cloaks, 'the thief who stole the script or I
who returned it.'

The traffic flowed quite well by London standards and our
journey home was uneventful until we got to Sadler Street.
'On two matters of business,' my guardian said, 'Inspector
Pound made enquiries of Mrs Dillinger and she told him that
she had burnt her son-in-law's clothing.'

'Can you blame her?'

There were people shouting in the distance.

'Yes. I find it easy to blame people but I blame the police
even more.' The shouting was getting louder. 'Also, I have
checked with Philby's Cutlers on Midden Street and they only
ever made two of those knives – a special order for William
Ashby.'

'So he was telling the truth about that.'

Sidney Grice tossed his head. 'The best lies are always flavoured with the truth but if the substance is rotten, it will stink no matter how much you try to disguise it.'

The hansom stopped and Sidney Grice tapped the roof with his cane and called up to the driver, 'What is the delay?'

The driver slid open his hatch and glared down at us. 'Road blocked.'

'Then turn round, man.'

'Can't back up with that lot behind me,' the driver said, 'and there's no room to turn.'

'Has there been an accident?'

'Trouble,' the driver said and slammed his hatch shut.

'What sort of trouble?' I asked and Sidney Grice looked out.

'A crowd,' he said. 'They have upturned a cart of barrels and set fire to it at the junction.'

The hatch slid open.

'My 'orse don't like it,' the driver said. We could feel it shifting restlessly and hear its hooves strike the cobbles.

I leaned out of my side.

'Keep your head in,' Sidney Grice said.

'I have as much right to look as you.'

There was a bonfire at the crossroads ahead and only one hansom between it and us. The fire must have been ten feet high, but it was growing by the minute. Men in rags were running out from an alleyway, throwing planks of wood on top, their faces lit crimson then white, then dissolving into the shadows as they ran back again.

'They must have looted a builder's yard,' my guardian said.

I could hear hammering and a squealing wrench and three

men appeared carrying a door, which they swung and tossed into the blaze.

'They will have the street on fire at this rate,' Sidney Grice said. 'Where are the police? Cosy behind their desks, no doubt.'

I heard the smashing of glass.

The driver shouted, 'You, behind, back your nag up and let us through.'

'Can't. It's blocked back to Onion Street,' the other driver shouted, 'and there's more coming up behind that.'

'Lord help us now.' Sidney Grice half stood to lean out further. 'They have broken into a vintner's. It is difficult to reason with any mob, but one with wine in its belly is a very unpredictable beast indeed.'

There was a loud crack as something burst in the middle of the fire and sparks sprayed high into the night, a shower of intense red stars crackling into the sky, glowing as they fell, floating over the rooftops. Then two men appeared, dragging a third between them. His face was down, but in the flaring lights I saw his head clearly. He had a great shock of red hair. The two men lifted him. His body was limp. They raised him higher and flung him on to the pyre. I bit my glove.

'It is a mannequin,' Sidney Grice said. 'They still think there is an Italian murderer on the loose.'

An elderly couple in evening-wear got out of the carriage in front and hurried away past my window.

'I suggest you do the same,' my guardian said. 'You will be quite safe if you go on to Onion Street and you should be able to hail a cab there.'

'What about you?'

'A gentleman never flees the rabble,' he told me. 'They are a pack of dogs and must be subdued or they will rampage through the city and anarchy shall prevail.'

'But—'

My guardian silenced me with a finger to his lips. 'And once you have anarchy the whole of society will be teetering on the brink,' he said, 'of *democracy*.'

'But what can you do?'

'Confront them.' Sidney Grice flung the flap open. He stood and waited to help me alight. 'Walk briskly but do not run,' he said. 'Keep your head up and speak to no one. I shall see you at home.'

'There's a couple of gentry,' a woman's voice called out from the crowd, and half a dozen of them broke away and ran towards us.

'You have money?'

'Yes but—'

'Quickly then, and tell Molly to put the kettle on.' Sidney Grice turned to face them. 'Stand back,' he shouted, his voice high and thin against the roar, 'or you shall get a taste of my cane.'

The front runner stopped two feet in front of him. He was a big man with strong bared arms and a face covered in circular tattoos, and he grinned at the little man in front of him.

'Try your twig against this, squire,' he said, raising an iron bar like a cudgel.

Sidney Grice darted forwards. He did not try to strike the man with his stick but lunged like a fencer, the tip of his cane catching the man under his chin. The man dropped his bar and clutched his throat.

'You shall all disperse immediately,' Sidney Grice shouted.

'I know you.' A wiry man in a long rabbit-skin coat grinned at him toothily. 'You're that detective geezer what started all this, getting an innocent man arrested and leaving our women at the mercy of a dago.'

'I shall not warn you again.' Sidney Grice waved his cane
and the man laughed and said, 'What, a pipsqueak like you?'
Sidney Grice sprang forwards, but the wiry man was ready
for him and batted the cane to one side. His fist lashed out
and caught my guardian on the temple, and Sidney Grice
reeled backwards, his hand to his head. A tall man came from
behind and clutched him in a bear hug, and another stepped
forwards with a broken bottle.

'Let's see how clever you are now,' he said, waving the
jagged edge in his face.

I picked up the bar. It was heavy and I did not want to kill
the man with the bottle, so I tapped him just once upon the
head. He fell like a dropped doll. I swung the bar at the man
who was holding my guardian and caught him on the shoulder. He yelped and let go, but I had only made him angrier.
The tall man reached behind himself and brought out a knife.
It had a broad straight blade and flashed as he lunged towards
me. I raised the bar, but somebody grabbed my wrist and
twisted hard. I cried out and the bar clattered on to the road.

Sidney Grice let his hand drop.

'My eye,' he screamed, his empty socket black in the fire-
light. 'They have cut it out.'

The thin man opened his hands and said, 'But how?'

'God help you all now.' Sidney Grice clutched his face
again. 'It is a hanging offence to put a man's eye out.'

The group looked uncertain.

I put my head down and my hand over my mouth and
squawked in my best cockney, 'Look awt, 'ere come the
peelers.'

The group looked about.

'Where?' The thin man tried to peer between them.

The tall man clambered to his feet. 'Never mind where.

Just get out of 'ere.' They ran back to the main group. 'Coppers. Scarper.'

'Damned eye fell out and smashed,' Sidney Grice said, 'and that was my best one. Come with me, March. This matter is getting out of control. The sooner we get Ashby convicted, the better for everyone.'

'Except him,' I said.

Sidney Grice primped his bow tie, brushed down his cape, looked about him and smiled. 'It was probably your accent that scared them more than anything.' But then his face fell. 'But I told you to get away.'

'They could have killed you.'

Sidney Grice snorted. 'I had the measure of them.'

'Well, of all the ungrateful—' I began, but my guardian put his hand to my arm.

'You did well,' he said. 'Very well… for a mere girl.'

19

The Uses of Gutta-percha

SIDNEY GRICE WAS in his study when I found him the next morning, bent low over a steaming copper pan balanced on a tripod over a spirit lamp.

'March.' He looked up. 'Do you know what this is?' He held up a brown stick about the size of my forefinger.

'Gutta-percha,' I said.

'One of the wonders of the modern age.' My guardian nodded. 'Do you know, this substance can be used to make jewellery or furniture and has even been wrapped round the underwater cable which connects us with the lost colonies of America – though why we should wish to communicate with them is a mystery even I could not solve.'

'My father used it sometimes to fill holes in soldiers' teeth,' I told him.

'Then you will know that it softens when heated in boiling water.' He dipped one end into the pan, swirled it around for a minute or so, lifted it out, prodded it and said, 'That should be soft enough.' My guardian pulled his left eyelids apart and pushed the stick between them and winced. 'A little warm perhaps.' He pulled it out and inspected it. 'Not too bad. A small air blow but I am sure they can fill that.'

'It will be deformed,' I said.

'What?'

'It will still be soft and will have distorted on removal,' I explained.

Sidney Grice huffed.

'Nonsense.' He wrapped the gutta-percha in a roll of cotton wool. 'I know exactly what I am doing.'

'But you are always having problems with the fit of your false eyes.'

'That is poor workmanship.' He blew the flame out and put a glass top over the wick. 'Anyway, I have other things to do.'

'So do I.'

Neither of us asked or said what.

Today was Tuesday the fifth of July.

One thousand and ninety-six days ago in another country in another continent, in what seemed like another world, you came to me. Tall and very smart in your second lieutenant's uniform. You were unusually quiet and serious, even a little nervous. Was something wrong?

'Oh, I am hopeless at this,' you said and I knew immediately.

You went down on one knee and your sword dipped into the white dust and there in the square in full view of the passers-by you brought out a little red cotton pouch.

'I don't even know which finger.'

'The third on my left hand,' I said.

'Is that a yes then?'

I looked into your eyes, the bluest I have ever seen, and they looked back at me with such love that I could not even speak. I nodded.

'I had to guess the size.'
Your hand trembled as it took mine.
'It fits perfectly.'
'Do you like it?'
'It is beautiful.'
People were applauding and the band began to play
– 'Lily Bolero', I think.
'And so are you.'
Oh, Edward, you were the beautiful one.
I held the ring to the sun. It did not glitter but it
shone all the brighter for that.

'Shall you be in for lunch?' my guardian asked so suddenly that I jumped.

20

The Name of the Game

THE TRAIN WAS pulling in when I arrived, and windows were dropping for heads to peer through and hands to reach out and twist handles. A slender figure in a blue coat and bonnet was disembarking at the rear of the train and I was hurrying towards it when I heard a voice cry, 'March,' and turned to see Harriet Fitzpatrick climbing down two yards behind me.

'I have not fallen on quite such hard times,' she said and, as the smoke thinned, I saw that I had been approaching a shabby old woman from a third-class carriage.

Harriet laughed and took my hands and kissed me. 'Why, March, I should hardly have recognized you from the mouse I left here a month ago. You are quite the fashionable lady now. Clearly London suits you. I assume it is me you have come to meet. Oh, I do love that little coat. We must have a drink together and we must have it now. How is the famous Mr Grice? Run along, porter. I do not need you and shall not tip. All my friends and enemies were simply emerald with envy when I told them I had met his protégée. You must tell me some thrilling stories about him. I am quite exhausted from inventing them.' All the time she was talking, Harriet had slipped her arm through mine and was propelling me on to the forecourt and through it, back on to the road. 'Oh fish. The sun is out and I did not think to bring a parasol.'

'Do we need a cab?'

'We can walk it quite easily,' Harriet said. 'Where did you get that sumptuous dress and what is that colour called? I am so out of touch, living in the wilds of Warwickshire.'

'It came from a shop on Regent Street that was recommended to me by Mr Grice,' I said. 'The lady in the shop described it as dusty rose satin.'

'What a clever name and how it complements your complexion. You do not call him Sidney?'

'No,' I said. 'He is very correct.'

'Then he is either a pompous ass or helplessly in love with you,' she told me, 'and, from the way you did not colour when you mentioned him, I should say the former. Oh, how disappointing. I had hoped he would have made you his mistress by now. How I could have entertained my tea-circle with that story. But do not worry, I shall anyway.'

'Really, Harriet,' I said, but she had suddenly stopped and paled. I took her hand. 'Whatever is the matter?'

'That is the second lady I have observed today wearing white lace,' she said. 'Please tell me it is not the style for I look ghastly in white, as if I have been decked out for my coffin.'

'That is a dreadful thing to say,' I told her, trying hard to keep a serious face, 'but no, I do not think it is in fashion.'

Harriet squeezed my hand and said, 'Then I am sorely tempted to tell my friends that it is.'

We crossed the road and turned right.

'Why, this is where I live.' I indicated up Gower Street. 'Why do you not come in for tea?'

Harriet stopped. 'Is your guardian at home?' she asked.

'I think so.'

'Then I shall not,' she said. 'I expect he is fat and bald, and I shall be unable to disguise my disappointment.'

'He is not.'

'But I shall still refuse your invitation.' Harriet pulled me on. 'Heroes are best imagined. I wish I never met mine every day of my life. So now we must make a little detour to avoid being seen.'

We carried on to the bottom of Tottenham Court Road and turned up it and then left into Beaumont Place, and along it into Huntley Street and a neat little house with a green-painted door.

'Is this a friend's house?' I asked.

'No, but it is a friendly house.' Harriet tugged the bell. 'Three quick rings. Remember that if you should come here again.'

The door was opened a crack and then fully by a slender middle-aged lady in a long red gown. 'Twinkle.' She threw out her arms. 'Come in. I see you have a companion.'

'Violet, this is Eve,' Harriet said as the lady put out her hand to greet me.

'Any friend of Twinkle's is welcome here,' she said and turned back to Harriet. 'Go through. Nobody else has arrived yet and I have one or two things to attend to, but I am sure you will make yourselves at home.'

Harriet led the way into a cosy sitting room and sat me on the chintz sofa.

'Why Eve?' I asked.

'It was the first name that came to my head.'

'But—'

'Nobody uses their real names here.'

Harriet took the stopper off a cut-glass decanter on the sideboard and poured two generous tumblers, handing me one as she sat beside me.

'What sort of a place is this?'

Harriet laughed. 'Don't be alarmed. You have heard of gentlemen's clubs; well, this is a ladies' club. We meet. We talk. We dine. It is a sanctuary from men.' She clinked my glass. 'And goodness knows we need one. Oh, Bombay, my favourite. Cheerio.'

'But why the secrecy?' I asked.

Harriet sipped her drink and said, 'Can you imagine the unwelcome attention we would get if our existence was made public – the men who would hang about outside – the innuendos? Now, tell me everything. Is your guardian kind to you?'

I took a large drink. 'Sidney Grice is not kind to anybody.'

'Does he abuse you?'

'No. He is aloof and cares only for money and his work.'

'Doubtless he is arrogant and overbearing too.'

'Yes, and he does not approve of alcohol.'

'The man is a monster.'

'And he will not let me smoke.'

'You have just described Mr Fitzpatrick perfectly,' Harriet said, 'and probably every man you will ever come across. Men are not like us. They are made of stronger but cruder materials.'

'My father was not severe.'

'Then you must miss him dreadfully.' Harriet put her hand on mine and let it lie there.

We put our glasses on a low rectangular table covered in red cloth.

'Have you heard of the Ashby case?' I asked.

'The Whitechapel Wife Killer? Who has not? In Rugby we talk of little else. Yet another triumph for Sidney Grice, it would seem.'

'I believe William Ashby is an innocent man,' I said, 'but I do not know what to do.'

Harriet was silent for a moment.

'The first thing you should do is have another gin and the second is to put your hair up.'

'But what of William Ashby?'

'You cannot help him.' She took a few loose strands of my hair and placed them behind my ear.

'It is all so horrible,' I said. 'I can hardly bear to be in the same room as my guardian, let alone stay in his house.'

'But where would you go and how would you support yourself?'

'I could find somewhere. I can typewrite.'

Harriet stroked my hand. 'The gutters are choked with girls who can typewrite.'

'But he will have William Ashby executed.'

'Have you considered that Mr Grice might be right?' Harriet asked. 'He is, after all, hugely experienced in these matters. Besides, if William Ashby is innocent, he will surely be acquitted. That is what the judge and jury are for.'

'You do not know how my guardian can distort the truth,' I said, 'and William Ashby is such a gentle person. He could never have been so savage.'

'You met him?'

'When he was being interrogated.'

Harriet went to the sideboard and recharged our glasses.

'If you had seen how wretched he was when his wife died,' I said.

'Perhaps he was filled with remorse.'

'No,' I told her. 'It was in his eyes. The real murderer is still free. I know it. There must be something I can do.'

Harriet handed me my glass and sat down close to me.

'Nothing,' she said. 'We are women. We can do nothing.'

21

The Trial

MONDAY 23 JUNE is marked in my journal as the start of the twenty-sixth week and the sixth full moon of the year. It was also the first and only day of the trial of William Daniel Ashby.

The courthouse was full and many disappointed sensation-seekers crowded the halls of the Old Bailey Criminal Courts in hope of news or even catching a glimpse of the man the press had branded a notorious murderer. It was said a space had already been prepared in Madame Tussauds' Chamber of Horrors and that the museum's agents were busy in the public gallery making sketches for his effigy. Inspector Pound had reserved seats for Sidney Grice and me in the front row on the left-hand side of the court next to the aisle. Mrs Dillinger sat on the right at the far end of the row, still in mourning, and accompanied by a cherubic priest. She nodded gently to me but did not glance at my companion.

William Ashby was brought in by two police constables and sat on a bench in the dock, aged and shrunken dreadfully in the few weeks since I had first met him. He was wearing a black suit. 'They will take his tie away when he goes back to his cell,' Sidney Grice whispered. 'Nothing upsets them more than a man making his own noose.'

William Ashby rose, entered a plea of Not Guilty and sat again. He coughed spasmodically but the judge refused the request of his lawyer, Mr Treadwell, for an adjournment.

'If we postponed hearings every time a convict had a spot of gaol fever we should never get anything done,' Mr Justice Peters said.

'With all due respect, my lord, my client is not a convict.'

'That remains to be seen.' The judge waved for him to be seated.

William Ashby was called first and cut a shambling figure as he hobbled to the witness box. His face was bruised. We learned later that he had had a fall, pushed down a flight of stone steps by a housebreaker. His voice was hoarse and wheezing and he kept having to clear his throat, and his eyes were puffy and red and made him look a little shifty.

He stuck to his story, neither adding nor retracting any details, and asserted his innocence quietly under the cross-examination of Sir Robert Finebray QC, but the case against him was strong and William Ashby's version of events fell apart under the weight of Inspector Pound's observations, as outlined for him by my guardian. The final question seemed a little odd to the judge. Did William Ashby ever frequent the Duke of Marlborough public house?

'No, sir. I prefer the company in the Black Boy.'

For a moment there seemed to be some hope. Professor Latingate's demonstration went wrong. His crystals reacted to three different solutions, but it transpired that his assistant had accidentally contaminated them with a cut finger.

And then the final nail was hammered in. I hardly recognized Sir Randolph Cosmo Napier as he took the oath. He stood erect and clean-shaven apart from a magnificent pair of waxed and curled moustaches. His clothes were tailored and decorated with a gorgeous red silk cravat, and his manner was authoritative. He had fallen on hard times, he admitted openly, and the suit had been bought for him, but a gentleman was always a gentleman and a gentleman's word was his bond. Even Judge Peters sat a little straighter as he heard the evidence. Sir Randolph had met William Ashby a number of times.

'Seemed a nice young man. Bought me a drink once in a while.'

'Did he ever mention his wife?'

'Never,' Sir Randolph said, 'except for the last time I saw him.'

'And when was that?'

'The Saturday night before he killed her.'

Mr Treadwell sprang up. 'Objection, my lord. This man was not a witness to the murder. He cannot assume that my client is guilty.'

'A man is entitled to his opinion,' Sir Randolph said, 'and this is still a free country, I believe.'

'Well spoken, Sir Randolph.' Mr Justice Peters scratched under his wig with a quill. 'Objection overruled.'

'Except when it comes to digging holes,' Sir Randolph said.

'Let us move on.' Sir Robert Finebray rustled his notes.

'They'd have let me dig if there were gold to be found.'

'Thank you, Sir Randolph,' Sir Robert Finebray said.

'Or coal even. Black gold, some call it.'

'On this last occasion, did you talk to the accused?'

'I have already said as much.' His voice rang out across the courtroom.

'And what line did the conversation take?'

'I observed to Ashby that my glass was empty,' Sir

Randolph said, 'and he offered to refill it for me, but not as graciously as he might have. Indeed, he seemed quite distracted.'

'In what way?'

'In every way.'

The audience chuckled.

'Please continue,' Sir Robert said.

'That is what I am trying to do,' Sir Randolph retorted.

'Then please do.'

'I shall. Did you not fag for me at Rugby?'

Sidney Grice was clicking halfpennies in his left hand.

'I was at Eton,' Sir Robert said.

'So was I,' the judge said. 'Did you fag for me, Finebray?'

'I did not, my lord.'

Mr Justice Peters banged his gavel to quell the laughter and signalled the witness to proceed.

'Ashby seemed agitated,' Sir Randolph said, 'and, when I asked him what the matter was, he told me he had had an argument with his wife.'

I watched William Ashby as this evidence was being given. He leaned forward, listening intently, but his face betrayed no particular concern.

'I asked him what the trouble was,' Sir Randolph said, 'and he told me that he had scolded her over her extravagance. She had bought some material for a curtain and was having it made up by a local seamstress. He thought the material too expensive and that his wife should have made it up herself.'

William Ashby nodded slightly.

'He told me that the money could have gone towards more stock,' Sir Randolph said, 'and that he had stormed out of the house when she refused to cancel the order.'

'Did he say anything else?' Sir Robert asked.

'Indeed, he did,' Sir Randolph said. 'We talked about the lack of respect modern youths have for their elders and we agreed that they lacked the discipline that a spell in the army would have given them. Ashby is an army man himself. He knows all about that.'

Sir Robert struggled to conceal his frustration. 'Yes, but did he mention his wife again?'

'He said she was a pretty little thing,' the witness said, and Sir Robert flapped his notes.

'Oh, for heaven's sake,' Sidney Grice said under his breath. He was rattling the halfpennies furiously now.

'Did he make any threats against her?' Sir Robert asked.

'None that I ever heard,' Sir Randolph said, and Sir Robert opened his mouth in dismay.

'But—'

'He made a vow, though,' Sir Randolph broke in. 'He swore that he would kill her if she did not mend her ways.'

William Ashby cried out, 'No!', but was silenced by a constable's hand on his shoulder.

'What were his exact words?' Sir Robert asked.

William Ashby had a choking fit, almost doubling as he spasmed with the effort to catch his breath.

'If the prisoner cannot be silent I shall have him removed from my court.' Mr Justice Peters banged his gavel as William Ashby tried to stifle his coughs with his hand. 'Proceed, Sir Randolph.'

Sir Randolph looked a little irritated. He glanced at his watch and muttered something about a horse.

'He swore that he would kill her if she did not mend her ways,' he said.

'No, Sir Randolph, please tell the court exactly the words that he used.'

'His exact words were that he would kill her if she did not mend her ways.'

Somebody hooted in derision.

'Silence,' the judge barked. 'I will have this court cleared if there are any more unseemly displays. Carry on, Sir Robert.'

'Imagine that you are he and I am you,' Sir Robert tried. 'I say something like *What's the trouble, old boy?* And you say...'

'My glass is empty.'

The judge brought down his gavel several times to restore order, and said to Sir Randolph, 'We need his words verbatim.'

'Then why did you not say so,' Sir Randolph asked, 'instead of all this silly playacting? He said, *I will kill her if she does not mend her ways*, and I said, *You do not mean that, surely?* And he said, *As sure as we are standing here. I have had more than enough of her. I will stick her with one of my knives if she does not improve.*'

The whole chamber erupted at this revelation and I looked across at William Ashby. He shook his head and clutched it with both hands. And, in the gradual quieting, a low sound emitted from him, the man with no face.

22

The Trained Monkey

THE INSTANT THE judge sent the jury to consider their verdict Sidney Grice was on his feet.

'Come, March,' he said. 'There is not a moment to lose.' And he was racing jerkily up the steps before most people had even stood up.

I caught up with him in the central hallway.

'This way.' He propelled me along a series of crowded corridors and through a door on to the pavement.

'What is so urgent?' I asked. Had he thought of another line of investigation? But Sidney Grice's face was set determinedly silent as he hurried me up an incline along a street opening into a wider, leafier road.

'Here we are.' The smell of coffee greeted us the moment he opened the door. 'Ceylon for three,' he called before the waitress had even reached our table, 'and hurry.'

I did not have to ask who the third tea was for because the bell tinkled and Inspector Pound came in, a little out of breath.

'Inspector,' Sidney Grice called, 'I have reserved you a place and ordered you a tea.'

'You always manage to beat me to it, Mr Grice.' Inspector Pound flopped down in a chair between us. 'And not a moment too soon by the look of it.'

The door was flung open and four men, one struggling with a large black-draped camera on a tripod, rushed in, followed by two couples chattering excitedly and a coachman in splendid livery.

'Bitter experience sped me here,' Sidney Grice said. 'I shall never forget the Nurse Raddison case.'

'Was she the one who drowned her elderly patients to pawn their clothes?' I asked. 'That was dreadful.'

'More dreadful than you know,' Sidney Grice said. 'There was such a crush for that one that I was unable to obtain a cup of tea for two consecutive days and my first Heat Retentive Bottle was smashed in the general mayhem.'

'He was almost in tears,' Inspector Pound told me as the waitress brought a tray and set its load upon our table. Sidney Grice lifted the lid from the teapot and asked, 'From what part of Ceylon did this tea come?'

'Don't know, sir.'

'Is it the part that mixes old leaves with new in the hope that the customer will not notice?'

'Don't know, sir.'

'Take it away and bring a fresh pot immediately.'

'It may take a while. I do have other people to see to, sir.'

'As you so rightly say, they are *other* people,' he told her. 'So we need not concern ourselves with them.'

She looked at him uncertainly. He pointed to the pot and she took it back to the kitchen.

'It seems we have Ashby well and truly kippered now,' the inspector said.

'Sir Randolph nearly let us down, though,' Sidney Grice commented, 'after all those rehearsals. The man is an absolute imbecile. The only wonder is he did not lose his fortune sooner.'

'You rehearsed the witness?' I asked.

'Only to tell the truth,' Inspector Pound said as the waitress brought another pot.

The bell clanged again and a large red-faced lady in a moss-green coat pushed through the gathering queue, her floral hat almost coming off her head.

'Whose truth?'

'You have been reading French philosophy.' My guardian felt the temperature of the pot and lifted off the lid. 'I must strongly advise you to desist before your brain is made complicated. The truth is the truth whatever its source. For example, it is indisputably true that that woman is fat whether I or a notorious liar say it and whether or not somebody has been reminded to say it.'

'She can probably hear you,' I said.

'Good.' He sniffed the steam and peered into the pot. 'There is little point in talking if you cannot be heard. I detest the modern fad for mumbling behind one's hand. It is very continental.'

'I am very sorry, madam,' the waitress said, 'but we do not have a table to spare.'

'We could invite her to join us,' I suggested.

'That would be the polite thing to do.' Sidney Grice replaced the lid. 'But, if word got about that I had started being polite, people might imagine that I had become thoughtful, rumours would spread that I was kind, and that is only one step away from being expected to perform acts of charity.' He shuddered.

'Little fear of that,' I said.

'I am not sure if I believe that the road to hell is paved with good intentions,' Sidney Grice said, 'but the road to ruin certainly is. The tea is stewing, Miss Middleton.'

I poured three cups through a silver strainer and splashed some milk into mine and the inspector's. He spooned two sugars into his and stirred vigorously.

'The water is flat,' Sidney said, and I raised my hand to attract the lady's attention.

'We have a free chair,' I called and my guardian groaned.

'I was about to point that out,' the lady said, and turned to the waitress. 'Fetch me a clean cup, miss, and more hot water.'

'Yes, madam.'

The lady sat heavily opposite me.

'And a big slice of pie,' she called. 'I do hope she heard. Oh, you are that horrid policeman.'

'Am I?' Inspector Pound smiled uneasily.

'You know you are.' She turned the pot so that the handle faced her. 'Trying to convince everybody that that sweet little man is a murderer. Well, you have not deceived the jury, I hope. One look at William Ashby tells you he is innocent.'

'But all the evidence points to his guilt,' Inspector Pound said.

'Evidence is a trained monkey.' The woman peeped into our milk jug. 'It will point wherever you want it to but it does not mean anything by it.' She sniffed the milk and poured a lot into her cup.

Sidney Grice laughed and said, 'I had not thought of it in those terms before. Might I help you with your hat, madam? It looks like it is about to escape.'

'Like an untrained monkey,' the inspector said, producing a neat meerschaum pipe and a small penknife to scrape it out.

'No, you may not.' The woman jerked her head away and her hat slipped a little further back.

The waitress returned with a jug of hot water and a cup

and saucer as the inspector tapped some tar-soaked strands into a brown china ashtray.

'No pie?' As the lady asked, Sidney Grice leaned towards her. 'Leave it alone, sir.'

Sidney Grice leaned back.

'I was merely trying to see how it was fastened, or not, in this case.'

'For goodness' sake,' I said. 'A man's life is in the balance and all you can worry about is tea and millinery.'

'It is from the seemingly trivial that some of our greatest advances have been made,' Sidney Grice said, and seemed about to take something from his inside breast pocket but then to think better of it.

'Quite so.' Inspector Pound brought out a scratched leather pouch and unbuttoned the flap. 'Where would we be today, for example, without James Watt's observations of the steam from a kettle?'

'It would be nice to see a bit more steam from the kettles in this cafe,' Sidney Grice said. 'This tea is cold as Sarah Ashby.'

Inspector Pound laughed and tamped some tobacco lightly into his pipe with his finger.

'That is a filthy thing to say,' I said as the doorbell clattered again and a police constable came in breathlessly, brushing past the waitress and straight to our table. He bent and whispered into Inspector Pound's ear.

'So soon?' The inspector raised his eyebrows and the constable mouthed, 'Yes, sir.'

Inspector Pound slipped an unstruck match back into its box and nodded to Sidney Grice.

'Come, Miss Middleton.' My guardian stood up abruptly.

'Are you going?' the woman asked.

'It would seem so,' I said, and she smiled contentedly and tapped the pot with her spoon, saying, 'All the more for me then.'

Sidney Grice slapped a shilling on to the table and said, 'Good day, madam. I hope your pie arrives soon or there shall be nothing left of you.'

There were still people queuing to get into the cafe as we hurried back down the street.

'Why the hurry?' I asked. 'The jury cannot have been out for half an hour yet.'

'Well, they are back in now.' Sidney Grice was limping badly. 'So we should be in time to see how Ashby takes the news.'

'Two to one says he tries to change his story,' Inspector Pound said.

'Not him,' Sidney Grice said. 'Besides, what could he change it to?'

'He could claim it was suicide,' the inspector said with a thin laugh.

I made no response as we re-entered the building. I was still hoping that the jury would see what the lady and I had seen – the innocence of his eyes.

23

The Verdict

WE HAD HARDLY reclaimed our seats when it was time for us to rise for the judge. The twelve men filed in and William Ashby was brought back into the dock. He stumbled as he climbed the steps and grabbed his escort's arm to steady himself.

'I beg your pardon,' he said and stood looking about him, at Grace Dillinger sitting anxiously with the priest, at the jury grave-faced in their box, at Inspector Pound, Sidney Grice and me, then back at Grace Dillinger who tried to force a smile.

'All be seated,' the usher called as the judge adjusted his wig.

The chairman of the jury handed a note to the usher, who gave it to the clerk, who passed it on to the judge, who unfolded it with a weary air.

'Members of the jury in the case of the Queen versus William Ashby, have you come to a verdict?'

The chairman stood, a petty thin-lipped man, suddenly finding himself important.

'We have, my lord.'

William Ashby coughed helplessly into a bloodstained handkerchief.

'And is it the decision of you all?'

'It is, my lord.'

'The prisoner will stand.'

William Ashby rose painfully, his eyes etched grey, his right hand holding the polished brass rail.

'On the charge of wilfully murdering his wife, one Sarah Ashby, how do you find the prisoner?'

The chairman paused to savour the greatest moment of his life and the words which decided William Ashby's rang out proudly. 'Guilty, my lord.' His face glowed with the death that he delivered and the courtroom burst into a fusillade of clapping and cheers.

'Oh dear God,' I whispered.

'Excellent.' My guardian clapped his hands together.

William Ashby swayed. He closed his eyes and flung back his head as the judge banged his gavel repeatedly.

Eventually the usher restored quiet and the judge addressed the prisoner. It was a foul deed that William Ashby had performed. He took a young and innocent wife, who looked to him for support and protection, and he slaughtered her with a savagery that would have been unworthy of a wild beast. And all in the false hope of filling his coffers with silver. To compound his felony, he had cruelly deceived the poor girl's mother into supporting him, the murderer of her child. Why, even the private detective who had been hired to clear his name was forced to the same conclusion as the court.

'*Personal* detective,' Sidney Grice muttered.

All the time the judge was speaking, William Ashby was fighting the spasms in his chest. 'No,' he said three times, his sandy hair falling over his eyes, his chest convulsing with infection.

Had the prisoner anything to say as to why the full penalty of the law should not be exercised upon him?

William Ashby whispered. 'I...' but shook his head and closed his eyes again.

A terrible silence crept over us as the black cloth was placed upon the judge's head.

'It is the sentence of this court that you be taken from this place to a place of detention and from thence to a place of execution, where you shall be hanged by the neck until you are dead. You should be grateful that your death will be more merciful than that of your wife, and may God have mercy upon your soul.'

The crowd applauded and William Ashby stood holding the rail of the dock shakily, and a woman cried out, 'Dear Lord. Please, no.' It was Mrs Dillinger. She had sat silently until then.

'Grace,' William Ashby cried back. 'You know I did not do it.' And she buried her face in her hands.

'It was an accident,' Ashby said almost to himself, but my guardian and the inspector heard him and laughed.

William Ashby was taken away but Sidney Grice hardly glanced at him. He was too busy fiddling with his notebook. The court was clearing, the crowd happily chatting, but we stayed in our seat and Grace Dillinger in hers. She looked lost when she stood at last, like a sleepwalker, as she came up the steps towards the exit.

'So much for your innocent son-in-law,' Sidney Grice jeered as she drew level, and Grace Dillinger stopped.

'It is an evil thing you have done,' she said. 'May you rot in hell.'

'Sweet William will be dancing his way there on the end of a rope long before me,' he crowed.

Mrs Dillinger raised her hand and, to my horror, Sidney Grice raised his hand above his head as though to strike back, but in reality to mime a rope round his neck, his head to one side and his tongue extruded.

'For the love of God,' I said. And Mrs Dillinger cried out, 'You are a monster!' as she launched herself into him, grasping his lapel in one hand and lashing out with the other. Sidney Grice moved quickly. He rose and grabbed her flailing arm by the wrist and pushed her with surprising strength away from him. Grace Dillinger stumbled backwards and would have fallen were it not for the priest coming up behind and steadying her.

Sidney Grice stood alert for another assault, but Grace Dillinger's face set hard as she turned away and rushed from the courtroom.

The priest's voice trembled as he said, 'If I were not a man of the cloth I should strike and break you like the venomous creature that you are, sir.'

'But we are in the same business, you and I,' Sidney Grice said, 'seeking out sinners.'

'I try to save them,' the priest said.

'Just as I have saved Ashby from murdering again,' Sidney Grice responded. 'Go tend to Mrs Dillinger, Father. She has more need of you than I.'

'You have more need of me than you know,' the priest said, and hurried after her.

Sidney Grice winced.

'She gouged my face,' he said, dabbing his cheek with his handkerchief.

Inspector Pound hurried over. 'You are lucky she did not take your other eye out.'

'And who would have blamed her?' I said. 'The poor woman

is carrying her dead husband's child. She has lost her daughter and is about to lose her son-in-law, and you chose that moment to taunt her. It was cruel and pointless.'

'I have to agree with your young lady on that point.' Inspector Pound stood aside to let some people past. 'What on earth came over you, Mr Grice?'

Sidney Grice smiled.

'My words may have been unkind and I have never claimed to be a kind person,' he said, 'but they were certainly not pointless.'

He inspected his handkerchief which was streaked red.

'It is only a scratch,' Inspector Pound said.

'A small price to pay then.' Sidney Grice brightened up. 'Well, we got the conviction, Inspector. I think you at least owe me a pot of tea.'

24

The Maze of Vice

TIME PASSED QUICKLY. There was a coolness between myself and my guardian after the day of the trial but we saw little of each other anyway, as he was occupied with an alleged suicide in Warren Street.

I found plenty to occupy myself, however. There were parks and squares to be explored, shop windows to be ogled, cafes where a young lady could sit and take coffee, with perhaps a nip of brandy to colour her cheeks, and watch the metropolis go by.

It was my guardian's suggestion that I visited an exhibition of paintings. He had been given a ticket by a grateful client but had neither the time nor the inclination to attend. It might amuse me, he told me one Tuesday over breakfast.

'Run up the green flag when you are ready but do not forget to run it down again. Molly forgot once and the whole of Gower Street became blocked with hansoms, their drivers arguing over who had seen the signal first.'

'I could easily walk there.'

Sidney Grice raised his eyebrows. His mother, he told me, would never have stepped out of her front door to cross the road if there were not a carriage waiting. It was a question of standards. I walked.

It was a lovely day and Oxford Street was choked with

traffic, hawkers and pedestrians. I stopped to watch a mangy monkey dancing in a red fez and waistcoat on a barrel organ. The music was raucous and the monkey was obviously poorly cared for, and I was just about to leave when I heard a man's voice very close by shout, 'Stop!' I turned and saw Inspector Pound grabbing a ragged little boy by the sleeve, but the boy dropped to the ground, twisting himself free, and scurried off between the legs of the other spectators.

'Stop, thief!' Inspector Pound shouted after him, but he was gone.

The inspector bent and picked something up.

'Your purse, Miss Middleton.' He handed it back to me. 'The filthy little tyke nearly made off with it.'

'I did not even notice it had gone.' The purse had been opened but nothing was missing.

'They are professionals, these rascals,' he told me. 'They could have your boots off your feet before you knew it but did I not warn you, when we first met, to be careful in London?'

'Of horses, with which I am very familiar, and foreigners, a variety of whom I have lived amongst for much of my life. You said nothing about children.'

Inspector Pound laughed and his usually sombre face brightened.

'If I were to warn you about every possible peril on the streets of this maze of vice, I should be lecturing you for years. May I take your arm, Miss Middleton?'

'It is nice to be in the company of a gentleman,' I said as he escorted me out of the crowd.

'My mother was not rich but she taught me my manners.'

'Mr Grice mentioned his mother this morning,' I said as a mule went by, pulling a wheeled sledge laden with building rubble.

'It is difficult to imagine him having a mother.' Inspector Pound grinned. 'But by all accounts he is devoted to her.' He pulled me back from the edge a little. 'And she to him, though I gather she never quite recovered from the shame of bringing a cripple into the world.'

'That is not fair,' I said. 'He may limp quite badly but he is hardly a cripple.'

'Why, even with his specially cobbled boots his right leg is several inches shorter than the left,' Inspector Pound said as we crossed the road. 'Legend has it that, whilst she was carrying him, Mr Grice's mother was terrified by a lobster falling from a passing fishmonger's tray into her lap, and lobsters, as you may be aware, have one leg very much longer than the other... It is no laughing matter, Miss Middleton.'

I put my hand over my mouth. 'You cannot believe that.'

'I most certainly do.' The inspector coloured a little. 'Why, there is a man by the name of John Merrick who makes a considerable living touring the country in sideshows. His mother was frightened by an escaped elephant whilst carrying him and he was born with a number of its characteristics. His head is enormous and misshapen. His nose forms the beginnings of a trunk. His hands and limbs are swollen and malformed. His skin is thick and lies in great grey folds and he even lumbers like a jungle beast. I have seen him myself and he is no forgery.'

'Well, Mr Grice certainly has a thick shell,' I said and Inspector Pound laughed.

We walked round four girls sifting through a pile of rubbish.

'May I enquire where you are heading for?' Inspector Pound asked.

I told him and he said, 'Well, what a coincidence. I am headed there myself.'

'Are you interested in painting?'

'I have never really thought about it, but a friend gave me a ticket and I thought I might take a look. We can cut through here.' He guided me down a side street. 'Never come along here at night, Miss Middleton. They call it Cut Throat Alley, but it is as safe as anywhere during the day. I trust Mr Grice's face is healing well.' The inspector chuckled. 'That is the first time I have seen anyone, let alone a woman, get the better of him.'

'Have you known him for very long?' I asked.

'About five years now.' A large grey cat came cantering by. 'He's a strange one but he does get results. I should probably have let that Ashby fellow go, if it were not for Mr Grice's help. How did you come under his care?'

I gave Inspector Pound a brief account of my history and he looked at me seriously and said, 'Then we have something in common. I lost both my parents before I was twelve years old and I was taken in by my uncle, who was a Robin.'

'A what?'

'It is what people called the mounted Bow Street Runners because they wore red waistcoats. It was he who guided me to my career.'

We walked on in silence and the alley narrowed again so that we were obliged to walk very close unless the inspector let go of my arm, and he showed no sign of doing that.

The alley widened out into a little square.

'Here we are.'

The exhibition was disappointing. Mr Rossetti's women all had small heads and green-tinted faces, large shoulders and necks like pillars.

The inspector did not stay long. He had work to do but would put me in a cab first. I told him not to trouble himself but he was insistent.

'And what of you?' he asked as we parted. 'You are quite a remarkable young lady. There are experienced men in my force who could not enter the mortuary as I hear you did.'

'It is the living who frighten me,' I said. 'There is nothing to fear from the dead.'

'Then you shall have nothing to fear from William Ashby soon,' the inspector said, 'for he is to hang on Friday.'

'So soon?'

Inspector Pound shrugged. 'You have seen some of the unrest for yourself. The sooner he is out of the way, the better. I for one shall not be sorry to see justice being done.'

'You will be there?'

Inspector Pound smiled and said, 'Wouldn't miss it for the world.'

He shut the door and the hansom set off, but I stopped it round the corner and walked.

There was a jewellery shop set back a little from the road. I stood for a while outside the window.

I had not had time to hang the ring around my neck. We had twelve patients to deal with and two of them needed amputations. I think it was while I was holding a corporal's leg down that I cracked the stone.

'Blast the man to hell,' you said when I showed you. 'I paid two months' salary for that ring and it turns out to be a fake and the blighter has disappeared. I am sorry, March. I shall save up to buy you another one.'

'No,' I said. 'This is my engagement ring. Any other, no matter what it cost, would be a fake.'

You kissed me.

'I did not think that I could love you more,' you said.

25

Sticks and Stones

IT WAS THURSDAY. I was in a hurry to get out that morning because I had run out of cigarettes and there is something about tobacco which I find almost addictive.

'March,' my guardian called as I scooted past his open study door, 'come and take a look at this.'

He was standing behind his desk with a top hat in front of him and a sheaf of papers in his hand. 'What do you make of this?'

I glanced down. 'It is a hat.'

'Not just any old hat,' he said. 'My hat.'

'Congratulations.' I was hungry for a smoke.

'What else is it?' He hopped from one foot to the other.

'A dromedary,' I guessed.

'Now you are being foolish. This,' he rotated it, 'is my latest invention – the Grice Patent Tea-maker.'

'And I thought it was a hat.'

'It is,' he said, 'and an excellent one at that. Note the subtly widened rim, designed to keep the sun out of one's eye in the summer and waxed to keep the rain off one's nose in the winter. See,' he flipped the hat upside down, 'how this black silk lining unbuttons to reveal compartments containing tea leaves, a box of vestas, a spoon, a strainer and a telescopic cup. Observe how this spirit lamp hinges down below the top compartment, a can of water. Everything a gentleman might need for that perfect emergency cup of tea.'

'Will it brew up whilst you are wearing it?' I asked, and Molly came in with the morning papers on a silver tray. She put it down and bobbed awkwardly.

'What are you doing?' Sidney Grice demanded.

'Curtsying, sir. Maude who lives in at number 112 told me they do it all the time there.'

The doorbell rang.

'It makes you look like a jackdaw.'

Molly grinned. 'Why, thank you, sir.'

'Door,' my guardian said and Molly looked blank. 'Answer the door,' he said.

Molly obediently left, then returned, crossing her legs in a jerky dip. 'Inspector Pound, sir.'

The inspector muttered a few pleasantries but he was clearly worried.

'You have not read the papers yet, Mr Grice?'

'No. Molly was delayed in ironing them. Apparently cook caught her hair alight.'

'Is she all right?' I asked and he shrugged.

'I expect luncheon will be delayed.'

'I had a visit from Father Brewster yesterday morning,' Inspector Pound said.

The two men sat and I pulled up a chair. Sidney Grice tilted his head quizzically.

'And?'

'He told me that Sir Randolph had called on him the night before.'

'And?'

'Sir Randolph had something on his conscience. He made

a confession that so disturbed Father Brewster that he persuaded Sir Randolph to repeat the information to him outside of the confession where it would not be sacrosanct.'

'And this information was?' My guardian made no attempt to cover his yawn.

Inspector Pound hesitated. 'He claims that you told him what to say in the witness box and paid him handsomely to do so, including putting him up in the Midlands Grand Hotel.'

Sidney Grice waved his hand airily. 'Stuff and nonsense.'

'But you admitted that you coached him,' I said and my guardian inhaled sharply.

'I merely helped him to organize his testimony,' he said.

'So you gave him no money?' I asked and my guardian stiffened.

'I was not aware that I was in the dock.'

'Not yet, at any rate,' the inspector murmured.

'I bought Sir Randolph a suit and paid for him to have a shave and haircut so that he would be a more presentable witness.'

'And the hotel?' Inspector Pound asked quietly.

'I put him up there for the night before the trial because I know the concierge. He arranged for a man to stay with Sir Randolph and make sure he turned up at court on time and sober. That is all.'

'That is not what the press are saying,' the inspector said, and I picked up *The Times*.

It was still warm and the front page, as always, was taken up by advertisements, but inside there was a grainy photograph of my guardian and another of Father Brewster, and a headline which proclaimed *Priest Speaks Out Against Private Detective*.

'Let me see.' My guardian snatched the paper and his face reddened. 'How many times? I am a *personal* detective.' He slapped the paper on to his desk and bent over it. 'That damned whey-faced puppy in a frock has been using his filthy pulpit to repeat his allegations. I shall go to his church this very Sunday and thrash him before his own congregation.'

'They are more likely to thrash you,' I said.

People were shouting on the street.

'I shall sue. I shall have him behind bars for criminal slander.' He took the paper in both hands and ripped it in two, screwing the halves up and throwing them in the direction of the fire on to the floor.

'Run up the flag, March. I know a couple of characters in Limehouse who owe me a favour. They will set him swimming in the river with his church bell chained to his scrawny neck.'

The front doorbell rang.

'You are lucky I did not hear any of that,' the inspector said.

Molly returned, crossing her legs unsteadily.

'Begging your pardon, sir, but there's a small to middling-sized mob in the street outside. They want to see you about William Ashby.'

'Tell them to clear off,' Sidney Grice said and went to the window to peer out. 'And bring more tea.'

'They are not the only ones to have concerns about the safety of the conviction,' Inspector Pound said. 'I was summoned to the chief constable's office this morning. He had had a meeting with the Home Secretary and in view of this new evidence...'

'Evidence?' My guardian swept back his hair. 'The ramblings of an inebriate as mouthed by a prejudiced idolater?'

'In view of this new allegation,' the inspector continued, 'Sir William has ruled that the execution be delayed until Sir Randolph has been interviewed.'

'Then go ahead and interview him.' Sidney Grice strode back to the window.

The crowd was chanting now, 'Ashby is innocent', over and over again.

'Where are the police when you need them?' my guardian asked.

'Standing by your fireplace,' I said.

'I mean uniformed men with truncheons on horseback to beat a bit of sense into their lice-laden skulls.'

'I shall go and speak to them presently,' the inspector said. 'But the problem is, Mr Grice, we cannot find Sir Randolph.'

'Down an alley with his throat cut, I hope,' Sidney Grice said.

At that moment there was a crash and a spray of shattered glass, and a brick crashed into the screen at my guardian's side. He put his forearm up to his face.

'Are you all right?' I asked and Sidney Grice turned to me. There was blood on his forehead.

'Sticks and stones may break my bones, Miss Middleton,' he said, 'but only words can hurt me. Do not trouble yourself, Inspector. The cowards are dispersing already.'

There was another crash and a stone struck him on the shoulder. I hurried to him and saw a youth running up the road. He turned and threw another stone, but it fell short and he ran away.

My guardian rubbed his shoulder – it was the one which always troubled him – and pointed out of the window.

'Those are your criminals, Inspector Pound,' he said. 'I suggest you start chasing them instead of hounding me.'

The inspector reddened. 'Would you like me to station a man outside your house, Mr Grice?'

Sidney Grice shook his head. 'No, Inspector. I would like you to put this matter to rest and you can start by finding Sir Randolph Cosmo Napier. I will give you two days.'

'Or what?' Inspector Pound was very pale.

Sidney Grice flapped his hand above his head.

'Two days,' he said, and turned back to the window.

26

Smoke

'THERE IS A strong aroma of cigarette smoke in here,' my guardian said as we went into the dining room. 'I hope Molly has not been indulging in that filthy habit. She will be looking for another position without a reference if she has.'

He had his patch on, as he often did in the evenings, to give his eye muscles a rest.

'It is probably my fault,' I said. 'I had tea in a very smoky cafe.'

He sniffed again. 'Is that gin I can smell?'

'Very likely,' I said. 'A man spilled something over me from a jug as I walked past him. I was not aware that it was gin, though.'

The dining room was chilly. It had a fireplace but it was never made up. That would have been an unwarranted extravagance.

'I would have sworn it was on your breath,' he said as we went to our chairs.

'I trust you would not have sworn in my presence,' I said.

'I only meant—'

'And I am not sure that you should be smelling my breath.' Molly brought in our dinner. 'It hardly seems decent.'

Molly suppressed a smile as she left. We had soft-boiled eggs and cold potatoes.

'How has your day been?' I asked.

Sidney Grice blew down the salt cellar.

'Most satisfactory.'

'In what way?'

He banged the cellar on the table. 'You will not have forgotten that I gave Pound two days to find Sir Randolph, and he has failed to come up with a single lead.' He salted his food. 'So I had a chat with the Home Secretary this afternoon.'

'Indeed?'

I poured myself a tumbler of water.

'Indeed.' Sidney Grice spread his napkin over his lap. 'I reminded him that Ashby had a fair trial, and Brewster's rantings from the pulpit were no more than uncorroborated hearsay and cannot constitute evidence. I pointed out that public order is at stake and the matter needs to be resolved as soon as possible. Sir William agreed and the execution is to be scheduled for the day after tomorrow. He owes me a favour, anyway.'

Sidney Grice tapped one of his eggs with a teaspoon.

'You regard the hanging of William Ashby as a personal favour?'

'Of course.' My guardian scooped his eggs out on to his plate. 'The whole thing has become an embarrassment.'

'So he is to die to spare your blushes?'

Sidney Grice nodded happily. 'I only wish I could witness the event myself.'

'But why?'

'If any man put William Ashby on the scaffold it is I.' He did his horrid smile. 'And I like to see my work completed.'

'You would enjoy it?'

'Why not?' He mashed his egg into his potato, shook some pepper on top and then some more salt, sowing it up and down his plate.

'But a man is to be killed.'

'You give him more consideration than he gave his wife, not to mention the suffering of her mother.'

'But are you sure?'

'The man is a brutal murderer, March. Twelve men good and true were sure of it too.'

My eggs had congealed into yellow strings around the pale potatoes. Sidney Grice tucked into his dinner and opened a book.

'You should read this.' He raised it briefly. 'It is quite fascinating. Apparently an American dentist called Southwick has devised a method of executing criminals by electrifying them. That sounds rather fun.'

I pushed my plate to one side.

'You are not hungry?'

'I feel sick.'

'You should try fletcherizing your food. Take tiny portions and chew each one thirty times before swallowing. It will improve your digestion no end and perhaps even your temperament a little.'

He wiped his mouth.

'It is not this muck masquerading as food that offends me,' I said. 'It is the monster masquerading as a human being that fills me with disgust.'

Sidney Grice put his napkin down and said almost tenderly, 'I quite understand but try not to upset yourself, March. The world shall be rid of him in thirty-six hours.'

I picked up my carafe and hurled it. I am a good shot as a rule but I did not take careful aim. My guardian glanced back at the shattered glass on the floor and the water on the wallpaper.

'You would have done better with the tumbler,' he said and returned to his book.

I once saw a man hang in Bombay. My father took me. I had heard that the man was an Indian mutineer and I said that he deserved to die. He had taken an oath to the Queen and betrayed her.

The man was brought into the square manacled and in leg chains, and dressed only in a loincloth. He shuffled to try to keep up with his escort. He was such a little man and he was crying. At the foot of the scaffold he stopped and fell to his knees. The guards put their arms under his and carried him up. He was wailing by then. They deposited him on the hatch and put a noose round his neck.

'Did he deserve this?' my father asked.

'How many people did he kill?'

'If it were ten did he deserve this?'

'Yes.'

I looked away but my father told me to watch, and the executioner pulled a lever and the man fell and his body jolted as the rope tightened. And then the struggles began. His hands went to his throat but the rope dug deep and he could not put his fingers under it. His legs were kicking. He swung from side to side.

'Did he deserve this?' my father asked but I could not answer.

The man was running now, his legs pumping in the air and some of the bystanders started to laugh. He soiled himself and the laughter grew. Some mocked him.

'No,' I said.

The hanged man tired. He slowed and slumped. His hands fell in front of him and his legs hung loosely. His chest quivered and he became limp.

'He spat at an officer,' my father said. 'If his comrades are to be believed, he was chewing betel leaves and just happened to spit as his captain came round the corner. The men laughed and the officer felt humiliated so he pressed charges. It was the word of an English captain against that of a native private judged by English officers. I am sorry to have put you through this but you have learnt the most important thing you will ever learn. No one has the right to say another man must die. Incarcerate him if you must, but it is for God to decide his allotted span.'

I picked up my tumbler and threw that too.

27

The Vigil

FATHER BREWSTER CAME to greet me, clothed in long white robes with a green stole, the moment I entered the church.

'I must tell you that I am not a Roman Catholic,' I said and he smiled. 'You are welcome all the more for that. Take a seat wherever you like and make yourself as comfortable as you can. We are in for a long night, if you choose to spend it with us.'

There were probably two hundred people seated in the pews already, most of them poorly dressed, and the majority were women, several with children.

I sat on the end of a pew at the back by myself. A grandfather clock had been set up before the altar. It was five minutes before twelve. Father Brewster went back to the front and bent to speak to somebody and, when she stood and turned, I saw that it was Grace Dillinger and that she was coming, tall and elegant, straight towards me. She was still in mourning, with no hat but a black gauze over her head hanging below her eyes, though her white face was still clearly visible.

'Miss Middleton.'

I stood and she took my hand and gave it a little squeeze.

'March.'

'Please call me Grace, and thank you for coming.'

There was a bleakness in her eyes that I had only seen in people before at the moment of their own deaths.

'I was not sure that I would be welcome after what my guardian has done and the part I played in persuading him to do it.'

Grace Dillinger touched my arm. 'You are always welcome. What you did was done out of kindness.'

A poorly dressed man in his twenties came in and dropped a coin through the slot of a black iron box.

'Is there an entrance fee?' I asked and she shook her head.

'He is lighting a votive candle. It is a small offering to the church and God for a special intention.'

'May I?'

I put a sixpence in the slot.

'A penny would have done,' Grace said.

'Then perhaps you will light one with me.' The candles were about the size of crayons, and as we held the waxed wicks into the flame I saw her hand shake and put out mine to steady it.

'Oh, March.' Her voice faltered. 'I am so frightened for him.' Her eyes closed briefly, then glistened through her veil in the yellow flicker. We pushed our candles into pronged holders on the stand, and she swallowed and said, 'Will you sit with me a while?'

'I feel I am intruding.'

'You are a good person and we have need of goodness tonight.'

We walked down the aisle. All eyes turned towards us as I slid into the front pew and Grace sat beside me, opening a prayer book on a page marked with a red ribbon but staring through it into the wastelands of all human suffering.

The clock stuck midnight and on the last chime Father Brewster said, 'One thousand, eight hundred and forty-nine years ago another innocent man awaited execution. He asked his followers to stay awake and pray. Was it possible, he begged, that the chalice of suffering be taken from him? If it were not possible, then he would bow to his Father's will. He did bow and through his death redeemed our souls. And so now we beseech thee, Father, God of infinite mercy, though we cannot see your will, if it be possible, to save our poor brother in Christ, William Ashby, from such a cruel fate. Just as Jesus enjoined his disciples in Gethsemane, let us, in obedience to his holy will, stay awake and say the rosary together.'

Many of the congregation brought out rosaries with crosses hanging from them and began to recite a prayer to Mary. Ten times they said it, then the Lord's Prayer but with the end omitted, then a short prayer starting with Glory Be, and then they began again. I sat quietly and watched the hands that counted the beads and the hands that counted the minutes and I listened to the chanting, and I was not even aware of falling asleep but I awoke with a start to see Jesus Christ hanging from the cross, his body pierced and twisted but his expression serene, high above the altar and a candle in a red glass cup.

'My brothers and sisters in Christ,' Father Brewster was saying, and I saw the hands at seven. 'We are past dawn.'

The morning was glowing through the round stained glass of the great east window. It cast its colours over the upturned faces.

'And, as we have had no news, we must accept that the deed has been done.'

Grace was on her knees beside me, her head resting on her intertwined hands.

'No,' she whispered. 'Please God. No.'

'I have put aside the green of hope,' Father Brewster said, and I saw that he had changed his vestments, 'for the purple of the passion of our Lord, for we must now accept that he has taken William Ashby into his Father's house.'

The quiet was torn by a choked wail.

'No.' Grace Dillinger raised her face to the ceiling.

'And we must commend his soul—'

'No.' She flung her missal skimming towards the altar.

'To God's eternal boundless love.'

Grace Dillinger rose. Her face was fixed in unutterable despair.

'God damn them all,' she said and swept away.

I rose to follow but Father Brewster put up his hand.

'God will find and comfort her and bring her back,' he said, but I could not reply for the disgust that filled my throat.

28

The Hanging

SIDNEY GRICE WAS out when I got home. He had left early, Molly told me, following some information about a stolen racehorse. Her apron was smudged with blacking.

Would I like breakfast? I would not.

I had a cup of tea and went into the small courtyard garden and sat for my first cigarette under the cherry tree. I put on my cloak and walked to Tavistock Square and smoked another cigarette there, until a scandalized gentleman in a tall top hat told me not to. I wandered to Brown and Sons and bought a packet of Willet's Empires.

''Orrible 'angin',' the news vendor called. ''Orrible 'angin'. Get all the gruesome details. See the artist's pictures. 'Orrible 'angin'.'

I had not a penny on me for the paper but if I had a hundred sovereigns in my purse, I should not have bought it. I hurried up Torrington Place and back along Gower Street, just in time to catch a glimpse of my guardian climbing out of a cab and walking briskly up the steps.

Molly was still taking his coat when I went into the house.

'Bring me a pot of tea,' he told her, 'and make it a strong one.' And, tossing his cane into the stand, he marched straight into his study.

The doorbell rang.

'What a waste,' he said. 'The bunglers who stole Nightjar broke his leg and he had to be destroyed.'

He flipped through a pile of letters on his desk but did not open any. Two were tossed straight into the bin.

'You worry about the life of an animal on such a day as this?'

'There were fifty guineas in it for me if he had been alive.'

'And one hundred and twenty-five pounds to send William Ashby to his death,' I told him, and swept out of the room.

I was halfway up the stairs when I heard a voice and turned to see Inspector Pound coming into the hallway. His face was grey as Molly took his things, and he did not even glance up as he went into the study.

The door was closed, but I was down and into the room just as the inspector slumped into an armchair. He stood and greeted me.

'You look rather pale, Inspector,' I said.

'He was just about to tell me about the fuss at the hanging,' my guardian said.

'Why? What happened?'

'A botched job.' The inspector tugged at his moustaches. 'The worst I have ever witnessed and I have seen a few poor ones. To give Ashby his due, he stepped on to that trap with as much quiet dignity as any man could muster. He was much the worse for his gaol fever but he walked and stood unaided to the spot. All the usual stuff about being innocent of the crime, of course, but you expect that. The Chaplain said his prayers. The sentence was read out. Everybody stood back and the hangman pulled the lever but nothing happened. The trap would not open. The hangman stamped on it. They even made Ashby jump up and down, but it was well and truly jammed.

'They took him off and brought in a carpenter. The wood had warped and he had to shave it down. Then the hangman started an argument. He had been delayed and relied on his assistant to assess the condemned man, but apparently Ashby had a stouter neck than he had been led to believe and he did not think the rope was long enough. There is a conflict at present between the short-drop stranglers and the long-drop neck-breakers. The hangman wanted a quick death and insisted on a longer rope, and it took twenty minutes to produce one, and all that time Ashby had to stand and listen to them quarrel while the carpenter planed the planks and tested the lever.

'Eventually they got him back on the trap and put the noose round his neck and the padre repeated his bunkum, and they all stood back and the lever was pulled and the trap dropped, but only by a foot. Ashby stumbled and was choking with one leg jammed in the gap, so they hauled him up by the neck and called the carpenter back to saw a larger piece off. Then they put Ashby back on the trap, by which time the observers were incensed and saying that his sentence should be commuted to life imprisonment, so the governor sent out for further instructions and Ashby stood another hour or more while Vernon Harcourt, the Home Secretary, was found riding on Rotten Row.

'Apparently he was very petulant at being disturbed and told them just to get on with it. When the news came back, Ashby's nerve broke. So at seven fifty-five, almost two hours after the prescribed time, he was dragged struggling and screaming on to the trap to fall so far that his head was ripped clean off his body. The hangman's assistant fainted and several other officials were unwell.'

'Excellent.' Sidney Grice clapped his hands.

'How so?' Inspector Pound asked quietly.

'He got a taste of his own medicine,' Sidney Grice said. 'Where is the deterrent or the punishment if the guilty man does not suffer?'

'What kind of people are we protecting if he does?' I asked, and Sidney Grice smirked and said, 'I have warned you already about reading philosophy books. They fill the head with ideas, and ideas in the feminine head can all too easily upset her mental equilibrium. This is not my opinion but the result of many years of scientific research by doctors in the Bedlam Royal Hospital for the Insane.'

'Then they are more in need of treatment than their patients,' I said, and my guardian sniffed.

'The strange thing is,' the inspector said, 'that Ashby was still insisting his wife's death was an accident.'

'Forty accidents.' My guardian snorted. 'But I see you are a little disturbed by the experience, Inspector. What you need is an intoxicatingly strong drink – of tea.'

29

The Pity

A WEEK HAD passed since the execution and Sidney Grice seemed somewhat subdued. He spoke to me even less than usual at mealtimes and immersed himself in his files in between times. He was called out once to deal with a fraudulent insurance claim and took me to the scene of the alleged burglary, but other than that our lives became very dull indeed.

It was on the Tuesday morning that Inspector Pound called on us next. I took him into the study and explained that my guardian was at the funeral of a friend but that he should be home shortly.

'I did not know he had any friends,' Inspector Pound said, standing by the window to the street.

'Are you not his friend?'

'I have a good opinion of his forensic skills.' The inspector peered round the fretwork screen. 'Look at that.'

I joined him at the window to see a landau pass, with a heraldic shield on the door, and the solitary passenger, a haughty young man with a weak chin and a tall silk hat.

'That is Edwin Lord Worlington. He is probably the most eligible bachelor in England and, therefore, the world, but he has still not settled upon a wife.'

'I do not suppose his amphibian eyes have helped.'

Inspector Pound laughed and said, 'An income of over forty thousand pounds would make most women overlook that.'

'But what about you?' I asked. 'I think you said you live with your sister. Do you not have a wife?'

'No.' He turned and surveyed my profile. 'And it is a pity you are so poor and plain. And a shame you have such intelligence and spirit, Miss Middleton. You might otherwise make a man an acceptable spouse. Even Mr Grice might be improved by having one.'

I laughed. 'I cannot imagine him ever taking a wife.'

'But,' the inspector raised his eyebrows, 'I have heard it said that he was engaged once to be married.'

'Really? But who was she and what happened?'

Inspector Pound shrugged. 'I know nothing else about it. She probably fled the country.'

I laughed and asked, 'Am I very plain then?'

'I will wager you have never even been kissed.'

'You would win your bet,' I said, and the inspector leaned towards me. At that moment we heard the front doorbell ring and, shortly afterwards, my guardian came in to find us sitting primly by the fire. He had a black suit on and his hair was plastered down.

'Did you get caught in the rain?' I asked.

'It would take more than rain to catch me out,' he said. 'I was fully expecting it.'

'But not prepared by taking an umbrella,' Inspector Pound said.

The two men shook hands and my guardian shuddered.

'I have a horror of umbrellas – great black things flapping over my head. They are one of the four things that truly

167

frighten me.' He tugged the bell rope. 'Well, Inspector, you would hardly want to visit Miss Middleton so I assume you are here on police business.'

Inspector Pound nodded.

'Would you like me to leave?' I asked, but Inspector Pound said, 'This may interest you too, though I hope it is of no interest at all.'

'How so?' Sidney Grice said, pulling up a chair to face the fire.

'It is probably nothing,' Inspector Pound said, 'but you remember William Ashby's description of the Italian who bought the knife?'

Sidney Grice's eyes narrowed and he leaned forwards.

'Of course,' he said quietly as Molly came in.

'Where is my tea?'

'I was just about to bring it when you rang, sir.'

'Then why did you not bring it with you?'

'I thought it might be urgent.'

My guardian snapped his fingers in her face. 'I do not pay you to think, lumpen girl. If I did I would want my money back. From now on I shall use a code. One ring means come instantly. Two rings – bring tea. Three rings – fill my flask. Got that?'

'I think so. Sorry, sir.'

'Go and get the tea.'

'Yes, sir, but what happens if you ring four times?'

'Now.'

Molly ran out and I said, 'You are so unreasonable to her,' and my guardian flapped his hand.

'I am always a reasonable man,' he said. 'Unfair, unkind and rude, I grant you, but my powers of reasoning have never failed me yet.' He tidied the black handkerchief in his breast pocket and turned back to our visitor.

'We had a report from Paddington,' Inspector Pound said. 'A trivial matter on the face of it, but apparently a street urchin went into a pawnbroker's shop off Star Street, trying to sell him a wig.'

'But—' I began.

'What of it?' Sidney Grice broke in.

'Probably nothing, but the broker was suspicious as to how the lad had come into possession of such an expensive item, and summoned a policeman.' Inspector Pound hesitated. 'It was a very curly wig with bright red hair.'

'And you think this somehow substantiates Ashby's fantastical tale?' Sidney Grice asked.

'It is a thought,' Inspector Pound said.

'And an absurd one. Where' – my guardian's eye fell out and he popped it back without a pause – 'is this ragamuffin now then?'

The inspector looked queasy. 'We have him at the station.'

'Well, I have nothing else to do.' He swivelled his eye around with one finger. 'Let us pay him a visit.'

Molly returned a little shakily with a laden tray.

'Have you ever heard of the saying *better late than never*?' my guardian asked her.

'Yes, sir.'

'It is a lie put about by indolent servants and you are too late. Take it away.'

Molly's lip quivered. 'Yes, sir.' And Sidney Grice snatched up his cane.

'You had better come too, March. All this sitting about moping is making you very plain indeed.'

30

The Boiling of Bones

IT WAS THE same interview room and the same constable stood behind the same chair, but this time the occupant of that chair was a skinny boy in a filthy grey shirt.

'Stand up when the gentlemen and lady come into the room,' the constable said, and the boy got up warily. His cut-down short trousers were much too large for him and tied around his jutting hips with a length of frayed rope, and his legs were badly bowed by rickets. His head too was characteristically large and square.

'Sit,' the policeman prodded him.

'Stop bullying him,' I said and the constable prodded him again.

The wig lay on the table like a dead animal. Sidney Grice went straight over and picked it up.

'Where did you come across this?' he asked and the boy sniffed.

'I told the prawnman and I told the peeler. I found it in the canal.'

'Where?'

'Round the back of Factory Street. If you can't find it use your snout. It don't 'arf pen when they boil up the bones. There's a bit sticks out near an old coal boat. I fought it might be worth somefink. I din't know it was part of the crowned jewels.'

Inspector Pound laughed and said, 'And that is as much as we got out of him this morning.'

Sidney Grice looked at him and said, 'Ever been in trouble with the law before?'

'Didn't know I was in it now,' the boy said. 'I've never done nuffink but fish a old syrup out and, if there's a reward, it's mine by rights but you'll be keeping that yourselfs I don't doubt.'

'Do you know who I am?' Sidney Grice asked, and the boy shrugged but did not reply.

'I am Sidney Grice. Do you know who I am now?'

The boy perked up. 'You're that geezer what 'unts people down.'

Sidney Grice's mouth twitched.

'I am indeed that geezer,' he said, 'and if I find out that you have been lying to me it will be your bones they are boiling in that factory next.'

'I 'aven't been lyink. Straight up, Mr Grice.'

'If I find out that you have,' Sidney Grice repeated slowly, fixing him with his eye, 'I shall track you down, however far and fast you run, whatever continent you flee to, whatever drain you hide in – be sure of it – I always get my man.'

The boy looked impressed but only said, 'Can I go now?'

'What is your name?' I asked.

'Albert, miss. Named for our dead Prince.'

'You need milk,' I told him and put a shilling in his hand.

'God bless you, miss,' he said as the inspector caught him by the wrist.

'Give the lady her brooch back, Albert.'

'It must 'ave fell orf.'

Albert opened his fingers to reveal my mother's cameo in his grubby palm.

'You have two choices,' Inspector Pound said. 'Either you stay here and get arrested or...'

'I'll take the second choice,' Albert said, and was out of his chair and through the door in an instant.

'Perky little chap,' Inspector Pound commented.

'He will die in the gutter or on the gallows,' Sidney Grice said, and looked at the wig again. 'There is a label in the lining here. It is quite faded but I think I can make it out.' He held it up to the light. '*Simon Grave, Wigmaker.* Can I borrow this, Inspector?'

Inspector Pound flicked his hand in the air.

'As long as you like, Mr Grice.' His lips struggled to stay straight. 'But I should not have thought it was your style.'

'I have no style, Inspector,' Sidney Grice said. 'You should know that by now.'

It was starting to rain, great plashing drops, when we went outside and there was not a hansom to be seen.

31

The Wigmaker's Shop

THE WIGMAKER'S SHOP was difficult to find. There were no street signs or numbers on the doors, and the window of the shop was boarded over so that we passed it twice, thinking it was derelict, before we realized what it was.

'They keep smashing them and Mr Grave cannot keep reglazing them,' Mr Grave, the owner, explained.

Sidney Grice showed him the wig.

'How could Mr Grave forget this one?' Mr Grave asked, picking it up and tidying the curls. 'The biggest head I have ever come across. Wanted a pair of matching moustaches as well. Fussy gent he was too. Well, you know what they are like.'

'Who?' Sidney Grice asked.

'These theatrical folk.'

'He was an actor?' I asked.

Mr Grave shook the wig and tutted. 'This has not been treated well at all. Drop it in a muddy puddle, did he? Criminal what—'

Sidney Grice rapped his stick on the counter. 'Do you have his name?'

'No.' Mr Grave picked at the wig sulkily.

'It is a great shame about the wig,' I said. 'It must have been beautiful when you made it. Do you have any idea who the man was?'

'Oh, Mr Grave certainly knows *who* he was.' Mr Grave smelled the wig and pulled a face. 'He just does not know his name.'

'Oh, for...' Sidney Grice threw up his hands.

'Who was he, Mr Grave?' I asked.

'Mr Grave told you. He was one of those theatrical dagos.'

'What do you mean by dago?' I asked. 'Spaniard or Italian?'

Mr Grave snorted. 'A dago is a dago. What's the difference?'

'The Spanish speak like theees,' I said, 'whereas the Italians speaka lika thisa.'

'That was almost as bad as your cockney,' my guardian muttered.

'The last one,' Mr Grave said. 'He was in that dago musical just off Drury Lane. The one with the stupid name.'

'*Rigoletto*,' I said.

'That's the one.'

'And you are sure he was Italian?'

''Course he was,' Mr Grave said. 'No Englishman would wear a wig like that. Speaking of which, hope you won't mind Mr Grave saying, but that hairpiece of yours does not look very natural, sir. Mr Grave could do you a very nice one for twenty guineas.'

'This is my own hair,' Sidney Grice said.

'You may fool your young lady but you will not fool a professional.' Mr Grave held a magnifying glass up to Sidney Grice's forehead. 'Mr Grave has been observing it sliding about since the moment you came in.'

'I do *not* wear a wig.'

'Let Mr Grave pull it then.'

His hand shot out but Sidney Grice whacked it aside with his cane. 'If you touch my hair...'

'Thank you for your help, Mr Grave,' I said. 'We had better leave you to your work.'

'Mr Grave understands,' he said. 'You are trying to make yourself look more youthful for the benefit of your young lady. Come back without her and Mr Grave can do you something much more realistic.'

Sidney Grice snatched the wig back.

'Good day,' he said and spun away.

'Would you like me to have it cleaned?' Mr Grave said and Sidney Grice turned on him.

'I should like you to go to your namesake. Come along, Miss Middleton.'

Sidney Grice glared at me when we got outside.

'This is certainly no laughing matter,' he said, but it seemed like one to me.

32

Broken Wings

THE NEW GLOUCESTER theatre was anything but new. Its most modern feature was the paintwork, which showered brown-red flakes when Sidney Grice rapped three times with the Face of Tragedy knocker.

'It looks deserted,' I said, and a panel in the door was opened by a very short man, so plump as to be almost spherical.

'You are late,' he said, admitting us through the opening into a large dusty foyer.

'We are not expected,' Sidney Grice said, and the round man looked him up and down.

'So you are not the comedy cow?'

My guardian raised his cane. 'How dare—'

'Neither comedy nor cow,' I said hastily. 'May we have a word?'

'So who are you?'

My guardian stepped forward. 'I am Sidney Grice, the personal detective. Are you the manager of this establishment?'

'If you have come to arrest me, I am not. Otherwise I might be.'

My guardian opened his satchel and brought out a brown paper bag.

'I am looking for the owner of this.' He produced the wig. 'And I have reason to believe that he played a part in your recent production of Verdi's dreary melodrama.'

'Not *a* part.' The manager took out a brilliant yellow handkerchief. '*The* part. This hairpiece was worn by Rigoletto himself. He was our greatest success before he ran off and left us in the lurch.'

'Do you remember his name?' I asked.

'How could I forget?' he replied, wiping his hands on the handkerchief.

'What was it?' Sidney Grice snapped.

'James Hoggart.'

'Hoggart does not sound very Italian,' my guardian said.

'Nor does it,' the manager agreed, leaning his shoulder against a mock marble pillar but pulling away when it wobbled.

'So he is not Italian,' I said.

'He was no more Italian than I, and I am not Italian,' the manager said. 'He did tend to talk like one, though – said it made it come more natural on the stage.'

'How well do you know him?' I asked.

'Enough not to want to know him better.' The manager picked up a broom. 'He was a deuced fine Rigoletto – his voice could blow the buttons off your shirt – and he could act the eyebrows off the rest of the cast, but was he ever happy?' He propped the broom, unused, against an autographed photograph on the wall.

'I imagine not,' I said.

'You have a good and accurate imagination then, miss,' the manager said. '*Not* is the very word. James Hoggart was *not* a happy man. His dressing room was too cold and he must have a fire lit. Then the fire is too smoky and we must have the chimney swept. Then he must have lilies brought in fresh every day. Then the pollen makes him sneeze and they must be removed and a bowl of lavender water put on his dressing table. And would he learn his lines like anybody else? Well, would he?' He threw out his arms.

'I would guess not,' I said, and he picked up the broom again and put it down.

'You are an exceedingly fine guesser, miss. Any tips for the two thirty?'

'Broken Wings might be worth a shilling each way at six to one,' I told him, and Sidney Grice shot a glance at me and said, 'Do you know where James Hoggart is now?'

'Dead,' the manager said, 'and buried for all I care. Though there's a lot of people would like to find him. I never knew a man so fond of gambling and so expert at losing. He owed money to every bookie this side of the English Channel, not counting the shopkeepers and publicans he had talked into opening a slate. Then he got involved with the moneylenders. That was when things turned nasty.'

'You have not heard anything from or about him since he went missing?' I asked.

'Not a cat's whisper.' The manager clicked his fingers. 'He could have gone back to Italy, for all I know.'

'But you told us he was not Italian,' Sidney Grice said.

'So I did and so he is not' – the manager whisked his handkerchief out again – 'but he trained in Italy and always said he might return.'

'Do you know where he lived?' Sidney Grice asked. 'Or the names of any of his friends?'

'No and no.' The manager tucked the handkerchief back into the same pocket.

'Do you know of any reason other than money why he might have disappeared?' Sidney Grice asked and the manager flapped his arms.

'What other reason could he need?'

'The possibilities are manifold,' my guardian said. 'I myself have written a paper entitled *Twenty-six Causes of Voluntary Concealment*.'

The manager pursed his lips. 'Don't think much of the title.'

'In what way would he not learn his lines like anybody else?' I asked, and Sidney Grice sighed and said, 'Does it matter?'

'I am interested,' I said, and there was a tap at the door.

'He always insisted that somebody read his lines out to him' – the manager found a pencil on the booking-office countertop – 'whilst he lay on his sofa with his eyes closed. He said he had to hear the words rather than see them. Broken Wings, you say?' He wrote the name on his shirt cuff.

'What did he look like?' Sidney Grice asked.

'Why, just like anybody else.' The manager pulled his sleeve down. 'He had a very big head and a very big nose, and when he wore his wig he had very big curly red hair indeed. Without his wig he did not. It was ratty like yours, miss.'

There was another tap at the door and the manager opened the panel, and a small woman came in with a cow's head under her arm.

'I know that face,' she said to my guardian. 'You play the hurdy-gurdy at King's Cross with a child dressed as an ape.'

'I would have thought you were sufficiently bovine without the need of a costume,' Sidney Grice said, stepping outside.

'Are you his new monkey?' she asked me.

'Something like that,' I said.

33

The Old Canal

JUST AS ALBERT had predicted, the glue factory was easy to find and the smell was truly appalling. We clamped our handkerchiefs over our noses and I wished I had had the foresight to perfume mine.

'Allow me.' Inspector Pound sprinkled a few drops from a dark blue bottle on to a white cloth for me.

'What is it?'

'Camphor.' He showed me the handwritten label. 'I always keep some with me. You come across some horrible things in my job.'

'But few more horrible than boiling bones,' Sidney Grice said. 'Do you have any of that to spare, Inspector?'

'I am afraid not, Mr Grice.' Inspector Pound slipped the bottle back into his brown coat pocket.

There were two constables with us as we made our way along the towpath. They carried coils of rope and grappling hooks.

'Not much of a place for soppy girls,' one of them said.

'Just as well there are no soppy girls here then,' I said.

'You won't get the better of her, Perkins.' Inspector Pound laughed. 'Do you really think this is worth pursuing, Mr Grice?' He hopped over a puddle. 'I've got a couple of very nasty murders and an attempted arson that need my urgent attention.'

'I am sure of it.' Sidney Grice flicked a maggot-ridden cat with his stick into the slimy black water where it came up to the surface and pitched on its back, grinning up at us. 'And this must be the barge.'

We made our way to the back of a rotten hulk, half-sunk in sludge, with a tawny tangle-haired mongrel standing on the broken prow.

'There were two families living in that last winter,' Inspector Pound told us, 'and they were being charged rent for it. The week before Christmas the collector came and found all twenty-four of them dead from the river fever. The owner tried to rent it out again, but the bottom caved in when the parish cleared their bodies and two men drowned.'

The dog barked and crouched and snarled and jack-in-the-boxed in our direction, but did not attempt to follow us.

'There's the jetty.' Inspector Pound pointed. 'So, if young Albert was telling the truth, he found the wig somewhere around here, and if there is a body it would not drift far in this stagnation.'

The canal widened into a circle about thirty feet across, where the narrow boats would have turned when the stretch was in use.

'What is that?' I pointed to a slight mound in the thick algae and weeds a yard or so from the far bank.

'Could be a log or a dead donkey,' Sidney Grice said, 'but I would not wager on it being either of those.'

Inspector Pound called one of his constables over. 'Think you can reach that, Perkins?'

'My granny could reach that,' the constable said, 'and she's not been out of bed these last three years. Excuse me, miss.'

I stood back and Perkins began to swing the grappling iron, four arrow-headed hooks on a thick rope. Faster and faster it windmilled at his side until with a faint grunt he let it go, sailing high in the air to splash into a patch of reeds just short of the target.

'Should have brought your granny,' the second constable said.

'I was just getting the measure of it,' Perkins said, hauling his iron back, clogged with soggy debris.

'Let me show you how it's done.' The second constable let his iron fly across the basin, over the mound and into a willow tree, jutting out of a tumbled-down shed on the opposite bank. He muttered under his breath and pulled, but the hooks were tangled in the branches and the tree shook and bent towards him but would not let it go.

Perkins laughed and said, 'My granny wouldn't have done that. Stand back, Maybury, and let the expert show you how it's done.'

Perkins swung again, higher but even shorter this time. He wound back in, his rope soaked with stinking water, while Maybury pulled harder but with no better results.

'The manager of the New Gloucester could use these two comedians,' Sidney Grice murmured to me and Inspector Pound looked at him sharply.

'Get on with it, Perkins.'

'Yes, sir.' Perkins swung his hook a third time and got the distance, but was over to the right of his target.

'You throw like a girl,' Maybury jeered.

'Would you like me to show you how a real girl can throw?' I asked and the inspector grimaced.

'Just do it, Perkins.' He was red with frustration. 'And, if you do not retrieve your equipment, Maybury, the cost of replacing it will be docked from your wages.'

Perkins fell short again and hauled in, while Maybury

went down the bank to wrench at his rope from a different angle.

'Perhaps we could hire a rowing boat,' I said as, with another grunt, Perkins let his missile go and this time it landed perfectly, plunging into the water about two feet beyond the mound.

'At last.' Inspector Pound exhaled. 'Reel it in, Perkins.'

Perkins pulled the rope and the end of the hook rose above the mound, but the barbs engaged and it began to float towards us.

'It's heavy.' Perkins adjusted his grip and Maybury took hold of the rope too.

The green surface broke, leaving a trail of muddy water in its wake as the mound ploughed steadily along now.

'It is about the right size,' Inspector Pound said and Perkins slipped, his foot going over the edge, letting go of the rope as he snatched at his colleague to save himself, and the two men tumbled backwards, falling into the nettles behind them. Inspector Pound put his foot on the rope as it snaked back into the canal.

'Imbeciles,' he said under his breath, but Sidney Grice was not even looking at them. His attention was fixed on the mound which had rotated a quarter turn with the sudden release of tension, and something reared out of the slime, grey and pocked with decay, unreal and yet unmistakeable, a mud-clogged nose and an eaten lip bobbing in the filth five yards away.

Sidney Grice's face was triumphant.

'Not a bad morning's fishing,' he said. 'Inspector, allow me to introduce you to the eponymous hero of *Rigoletto*, otherwise known as the late Mr James Hoggart.'

34

Buckets and Sacks

'AND I THOUGHT the canal smelled bad,' Sidney Grice said, clamping his handkerchief firmly over his nose and mouth as the body was heaved up out of the water and deposited supine on the weed-choked towpath.

Perkins and Maybury turned away and Inspector Pound took a few steps backwards, but I had smelled death before many times, fresh on my father's table and old in the dysenteric field hospitals of Natal, and I would not let it overcome me. I swallowed hard but stayed my ground. If Sidney Grice could stand with the rotting man at his feet, so could and so would I. If only it had not been the face.

His face was half-eaten by rats and decay. The eyes and their lids had gone as had the upper lip and half the lower and most of the nose, the cavity in its place bubbling with a brown froth, and the left ear was missing and something slug-like oozed out of the crater in its place.

I could probably have coped with that face but it was the vapours of corruption that really unbalanced me. They hissed out of him in a last lost word.

I stumbled back. 'I did not know.' But nobody was listening to me.

'Send into the factory for some buckets of water,' Sidney Grice called to the inspector, who jerked his head towards his men, who ran back the way we had come and across a wooden bridge over a bricked drainage ditch.

The body wore tails and a high-collared shirt with a black tie, sagging but still in an extravagant bow. His boots were still on his feet.

'Looks like he was going to the opera.' Inspector Pound leaned forwards but stayed well back.

'He was.' Sidney Grice suppressed a choke.

The inspector produced his bottle of camphor oil and emptied it on to his handkerchief.

'You said you had none left,' my guardian said.

'Not so.' Inspector Pound's voice was muffled. 'I said I had none to spare.'

The constables returned with two metal pails and dowsed the face and hands and upper body carefully, under Sidney Grice's instruction. Several of the dead man's fingers had been chewed off, and he was wearing a canary yellow waistcoat, badly shredded.

Sidney Grice walked clockwise slowly round the body, stopped, and then walked counter-clockwise.

'No obvious frontal wounds.' He turned to Inspector Pound. 'You might as well take him to the morgue, but please make sure that the clothes are not thrown away this time and that the pockets are searched.'

The inspector's mouth tensed.

'All right, men, get this body moved.'

'What?' Perkins asked in horror.

'How?' Maybury asked.

'Take the buckets back to the factory,' Inspector Pound said patiently, 'and ask for some spare sacks to roll it on to.'

'I think we will leave them to it,' Sidney Grice said to me. 'I expect you could do with a cup of tea.'

Back at Gower Street I rushed to my room to get out of my boots and dress. I went to the bathroom and washed my hands and face and blew my nose, and went back to my room and smoked a cigarette out of the window and drank a large gin very quickly, then another more slowly with a second cigarette. I sprayed myself with Fougère, but the stench still filled my nostrils and a taste clung in my mouth. My living flesh was saturated with putrefaction.

35

Caligula

INSPECTOR POUND CLEARED his desk. He pushed everything on to the floor, instantly turning a mess into chaos. He sat behind the desk in a creaky swivel chair as we sat facing him on two old uprights.

'Well, we have found out how he was killed.' He put down a plain brown cardboard folder. 'I was worried that the corpse would be too decayed for that but the surgeon tells me there is no doubt about it – a stab wound in the back of his neck. The skin and muscles were too rotted to tell him anything, but the bones of his spine had been separated from the base of the skull by a short sharp blade.'

'A professional job then,' Sidney Grice said and the inspector nodded.

'It reminds me of a murder we had in seventy-eight. A Sicilian steamer captain found floating in the East India Docks with the same sort of wound. We never caught the culprit and the crew were very nervous about talking to us but, from what we could piece together, it was the work of a hired assassin. There is a lot of rivalry between the various family gangs there.'

'*Rivincita*,' I said, but my guardian brushed the word aside.

'No other obvious injuries – broken bones, for example?' he asked.

'None that he could find.' Inspector Pound brought out his meerschaum pipe. The bowl had been carved into a woman's face, her hair flowing backwards. He blew experimentally down the stem.

'Who performed the post-mortem examination?'

'Mr Rawlings.'

'He is a thorough man.' Sidney Grice leaned back. 'Anything in the dead man's pockets? Any identification, for example?'

'All his pockets were empty save one,' Inspector Pound said. 'In fact most of them were sewn up.'

'Now why would that be?'

'I could not say.' He opened his leather pouch and fed some tobacco into the pipe.

'They were obviously his stage clothes,' I said. 'So he would not have any use for pockets and stitching them keeps the costume in better shape.'

If either man heard me they gave no sign of it.

'You said *save one*,' Sidney Grice said, and Inspector Pound opened the folder grimly.

'I think you need to see this,' he said, and placed an oblong brown envelope on to the gouged wooden desktop. 'Mr Rawlings found it in the inside jacket pocket.'

'Left or right?'

'Left.'

Sidney Grice picked it up and shot one hand to his eye.

'It is addressed to you,' he said and read out, '*For the urgent attention of Inspector Pound, Marylebone Police Station.*'

'Just as well it is in pencil,' the inspector said. 'Ink would have run and be completely unreadable.'

'Was the envelope sealed?'

'I believe so.' He tamped the tobacco lightly with an oval disc on the end of his penknife.

Sidney Grice folded back the flap and took out a single piece of paper and laid it out flat.

'The handwriting and spelling are good,' he said.

'A man's hand,' Inspector Pound said, and Sidney Grice paled.

'Some sort of trick,' he said.

'None that I can see.' Inspector Pound pulled a straying strand of tobacco from the bowl and placed it back in the pouch.

'What is it?' I asked and Sidney Grice said quietly, 'Read it out, Miss Middleton. I need to think.'

I picked up the letter. It was stained and slightly torn but still clearly legible. The writing was small and neat, in strong square letters, and both sides of the paper were filled.

'Dear Inspector Pound

'I am writing to you because I know you to be a man of honour who will not hesitate to admit he has made a mistake if it will save an innocent man from the Gallows and, be in no doubt about it, WILLIAM ASHBEY IS INNOCENT.

'How do I know this? Because I AM THE MURDERER OF SARAH ASHBEY. I crept into her sitting room and killed her with a crinkle-bladed knife I bought in their shop. I put my hand over her mouth and stabbed her in the heart before she could make a sound, and then I stabbed her again and again, forty times in all. I counted every cut. She never did me any wrong except for one thing. I saw her walking down the street. She had beautiful full lips and I smiled at her, but she walked straight past without even giving me a glance and I do not take kindly to being ignored. So I decided to make sure she would remember me FOR THE REST OF HER LIFE.

'The last person she ever saw was me, while her simpleton husband snored in the next room. I wanted to wake him up and tell him that he sold me the knife that killed his wife but he will know soon enough, when he reads this. I crept out of the front door. The stupid match girl was asleep outside. I stole a box of vespers from her tray.

'My bloodlust was up after I did it. I went home but I could not sit down. I was so excited and I thought – *why stop at one?* – so I went out and did it again. This one was younger and I enjoyed the cutting of her all the more – the surprise when she saw me turning to terror when she saw the knife – the way she tried to fight me off and escape, the way she begged. Lord, how she squealed, but that only made it better. I did not have to worry about the noise this time.

'And when it was over I thought I would play a little game. So I put her body in a box. Nobody has found her yet, though, so I had better tell you where she is. She lived and died in the basement of 37 Chandler Street. The number is on the front door. Even your lot should be able to find that.'

The inspector struck a vesper and I carried on reading.

'Why am I telling you this? Because I do not want that lumbering idiot of a shopkeeper to get the credit for my artistry. I shall kill a dozen women before you catch me, IF you ever catch me. Maybe I shall make it a hundred – all that hot blood on my hands – I have the taste for it now.

'I started with those two whores on Slurry Street. Who knows where it might end?

'Do not waste your time listening to Mr Grice. He will try to steal your glory and he will never catch me, but you might, and here is a little clue to put you on the scent.

'You will know me as CALLIGULLA.'

Inspector Pound held the flame over his pipe and sucked it down two or three times before he blew it out. Grey wisps curled over the rim, thickening into small fragrant clouds that reminded me of my father in the long evenings we shared by the fire when his sight was failing and I would read to him. The inspector snapped the match and tossed it into a bin on the floor. He sat back to watch my guardian lost in thought, and it must have been the smoke that brought a tear to my eye.

My father did not approve of schools. He had been bullied at his and my mother, he told me, had been made miserable by her governess. And so he decided to teach me himself. But my father was a busy man. He had thrown himself into his medical and military duties and, whilst they brought him no consolation, they did distract him from his grief. He taught me the three R's and gave me a free rein in his library. I pored over atlases and anatomical textbooks. I fell in love with Horace and Shakespeare's sonnets. I studied military campaigns and astronomy. It was, perhaps, an eccentric education but, I believe, a good one. I never learned the pianoforte or sewing. I was not taught deportment but you were glad of that, you told me. I moved like a woman, you said, not like a standard lamp on castors.

36

Easy Tricks

SIDNEY GRICE LISTENED in silence. He was even paler than usual.

He held the letter up to the light and said, 'No water-mark.' He put his elbow on the desk and tapped his forehead. 'Cheap paper. HB pencil not sharpened during the writing. See how the lines progressively thicken.'

'These are easy tricks, Mr Grice,' Inspector Pound said, 'but what are we to make of the contents?'

'There is no doubt that it came from James Hoggart's pocket?'

'Mr Rawlings found it himself.'

Sidney Grice sniffed the letter.

'And it has certainly had a long soak in foul water. Who else has read this?'

'Only Mr Rawlings and he gave it directly to me.'

'This must be kept quiet at all costs,' Sidney Grice said urgently. 'It would be a powder keg in the hands of agitators.'

'We can depend upon Mr Rawlings' discretion.'

My guardian looked at the letter again. 'May I borrow it?'

The inspector shook his head. 'It could be crucial evidence, Mr Grice.'

'Of what?' Sidney Grice said. 'We have already caught and hanged the murderer of Sarah Ashby.'

'I hope so,' Inspector Pound said quietly.

'Miss Middleton will make a good copy,' Sidney Grice said. 'I trust you have no objection to that?'

'None whatsoever.' Inspector Pound opened a drawer and gave me a sheet of blank paper, and indicated to the inkstand and brass-tipped pen. 'Caligula,' he said as I set to work. 'That is an Italian name, is it not?'

'It was the nickname of a Roman emperor infamous for his cruelty,' I said. 'It is said he murdered his own mother and had knowledge of her and his three sisters. He is supposed—'

'Is that what they teach young ladies these days?' Inspector Pound broke in.

'They taught me how to read,' I said, 'and my father had a volume of *The Twelve Caesars* by Suetonius. Do you want me to copy this exactly?'

'Of course,' my guardian said.

'Including the spelling mistakes? He has spelled Ashby as *Ashbey*.'

'Let me see.' Sidney Grice took the letter from me. 'Why would he do that?'

'Because he was Italian,' the inspector suggested.

'He was *not* Italian,' Sidney Grice said.

'And he has spelled Caligula with two double L's.'

'Not very Italian of him,' my guardian said sourly.

'This blood test of yours...' Inspector Pound brought out a box of matches. 'I suppose there is no possibility of a mistake?'

'It is not *my* test.' Sidney Grice fiddled with his eye. 'And Professor Latingate is respected throughout the Empire.

Besides which, the case against Ashby was based on a whole gamut of forensic and circumstantial evidence. Even if I had never found the knife, he would have hanged, and rightly so.'

I dried my copy carefully on a much used blotter and turned it over.

'All the same, it was the test that clinched it,' the inspector said.

'What are you implying, Inspector?'

Inspector Pound rubbed the back of his neck and hesitated. 'Just that I would feel more comfortable if we had had more evidence, and if Ashby had not been such an unlikely murderer and this letter had not turned up to corroborate his story.'

Sidney Grice laid his palms upon the desk and tensed his lips. He started to say something but no sound came. His fingers drummed the wood and he blew out slowly.

I re-dipped the pen. The ink was India Blue, almost black in my shadow.

'We thought there was trouble *before* William Ashby was hanged,' the inspector said. 'My God, if it got out that he was innocent...'

'I hardly think...' Sidney Grice's voice wandered off.

'You were nearly lynched last time,' I said, but he did not seem to hear me. He brought out his halfpennies and flipped them absently.

I turned to the inspector. 'Have you sent anyone to investigate Chandler Street?'

'Not yet,' he said. 'I only received this an hour before you came and I wanted Mr Grice to see it first. I was hoping he would be able to dismiss it.'

My guardian roused himself from his thoughts.

'Then we must go there immediately.' He pushed his chair back. 'And give the lie to this tasteless prank.'

I finished and dried my copy, and my guardian slipped it into his satchel. On the way out we saw the constable who had stood over William Ashby in the interview room.

'Good morning, sirs, miss.'

The men replied and walked on, but something was troubling me.

'Do you remember fetching that bowl of water?' I asked.

'Of course, miss.' His shoes were scuffed on the toes and his trousers a fraction too short.

'Why did it take so long?'

The constable stiffened indignantly.

'We don't keep that kind of thing here. I had to borrow it from the shop next door.'

'Drayton and Son?'

'Yes, miss.'

'Thank you,' I said. 'I meant no offence.'

'That's all right, miss,' he said but I could see it was not, so I said, 'You look very smart in that uniform.' And the constable simpered just in time for Sidney Grice to come back and drag me away.

37

The House on Chandler Street

CHANDLER STREET WAS little more than a narrow cobbled walkway, almost a tunnel at times where the upper floors of houses nearly met over our heads.

We stopped at a door hanging inwards on broken hinges, and Inspector Pound pushed but it would not budge. He climbed in through the gap and I followed.

'Hell,' I said as my hem snagged on a rusty screw, and Sidney Grice pointed to the gutter.

'Kindly leave such language where it belongs, Miss Middleton.'

'You should try scrambling through in a dress,' I said and Inspector Pound chuckled.

'I would give a guinea to see him try.'

He took my hand to help me through, and in the dim light filtering between the planked windows I saw we were in a large high hallway. A staircase tumbled upwards and the floor looked in no better condition. Inspector Pound put one foot forwards and leaned his weight on it.

'Hear that creak?' He leaned again. 'The joists are rotten. We must keep to the sides and well apart. I shall go first.' He edged his way round the room on the right-hand side. 'And you must stay there, Miss Middleton.'

'You should know by now that I am not a girl who does what she must,' I said, and made my way after him.

The walls were bulging with laths jutting through in places, and I caught the back of my dress this time, but I had resigned myself to ruining my clothes now. The inspector reached an archway on the wall opposite the front door and passed through it.

'The stairs are here,' he said as I caught up with him.

They went disjointedly down an unlit passage.

'And in equally poor condition by the look of them,' Sidney Grice said as he joined us. 'See all those holes? They are riddled with woodworm. It would be safer for you both to stay here.'

Upstairs a baby cried weak hungry wails, but I heard no mother soothing it.

'I have a better idea,' I said. 'Being the lightest, since I do not have a huge masculine brain to weigh me down, I shall go first.'

'I am afraid I cannot allow that.' The inspector held up his hand but I was already on my way down.

The stairs groaned and sagged under my feet, but I made my way easily enough down them to a plain pine-plank door at the bottom.

'I cannot think a man the size of James Hoggart came along this way,' the inspector said. 'He was more heavily built than us.'

'Wait there,' Sidney Grice called from the top, but I had the handle in my hand and turned it.

There was a faint humming, getting louder as I pushed the door open, and it did not take me long to recognize the source of that sound. The cellar room I was entering was swarming with flies.

38

The Plague of Flies

THE AIR WAS thick with them – fat buzzing blowflies. They swarmed around my face, metallic blue, bristly and loathsome.

I gagged on the rankness of rotting meat.

The inspector came clattering down and, more cautiously behind him, my guardian, who peered in. 'Carrion flies.' He tried to bat some away. 'And look,' he pointed, 'over there.'

On a sack blanket on the floor in the far right corner was a rounded lump. It was shrouded in a swarm of big slow flies but, even in the half-light, we could see that this thing was not a woman's body. It looked more like a head, hacked off and covered in thick black hair. Inspector Pound went over.

'Some mangy old cur,' he said, 'and crawling with maggots… And that would be how our man got in.' He strode across and threw open an unbolted door at the back, which led to a small sunken area with iron steps. The floor was smeared with footprints and littered with dead bluebottles crunching under his feet. 'I think I will get this outside.' He picked up the sacking by its corners with undisguised distaste and took it up the steps.

It was a bare brick room with a sagging ceiling and the only furniture was a low unmade bed. In one corner, floor to ceiling, was a wire-netted cupboard which would have been a meat safe when the house belonged to a family. A dried puddle had oozed from it into a dip in the floor.

'Her wardrobe.' My guardian opened the door, revealing a few scraps of clothing hanging from butchers' hooks above a pine blanket box.

'Watch out,' Inspector Pound called, 'if you come up here. There is a sewer with the manhole cover missing and that, I think, is the best place for this.'

'No!' Sidney Grice rushed to the door.

I followed him up into a high-walled courtyard bordered by straggling shrubs. An iron-gated arch led into a backstreet.

'Too late.' The inspector wiped his hands on a handkerchief. 'I did not realize you wanted to give it a Christian burial.'

'That animal could have been evidence,' Sidney Grice said, but the inspector shook his head.

'I do not investigate dog murders, and if it was a witness it was not going to tell us anything.'

My guardian hunted about for something to fish it out with but, as I looked down the oblong metal-rimmed hole into the swirling sludge two yards below, a yellowed ragged mongrel turned a half-circle and drifted away.

'It could have told us all sorts of things.' Sidney Grice rubbed his left shoulder. 'How did it die, for example?'

'I neither know nor care,' Inspector Pound said, 'and I do not think Mr Rawlings would want to do a post-mortem on it. He has a hundred human corpses to worry about first.'

The slabs were thick with weeds and moss between and over them, but enough stone was exposed to show dozens of bloody footprints.

'What do you make of those?' my guardian asked.

'It looks like a few people were here,' I said. 'The prints are all over the place.'

Sidney Grice shook his head. 'Just one man.'

'There are at least two sets of prints coming out.' Inspector Pound pointed. 'And they overlap in places.'

'One man,' Sidney Grice repeated, 'but you are right that there are two sets. See how clear they are near the house, but they fade towards the gateway and the ones coming towards the house are very faint indeed. Obviously, our man ran out of the house – the long strides on the toes.' We followed the course of the prints. 'He stopped near the gate here, turned and walked back – these shorter strides. He is putting his heels down but his toes are almost clear of blood. He went back in, got them wet again, and finally ran off. The prints go to the left of the alley before they disappear.' Sidney Grice pinched his upper lip and paced round the courtyard. He poked around in the bushes half-heartedly with his cane, and when he spoke it was probably to himself. 'But why would he go back into the cellar?'

'Perhaps he forgot something and went to get it,' I suggested.

'Yes, but what? And, more importantly, what or who was the source of that blood?'

We all went back down into the room. It seemed darker than when we had first entered it, but our eyes soon adjusted themselves.

'Well, at least most of the flies went with the dog,' Inspector Pound said, 'and that must be the box our friend Caligula wrote about. Excuse me, Mr Grice. I think this is a police matter.'

Sidney Grice had his hand to the box, but stepped away as Inspector Pound approached it and gingerly lifted the lid.

'Sweet Jesus,' he said. He closed his eyes briefly and exhaled slowly.

'Dear God.' I looked into the box. 'She is little more than a child.'

The body of a girl had been twisted and stuffed into it, her head wrenched at an unnatural angle so that the face was looking over the shoulder, the big eyes staring blindly, glazed like stale fish, the jaw hanging open and the corner of the mouth hacked into the grotesque grin of a clown, the fingers of one hand reaching towards the lid as if she were about to clamber out, the body clothed in a dark garment and everything encrusted in the rust of old blood.

'How old would you say she is?' Sidney Grice said, not taking his eyes off her.

'Fifteen or sixteen,' I said. 'Oh, the poor girl. Do you think she lived alone?'

'Who knows?' Inspector Pound said. 'She is alone now, though.'

If I were not with men I should have cried.

'She was a pretty thing,' Sidney Grice said.

'Is that important?' I asked.

'It could be,' he said. 'Many a girl has died for less reason than that.'

'Look at this.' Inspector Pound indicated a patch of damp plaster on the wall at the back of the cupboard.

'*Rivincita*,' I read out, 'and it looks like the same handwriting.'

'Similar,' Sidney Grice said.

'There is the same unusual capital R,' I pointed out.

'Very similar.' Sidney Grice put his hand to his eye. 'So, we might as well have a proper look at her.'

'You cannot expect us to pull her out,' the inspector said.

'No need. The sides are clipped.'

Sidney Grice slid two wooden pegs out and stepped back, and the girl's body came tumbling half on to the brick floor. We could see her wounds now. Her face and neck were cut in several places, as were her hands and arms. The cloth was ripped from her left shoulder to the top of her breast, where there was a wide and deep laceration.

'That would be fatal in itself,' the inspector said.

Sidney Grice rooted in his satchel, struck a Lucifer and lit a stubby candle, holding it over the body and bending so close that his nose almost touched her.

'What have we here?' he said. 'Hand me my bag, Miss Middleton.'

I passed it over to him and he put the candle down, brought out a small cloth roll, untied it and unrolled it on the floor to reveal a small set of surgeon's instruments.

'What are you doing, Mr Grice?' Inspector Pound asked, but my guardian did not reply. He took a pair of sturdy locking tweezers, pushed them into the wound and clamped them shut.

'You cannot interfere with the body like that,' Inspector Pound said, but Sidney Grice was not listening. He was rocking the tweezers and pulling them firmly and steadily out, and it was obvious he had something in their grasp.

'There we are,' he cried out in triumph. 'What do you make of that?'

It was an elongated triangle of steel. Sidney Grice held it up and rotated it, the tip of a knife, two, perhaps three inches long, glittering in the dancing flame and undulating along its edges.

'It snapped off on a rib,' he said, 'but the force of the blow pushed the rest of the knife through.'

'Dear God,' Inspector Pound said. 'It looks exactly like the one that killed Sarah Ashby, the one that William Ashby swore he had sold to the Italian. It all ties in with the letter.'

'Precisely,' Sidney Grice said. 'Which all goes to prove that the two murders were committed by two different people.'

Inspector Pound stood up and his voice was sharp and hard. 'I cannot argue with you now, Mr Grice. I am going to summon assistance and have this poor girl taken to the mortuary. Then you and I need to have a long talk. As if it were not enough to be investigating a maniac, I am beginning to think that either you or I must be completely and incurably insane.'

'Which of you is right does not matter very much at the moment,' I said. 'Either way there is a madman on the loose. He could be hacking another defenceless girl to death this very minute, and all you can do is stand here squabbling.'

'Now see here...' the inspector said, but did not finish his sentence.

Sidney Grice stepped back and stared at the dead girl. He clicked his tongue, rubbed the back of his neck, and said nothing.

39

Judas

MY GUARDIAN WAS thoughtful as we rode home in a hansom, but after a few minutes he brightened and began to tap his knee almost rhythmically.

'You seem very cheerful,' I observed and Sidney Grice smiled.

'I am.'

'How on earth can you be happy after what we have just seen?'

'Because it gives me the opportunity to silence my critics once and for all,' he said and started to hum.

I took a breath and said as calmly as I could, 'Is that all it means to you? Do you not feel anything for that poor girl?'

'She knows nothing now,' he said. 'No pain. No fear. My feelings cannot help her.' He looked down for a moment and then straight ahead. 'But you were right about one thing, March. Whoever did this will certainly strike again – unless he is stopped. And there is only one hope for that – me.'

'So what are you going to do?'

'I have not the faintest idea.' Sidney Grice smiled and twiddled his cane. 'But rest assured I shall do it.'

I was beginning to think that Inspector Pound must be right.

'Have you ever been wrong?'

He looked deeply puzzled. 'Why on earth should I want to be that?'

We passed an old woman lying by the other side of the road unattended.

'May I ask you another question?'

'By all means,' he said, breaking off from a tuneless hum to polish the top of his cane with his glove.

'Ge' owov the way,' the cabby shouted, but I could not see at whom. He cracked his whip and we shot forwards.

'Do you know where the basin which you used to test William Ashby's knife came from?'

'Probably one of the lesser Stoke potteries,' my guardian said. 'It was asymmetrically cast and the quality of the glaze was poor, but I did not look at the stamp on the base. The bowl was full of water as even you will have observed.'

A pigeon landed on the sill and he shooed it away.

'I mean where the policeman fetched it from.'

'No, but I sense that you wish to tell me.'

'Drayton and Son,' I said.

Sidney Grice's cheek ticked and he caught his eye.

'Blast this thing. Blast that quack Goldman and his stupid gutta-percha and all his glass-blowing nincompoops.' He slipped it into his waistcoat pocket. 'The butcher's shop next door to the police station?' he asked, a little too casually, I thought.

'Yes.'

My guardian took a patch from his satchel and turned to look at me. 'And what are you inferring from that?'

I drew a breath and said, 'Do you not think it possible, indeed likely, that the bowl itself could have been contaminated by blood either by being used to store raw meat, or even just from being touched by a bloodstained hand?'

'Yes.' He tied the cord behind his head.

'And that does not worry you?'

'Not in the least.'

'Might I ask why not?'

'Certainly you might.' He straightened his patch.

'Why not?'

Sidney Grice sighed.

'Because, my dear girl, if there had been blood in the bowl, even the slightest trace of it, the crystals would have changed colour when they were put into the water whereas, as you will recollect, they did not do so until the knife was put into the water.'

'And swirled around,' I said.

'And swirled around,' he agreed.

The cab rocked violently and we heard a few shrill barks.

'Ge' owovit,' the cabby bellowed as his horse shied towards the pavement. The hansom stopped, one wheel up on the kerb, and we heard the crack of a whip and a yelp. 'Blasted strays,' he shouted, 'gettin' under my 'orse's 'ooves. I run 'em over when I can. Blast the blasted fings.'

'Ladies,' my guardian called.

We straightened ourselves up and the cab set off again, a little unsteadily at first, jolting over a pothole.

'Do you remember remarking that the water was very cold?' I asked.

'My powers of recall are more than the equal of yours,' he said. 'I remember it perfectly.'

I hesitated again. 'Do you think it possible that any blood on the bowl did not wash into the water until you swirled it?'

'I do not.'

'Or that the crystals did not dissolve in the water until you stirred it with the knife?'

'No.' Sidney Grice banged on the roof with the silvered ferrule of his cane and called, 'Pull over, cabby. I shall walk from here.' He flung open the flap. 'I have supported you out of the charity of my heart, Miss Middleton. It would be pretty to receive a little loyalty in return.'

'Even at the cost of a miscarriage of justice?' I asked, my voice rising above the noise of the street.

Sidney Grice thrust some coins into my hand and said, as he alighted, 'That should pay your fare back to my home, or do you want your forty pieces of silver?' He slammed the door and shouted, 'Drive on, cabby.' And the hansom lurched forwards, flinging me back into my seat.

I leaned over and looked out, and saw a head bobbing jerkily to the right, but the crowd closed in and Sidney Grice was lost from view. Swamped, for the first time I had known, by humanity.

40

Diogenes

I WAITED FOR two hours in the study but my guardian did not return.

'Gone to his club, most likely,' Molly said, tucking one stray strand of hair under her hat and making two more fall out.

'What club is that?'

'Why, the Diogenes. Mr Grice taught me how to say that,' she told me, tossing her head proudly. 'He often stays there when he is perplexicated. They have no women and no talking. He likes both those rules a great deal.'

'I imagine he does,' I said. 'Turn round.' I tied the bow of her apron for her. 'How long have you worked for Mr Grice now?'

'Two years and two months.' She flicked the hallstand half-heartedly with a feather duster. 'Which cook says is two years and one month longer than anybody else ever.'

'So why do you stay?' I pinned her hair back up.

Molly wrinkled her nose. 'Well, I know he shouts a lot and says cruel things, but I like that. I can't abide masters or mistresses who think you are the best of friends. If I am their friend, why do I have to fetch and carry for them? Mr Grice knows my place and so do I. Also, he is very kind at heart.'

'Kind?'

'Very.'

I went to my room, where I wrote my journal. I took the letters out and held them but I could not read them that night. I touched the gold and put them away to smoke a cigarette out of the window. The city was curiously quiet and there were a thousand stars glinting. At about midnight the front door slammed and heavy jerky footsteps came up the stairs. A few minutes later I heard the bath filling, the pipes clattering against my wall, and an hour later I heard it emptying, the water rushing down the drainpipe. I stood by my door and flung it open the moment I heard his.

'Oh,' I said, 'I did not realize you were home.'

My guardian stood in a full-length red silk dressing gown. He had matching slippers on and a turban made from a white towel. He did not have his eye in or a patch on.

'Well, you do now,' he said, and turned towards his room.

'Why did you take me in?'

Sidney Grice stopped with his hand on the doorknob, but kept his back to me.

'As I told you, from the charity of my heart.'

'But as you have also told me many times you have no charity and precious little heart.'

He kept hold of the handle but turned to face me.

'Out of vanity,' he said.

He looked so comical, seeming to wink at me with his headdress bobbing about, that I wanted to laugh, but I only said, 'How does my presence flatter that?'

For a moment I thought he would say that he had come across my photograph and that he wanted to be seen about town with a beautiful young ward, but he shrugged and said, 'There are so many downright lies written about me. I read your book about your father. It was more than a little naive and had a number of factual errors and omissions but—'

'Errors and omissions?'

'Yes.' He wiped a trickle from his temple. 'But it made me wish that I had known him… better. I thought you might do the same for me – record my cases – be my Boswell, as it were. Your diaries are not very flattering, but they describe my methods and character far better than anything I have—'

'You have been reading my diaries?'

'Every day.'

I drew myself up and looked him in the eye, but he did not seem the least bit abashed.

'How could you? I suppose you will try to tell me it is part of your duty in caring for me.'

He shook his head and the towel unravelled a little.

'Certainly not. I have little or no right at all to read them, but I have always been inquisitive. It is the fuel of my profession.'

I said, 'My diaries are private. I confide things to them that I would not disclose to any man or woman alive. You have gone too far this time, Mr Grice. I cannot stay here to be spied upon. I shall leave in the morning.'

His face fell.

'That would be a great pity.'

'Do not pretend you would miss me.'

'I should not pretend that,' he said, 'but it would be a pity for both of us. I should lose my honest chronicler and you, who have nowhere else to go, incidentally, would lose the chance to see that poor girl's murderer brought to justice.'

'I shall stay until the case is solved,' I said, 'but you had better be quick about it.'

My guardian's mouth twitched.

'I shall do my best.'

'What errors and omissions?'

Sidney Grice smiled.

'Goodnight, March,' he said. 'I shall see you in the morning.' And he turned the handle of his bedroom door.

I went to bed and tried to stay awake, but sleep conquers all in the end.

I see you every day. But in the night I can touch you. We hold hands and walk, and the sun pounds on our bare heads. The earth is hard and the grass withered. We never talk. Sometimes we are happy – though we never laugh – and sometimes unbearably sad.

But it is always the same at the end. We stop and you turn to me and all I see is a confusion of black gouts and splinters of white bone, and it is only when my name breathes hollow through those raw lips that I know. And that is all you ever say because it is all you can say. That last lost word empties you of air and fills you with blood. It sprays in my face as I lean over you, and flows on to my hand, and I cannot wipe it off.

I sit up and the air is thick with terror.

Then I open my eyes and know what it was, but there is no relief. The cruelty of dreams cannot begin to match the savagery of being alive.

And I hold it inside me like a dead child, the heaviness of my guilt.

41

Reasonable Doubt

INSPECTOR POUND HAD been drinking – I could smell the whisky on his breath – but he was not drunk. He was wet, however, for it was raining heavily.

'Miss Middleton.' He bobbed his head unsmilingly.

'A vile night.' My guardian shook his hand. 'Will you take tea, Inspector?'

'Do you never have anything stronger?'

'On special occasions I am not averse to a drink,' Sidney Grice said, 'of coffee.'

'Then I shall take tea.'

I poured for the three of us.

'Thank you.' Inspector Pound cleared his throat. 'Well, this is a pretty thing, Mr Grice.'

'How so?'

'Because everything that happened yesterday supports William Ashby's protestations of innocence.'

'On the contrary,' Sidney Grice said. 'I have neither seen nor heard anything to give me the slightest doubt that we hanged a murderer when we put a rope round William Ashby's neck.'

'How can you say that?' I asked and Sidney Grice smiled.

'Let me summarize the case against Ashby,' he said. 'His story was absurd from start to finish. He expected—'

'We have been through all this at the trial,' Inspector Pound broke in, 'but, as you are well aware, there have been developments since then.'

'Which are?' Sidney Grice stirred his black tea.

'Firstly' – the inspector dug his spoon into the sugar – 'William Ashby told us that he had sold a knife identical to the murder weapon to an Italian with extravagant clothing and bright red hair. You and I and the prosecution ridiculed this account. It seemed so patently silly that it went very heavily against him. Now we have discovered the body of such a man, who may not have been Italian but made his living pretending to be one. Not only that but he has in his pocket a letter which he himself wrote, admitting—'

'How do you know he wrote it?' Sidney Grice asked.

'Who else could have written it?' I asked.

'The murderer or a confidant,' Sidney Grice said.

'But I am coming to that,' Inspector Pound said. 'James Hoggart *was* the murderer.'

'That is an enormous leap of faith,' Sidney Grice said, 'so great that its logic shatters the moment it hits the ground.'

'But surely,' I said, 'he gave us details of the murder which only the murderer could have known.'

'No.' Sidney Grice leaned forwards. 'The writer of that letter knew details which must have come from somebody who knew a great deal about the crime.'

'The murderer.' Inspector Pound brought out his pipe.

Sidney Grice raised his hand and said, 'I do not permit the smoking of tobacco in this house. It deadens one's senses of smell and taste, muffles one's hearing and weakens the eyes and brain, and I intend to keep my senses as acute as possible for as long as possible but, to stay with the subject of the letter writer's identity, let us see who we can exclude. The man who knew most about the crime was the criminal himself. That much is obvious. You have not forgotten that I received a letter from Ashby, asking for my help?'

The inspector pointed with his pipe. 'You have not forgotten that I was there when he wrote it?'

'You told me you saw him actually writing the letter.'

'I came in as he was finishing it and I read it. In fact I pointed out that he had misspelled your name, but he said it did not matter, that you would not ignore his plea. Lord, how he must have wished you had.' He rammed his pipe back into his outer breast pocket.

Sidney Grice lifted a small cardboard filing box from the table at his side and hinged open the lid.

'This is the letter?'

The inspector glanced at it and said, 'You know it is.'

'Whose idea was it to write it?' My guardian put on his pince-nez.

'His mother-in-law's. She said if anyone could help him, you could, and that she would bring the letter personally to this house. She was overwrought, as one would expect, so much that when she stood to receive the letter she fainted. I believe I mentioned it at the time.'

'Did she hurt herself?' I asked.

'Thank God she did not, for she is with child.'

'I only asked because—' I began, but my guardian batted me away.

'Who went to her assistance?' he asked.

'Why, I did' – the inspector stirred his tea – 'while the constable kept Ashby firmly in his seat. We are not innocents, Mr Grice. I am fully aware that these situations can be faked to give one party the opportunity to pass notes or weapons or lockpicks to the other.'

'Did it take her long to recover?' I asked.

Pound took his cup. 'A minute or so. Is all this important?'

'Yes,' Sidney Grice said. 'I wished to be absolutely certain that there was no trickery and that Ashby wrote the letter himself. Having satisfied myself as to that point, we can rule him out as the writer who calls himself Caligula, for the two hands were completely different. Ashby's is large and ungainly whereas Caligula's is small and neat.'

'Another point in Ashby's favour,' Inspector Pound said, but Sidney Grice sipped his own tea and responded, 'I beg to differ, but we will leave that to one side for the moment. How do we know the letter found on Hoggart was not written after the trial?'

Inspector Pound put his tea down untouched, slopping a little in his saucer. 'Because the state of decay of the body showed it had been in the water for longer than that.'

I mopped his saucer and the underneath of the cup.

'What if somebody took the body out of the water, put the letter in its pocket and replaced the body?' Sidney Grice said and the inspector blinked.

'Now you are clutching at straws, Mr Grice. That body had not been disturbed for weeks, the weeds had grown around and over it, and they would not do that overnight. Also, the theft of a box of vestas from the match girl was never mentioned at the trial but the writer knew about it.'

'As did I, you, your constable and Miss Middleton,' Sidney Grice said.

'Now you are being absurd.'

Sidney Grice put his hand to his eye and held it there for a moment and said, 'I am trying to make two simple points, Inspector. Firstly, that the finding of a letter in a man's pocket does not prove that he wrote it and, secondly, that people other than the murderer had an intimate knowledge of the circumstances of the crime. Ring for more tea, please, Miss Middleton. This pot is getting stewed.'

'What about the blade you found in that girl's body?' I went to the bell rope and pulled it twice. 'It matches exactly the one which Ashby said he sold and the one which killed his wife, and yet you claim that this proved the murders were committed by two different people. I cannot see the logic in that.'

Sidney Grice drummed the arm of his chair with his fingers.

'All murderers have a modus operandi,' he said. 'You know that as well as I. A woman who poisons for profit will, if she kills again, use the same poison. It is her tried and tested method. A garrotter does not become a bludgeoner, nor a strangler an axe-man.'

'But these two women were killed in exactly the same way,' Inspector Pound said. 'They were both stabbed repeatedly with their throats cut, and through the heart, using the same or an identical knife.'

'Sarah Ashby was murdered by an experienced killer,' Sidney Grice said. 'The fatal blow was the first. I asked at the mortuary if the body had been washed. It had not and yet there was surprisingly little blood from some of the deeper wounds, including the one to her throat. She was killed quickly and cleanly and then her body mutilated.'

'But William Ashby was a shopkeeper,' I pointed out.

'Ashby was a trained soldier,' Sidney Grice said.

'What makes you so sure it was a professional killing?' I asked as Molly came and took away the teapot. The bow of her apron was coming undone.

Sidney Grice stood up.

'Stand and face me,' he said. 'Now take this ebony rule and stab me in the chest with it.'

'Oh, can I watch?' Molly asked.

'Go away,' my guardian said.

This was too good an opportunity to miss. I grasped the rule firmly and took a step towards him, bringing it down as hard and fast as I could.

'Ow.' My guardian winced and rubbed his arm as I drew the rule back for another assault. 'Thank you, Miss Middleton. That is enough to prove my point.' He took the rule from me and rolled up his sleeve to examine the damage. 'No one used to fighting with a knife would use it like that. First, you held the knife high so that your victim could see it and have time to prepare an escape, defence or even counter-attack. Second, you delivered a swinging blow. This is slow. The victim can see it coming and, most commonly, raises her arm to fend off the blow. Also, you know enough anatomy, I should imagine, to have learned that the ribs are arranged in a louvred fashion, the slats pointing down so that a knife coming from above in an arc is more likely to hit a rib than to slide between them, and this is exactly what happened to our second victim.' He rolled down his sleeve and re-buttoned the cuff. 'The knife caught on the seventh rib, twisted and snapped off. An expert holds the knife low where it is more easily concealed – he can hold it at his side, for example – and he stabs upwards in an almost straight line, though there is always a slight bias from the killer's shoulder towards the midline. The thrust is much faster, more difficult to anticipate and to ward off and, if he makes contact,' Sidney Grice demonstrated with the rule on me, 'the blade slides easily between the ribs and is directed straight to the heart. Death is instantaneous. The second nameless girl—'

'She had a name,' I broke in, 'even if we don't know it.' He tutted.

'The second girl had several lacerations to her arms where she had raised them to defend herself. Her killing was the botched job of a bungling amateur who was, judging – as one must – by the angle of the wounds, left-handed.'

'As was William Ashby,' I reminded him, and Sidney Grice sniffed.

'That is the only similarity.'

Inspector Pound drank his tea in one movement and I refilled his cup for him. He stirred the sugar in thoughtfully.

'I have the greatest of respect for you, Mr Grice,' he said, 'and I would be the first to admit that you have been of great assistance to me over the years, but are you absolutely convinced that you are not saying these things to stop yourself from admitting that we made a mistake?'

Sidney Grice sipped his tea. The cup looked quite large in his elegant hand. He said, 'Admittedly, it would not do our reputations any good if we were wrong. It would destroy your hopes of promotion and it has not done my business any good to send a client to the hangman. Think what damage would be done if it were to transpire that he was an innocent man. But I have two engines propelling my life. The first is a love of money and the second is a hatred of lies, and I would sooner send myself to the gallows than sacrifice the truth. Remember how we let Samuel Wesley walk free, though we knew he had broken his own mother's neck? If I had been prepared to swear that his handkerchief was found in the stables and not in the yard, we could have swung him and not lost a wink of sleep, and I would have pocketed the large reward that his sister was offering for his conviction.'

'I admit I did try to persuade you to alter your evidence.' Inspector Pound looked at the hearthrug.

'Two murders,' Sidney Grice said. 'Two murderers.'

Molly returned with a fresh pot of tea and three clean cups.

'But why would Caligula confess to killing Mrs Ashby?' I asked.

Molly changed our cups.

'For the same reason that he confessed to the Slurry Street killings,' Sidney Grice said. 'He wants the notoriety. It is what the French call a *crime de copié*. It all began with Springheel Jack. Every cutthroat in England claimed to be him as they stood on the trapdoor. It was their only hope of being remembered. How do we know that he did not murder the girl in the cellar before Sarah Ashby was killed and added her to his list when he heard about it? You wait until this latest murder reaches the Penny Dreadfuls and see how many lunatics and attention-seekers will confess to it. Go away, Molly.'

Molly had been loitering behind him. She bobbed lopsidedly and went out slowly, leaving the door slightly open.

'I hope you are right,' Inspector Pound said. 'All hell will break loose if you are not.'

'I *am* right and, if you will let me, I will help you find that unfortunate girl's killer.'

'I will drink to that,' Inspector Pound said as I poured us all another cup of tea.

'Go away, Molly,' my guardian shouted, and the door softly closed.

42

Boots

INSPECTOR POUND'S EYES were puffy and darkly rimmed. He was eating a pork pie over a gingham cloth when we arrived at his office.

'Breakfast,' he said.

'The flesh of swine in the jelly of their boiled bones,' my guardian said, 'all encased in wheat and animal fat.'

'The wheat sounds a bit disgusting, I grant you.' Inspector Pound wiped his lips with a napkin tucked into his collar. 'It tastes good, though.'

The pie looked wonderful and after weeks of boiled vegetables and eggs, I would happily have eaten the scraps he deposited in his bin.

'What news?' Sidney Grice asked.

The inspector put his napkin in a drawer.

'The dead girl in Chandler Street,' he said. 'We have her name. Alice Hawkins.'

'And how did you find that out?'

Inspector Pound suppressed a smile.

'Basic police work, Mr Grice. We asked her landlord. He lives in the house opposite.'

'Did he identify the body?'

'Yes. He was not very keen but when I told him that he

could not let out the room again until the case was solved, he became more cooperative.'

'Did he tell you anything about her?' I asked.

'Not much.' The inspector tidied his moustaches with a thumb and forefinger. 'She lived there about a year and he last saw her three days before the Ashby murder, when she paid the rent. Had an Irish accent and never gave him any trouble.'

'Has Mr Rawlings examined her yet?' Sidney Grice asked.

'I had a word with him last night. Nothing surprising. Alice Hawkins died of her stab wounds some weeks before we found her. Twenty-seven to be precise. Chest, stomach, hands and arms, face.'

'Not forty then?' I said, but neither man replied.

'And all from above by a left-handed man,' Sidney Grice said.

'Or woman,' I said, and Inspector Pound looked at me sharply.

'You have a poor opinion of your sex.'

'Marat, the French revolutionary, was stabbed to death by a woman,' I pointed out, 'and the Bible tells how Judith cut off Holofernes' head.'

'It was a man,' Sidney Grice said.

'How can you be sure?' I asked.

'Because whilst the inspector was questioning my sanity I was looking at the floor. Blood is nature's ink and there were, as we noted at the time, several prints on the flagstones, including a clear one of a left boot. I have rarely seen a woman with feet larger than Miss Middleton's, but this was larger even than yours, Inspector, and your feet are enormous.'

'My feet are not big,' I said.

'They would be if you did not squeeze them into such silly little boots.'

'And mine are not enormous,' the inspector said.

'The same goes for you,' Sidney Grice told him.

Inspector Pound frowned. 'Just a thought, Mr Grice, but do you think it possible that William Ashby also murdered Alice Hawkins? He had large feet as I recall.'

'It would be very tidy if he had,' Sidney Grice said, 'but, as I have already explained, the two crimes were committed by different people. Quite apart from the different modus operandi, the best footprint on Miss Hawkins' floor showed a small horseshoe-shaped defect. You will recall that I examined the soles of Ashby's boots when we interviewed him. They had a number of gashes and scuffs as one would expect in well-worn footwear, but there was nothing of that shape on them nor, I might add, on the soles of James Hoggart's boots either.'

The inspector pursed his lips and said, 'Hoggart could have had more than one pair of boots.' And Sidney Grice raised his eyes and said, 'I have thought of that, but Hoggart had small feet like mine. Find a man in large boots with a U-shape cut out of the left sole and I will wager that you have your man.'

'I cannot send my men out examining the feet of every man in London,' the inspector said.

'Why not?' my guardian asked. 'They would be more usefully employed than they are at present. But we are wasting time. Come, Miss Middleton. There is obviously no tea on offer so we must find our own, and then we have work to do.'

43

Throats

THE FRONT DOOR was still hanging on one hinge when we went back to Chandler Street, and Sidney Grice was halfway through the gap when he froze and said, 'I have a policeman with me and cutting a man's throat is a capital offence even in this godforsaken area.'

'Stay where you are,' a woman's voice said. 'It ain't me what's planning on cutting throats. Who are you?'

'My name is Sidney Grice.'

'I know you. The man what 'ung poor Ashby.'

'I did not have the pleasure personally but—'

'What d'you want?' Her voice was hoarse and broken by coughing.

'Alice Hawkins.'

'She's dead and well you know it.'

'And I intend to find the man that killed her.'

There was a pause and then she said, 'Come in.'

Sidney Grice scrambled through and I followed, to see a girl, thirteen or fourteen years old, a baby cradled in her left arm and holding a long carving knife towards my guardian's neck. She frowned when she saw me and said, 'Some peeler you are.'

'I am in disguise,' I said and she laughed hoarsely, black-mouthed, before lowering the knife.

'Can't be too careful,' she said. 'That mad dago what did for Alice could come back any time for all I know.'

Her dress was a patchwork of different materials, torn rags stitched clumsily together with string, and her feet were bare, black and scarred with two toes missing from the left. Her baby was parcelled in a piece of shredded cloth, only the back of its scabbed head visible.

'How do you know he was a dago?' my guardian asked and the girl rolled her eyes.

'Everyone knows 'e is.'

'Have you seen him?'

She broke into a violent coughing fit, bending double to catch her breath. 'Wouldn't be 'ere to tell if I 'ad.'

'Did you see or hear anything on the day she was killed?'

'What day was that then?'

Sidney Grice took a step backwards and scrutinized her.

'When did you last see Alice?' I asked.

She tucked the knife into the rope belt around her waist and pulled her hair away from her face, pocked by disease.

'Weeks ago.'

'How many?'

She twisted her mouth up.

''Oo counts? The weeks don't mean nuffink to me. Oh yeah, I remember. It was just after we went to tea with the queen of China.'

Sidney Grice looked heavenwards.

'Do you live upstairs?' I asked.

'Sort of.'

'How well did you know Alice?'

She picked her ear.

'She was too posh for me, 'ad her own room and a regular job she did. Always saying she was going to save up and get out of 'ere. Well, she got out all right, didn't she? Cow.' She bent over in another coughing fit. 'When I was so starved I couldn't do no milk she wouldn't give me a penny to feed myself or the baby. Pissing cow.' She spat on to the floor, white worm casts floating in a dark froth of blood.

'What sort of work did she do?' I asked.

'Shopgirl.'

Sidney Grice jerked to attention. 'Where?'

The girl looked at her finger and wiped it on her hair. She sneered her smeared lips and said, 'Well, you ain't much of a detective, are you? She worked in Finnegan's.'

Sidney Grice's cheek ticked.

'The curio shop on Mangle Street?'

'That's the one.' She spat again.

'Hell,' he said and tugged at his ear.

'Your baby is very quiet,' I said and she looked blank, her eyes almost as dead as the child she was holding.

44

The Curious Curio Shop of Childe Finnegan

THE DOORS AND windows of the Ashbys' shop were
boarded over now and there was no policeman on
guard as we went into the curio shop across the road.
My guardian picked up a stuffed monkey and said, 'Are
you the proprietor of this shop?' The man behind the counter
nodded enthusiastically.

'Childe Finnegan.' He bowed. 'At your service, sir.'

Sidney Grice put the monkey down and said, 'Alice
Hawkins.'

'Now there is a coincidence.' Childe Finnegan straightened
the funnel of a tin model steamer. 'For I had a girl by that very
same name work here until quite recently.'

Sidney Grice rolled his eye and said, 'And how long did
Alice Hawkins work for you?'

'Why from eight in the morning until eight in the evening.'
Childe Finnegan pulled the funnel up again and Sidney Grice
groaned.

'Is the whole world full of imbeciles?'

'I myself have often thought so, sir.' The mast collapsed.

'How long ago did she start working here?' I asked.

'Last October as I recall,' Childe Finnegan said. 'The piece you are holding now is a magnificent shrunken head all the way from the Cannibal Islands of darkest Portugal.'

I put it down. 'And when did she leave?'

Sidney Grice picked up a spear.

'Oh, but she herself did not leave as such, miss.' Childe Finnegan pushed the steamer away and put a Toby jug in its place. 'She just never came back. That, sir, is a rhinoceros hunting spear from the island of Armenia.'

'And I shall plunge it into your heart if you do not start making sense,' Sidney Grice said.

Childe Finnegan laughed. 'You can try, sir, and are most welcome to do so, but I have to tell you that I have no heart and never did for I was born without one.'

'Then you two have something in common,' I said. 'But surely that is not possible.'

'Indeed it is not,' Childe Finnegan agreed. 'The doctors were astonished for by rights I should have been dead before I was alive, but as you can see for yourself, madam, I am not.'

I opened the lid of a music box and a rusty ballerina creaked upright.

'What date did you last see Alice?' I asked.

'Why, the fifth of last month.' Childe Finnegan frowned. 'Careful with that genuine club of Hercules, sir. She came as usual, worked as usual and left as usual, and I was quite surprised that she did not come back as usual. I often wondered if she might have had an accident.'

'Did you not try to find out?' I asked.

'No,' Childe Finnegan said, 'for I have never cared what happens to other people. It comes from having no heart, you see.'

'Did you know William and Sarah Ashby?' I asked.

'That depends what you mean by *know*,' Childe Finnegan

said. 'We would nod to each other across the street occasionally.'

'Did Alice know them?'

Childe Finnegan screwed up his nose and said, 'There again, it depends what you mean by *know*. She would go over and chatter to them and I believe that she sometimes had supper at their house.'

'So they were good friends?' I asked.

'We have no time for idle chitchat,' Sidney Grice broke in, peering at a pickled cobra in a jar.

'Three guineas to you, sir, for the very asp that killed Lady Godiva. No, madam, I could not say if they were good or not for if truth be told, I never liked her.'

'Alice?'

'Mrs Ashby. Goodness' – Childe Finnegan threw out his arms so vigorously that he upset a basket of stuffed mice into a bamboo umbrella stand – 'but she had a tongue. Sharp enough to shave a badger it was, always yelling and yawling at poor Mr Ashby. He held up a couple of mouldy specimens by their tails. 'The actual mice that saved Rome.'

'What did they argue about?' I asked.

'Money,' Childe Finnegan said, so simply that I waited for more but no more came.

'Come, Miss Middleton,' my guardian said. 'We have suffered enough for one day.'

'Have you ever had any strange Italians in the shop?' I asked, and Childe Finnegan rattled his fingernails on the countertop while he considered the question.

'No,' he said at last. 'And I do not think there would be any call for one.'

My guardian opened the door but as I turned to close it I asked, 'Do you know what has happened to Tilly, the match girl that used to sit outside their shop?'

Childe Finnegan's face lit up. 'Died,' he said with a dreamy smile. 'Died of being too lazy to wrap up warm. Stiff as a fish when they found her still sitting on her box in the morning.'

'Oh,' I said. 'How awful.'

'Dreadful,' my guardian agreed. 'Yet another expense for the parish council.'

I slammed the door.

'Careful,' Sidney Grice said. 'You nearly caught my fingers.'

I looked at the Ashbys' shop. It still had William Ashby's name over the door.

'Pity he could tell us nothing,' my guardian said.

'But surely—'

'Did you observe that he did not have a device for removing the seeds from strawberries?' he asked. 'That has given me the idea for an invention.'

45

Dogs

FOR ONCE MY guardian did not complain about our tea, though I thought it very weak. He did not even mention the tablecloth, which had obviously not been changed for a while, and he forgot to be rude to the waitress. He seemed preoccupied with flattening the sugar with the back of a teaspoon.

'Grace Dillinger.' He spoke her name carefully as though it held a secret meaning which he had yet to discover. 'She is our only living link between the Ashbys and Alice Hawkins.'

'Perhaps it is just a coincidence that Alice worked in the shop opposite theirs,' I suggested.

He dug a little hole in the sugar and asked, 'Do you believe in coincidences?'

'Sometimes, yes.'

'So do I.' He filled the hole and smoothed it over. 'But I do not think that this is one.'

'Neither do I,' I said and finished my tea. 'Do you think Grace Dillinger might know something about Alice Hawkins?'

My guardian held his pince-nez up to the light.

'That is what I need to find out.'

He produced a small white cloth from his inner breast pocket.

'I cannot imagine she would want to speak to *you*.'

'Neither can I.' He huffed on the lenses and polished them. 'Will you take another cup?'

'No, thank you.'

Sidney Grice nodded and separated the chintz curtains to gaze on to the street with no apparent interest.

'Very wise. There is something known by scientists as a *chemical* in tea which destabilizes the delicate female nervous system.'

Sidney Grice lifted the lid of the hot-water pot and let it fall noisily.

'Oh, this is a conundrum.' He plucked the petals from a violet that was wilting in a little green glass vase in the centre of the table. 'If only I knew a young lady who was on good terms with Mrs Dillinger and had the intelligence to ask her a few simple questions.'

My guardian put on his wire-framed pince-nez for the sole purpose, it seemed, of peering over it at me.

'I think I *shall* have another cup of tea,' I said, and signalled to the waitress.

46

The Strewing of Straw

MY GUARDIAN WAS standing at his desk, levering the lid off a wooden box.

'Ah, March. I was hoping to see you.' He was wearing one of his black eye patches. 'You are seeing Mrs Dillinger today, I believe?'

The lid creaked up and he put it to one side.

'We are having lunch together at twelve.'

'Good.' He tossed a few handfuls of straw on to the desk. 'Because I have made a list of questions that I wish you to ask her.'

'I have thought of a few things,' I said.

'I daresay you have, young lady.' He strewed some straw on to the floor. 'But you can hardly expect that your thoughts will be as relevant to the matter as mine. I do not want her views on the demise of the crinoline, for example. What did you think of asking her?'

'I was going to ask whether she had heard of Alice Hawkins, if she had met her and, if so, how well she knew her and when she last saw her. Did she know of any reason why anybody should want to kill Alice? Had Alice mentioned receiving any threats, for instance, or noticed anyone suspicious, or did she seem frightened?'

Sidney Grice huffed and said, 'I suppose those questions will suffice for now. Ah, here we are.' He brought out a smaller box and hinged open the lid. 'At last.' He lifted the top layer of cotton wool off to reveal an eye staring out at me. 'Is she not a beauty?' He held it up for me to admire.

'Lovely,' I said as he lifted the patch from his forehead. He seemed to have some difficulty inserting the new eye and grunted a few times in discomfort. 'Is it too large?'

'Of course not.' He wrenched his lids further apart and pressed harder. 'As you are well aware, I made the impression myself. It is probably that the tissues have swollen a little into my socket whilst it was empty. Blast.' He bent over away from me and took a sharp breath as he rammed his hand upwards. 'Blast. Blast. Blast. Blast. Blast. There we are.' He straightened up and faced me. 'You see.'

'Indeed I do,' I said. His eyelids were stretched wide apart and purpled and the eye itself was enormous. 'It makes you look like a giant squid.'

'Nonsense.' Sidney Grice looked in the mirror over the fire mantle. 'It will just take a while to bed in.'

'I had better be going,' I said. 'Does it hurt you?'

'Not in the least.' The tears were streaming down his cheek. 'I hope you do not imagine that I will reimburse you for this lunch.'

'I do not see why not. I am investigating the case on your behalf.'

My guardian brought out a handkerchief to wipe his face and said, 'As I see it, this meeting concerns the possible connection of Alice Hawkins' murder to the Ashby case.'

'Yes, I agree with that.'

'And since you are responsible for the cost of investigating the Ashby case, you may claim all the expenses you wish by presenting a report and written receipt to yourself, and if you are not happy with that you may consult a solicitor and take yourself to court. Excuse me, March. I have something to attend to upstairs.'

Sidney Grice rushed past me, clutching the handkerchief to his eye.

I took my cape from the coat hook and set off. It was cool and breezy with a heavy drizzle, but I did not care. I was setting off on my first solitary assignment.

47

Lamb Chops

GRACE DILLINGER WAS already at the table when I arrived at Brown's Grill House. She rose and kissed my cheek and we sat opposite each other in a little kiosk.

'How are you?' I asked.

'I am well,' she said, but one look at her face, drained of life, told me she was not.

'And your baby?'

'Quiet.'

'Are you sleeping all right?'

She twisted her wedding ring. 'I try *not* to sleep. In my dreams the three people I loved are still alive, but even in my dreams they are murdered all over again. I shall never take off this mourning.'

A waiter tossed two menu cards down. He had close-cropped hair.

'This table is filthy,' I told him and he turned up his nose.

'So it is,' he said in a German accent and stalked off.

'I have to ask you something,' I said and her eyes flickered.

'Have you been sent here?'

'He did ask me to meet you but I—'

'Is your guardian too stricken by remorse to ask me himself? Or is he too much of a coward?'

'I do not think he is a coward and I am not sure that he is capable of remorse,' I said, 'but he thought you would not be willing to speak to him.'

'He was right in that,' she said and then suddenly flared. 'What is it now? He has let my daughter's murderer go free and put my son-in-law into a pit of quicklime. Is he not satisfied with that?'

'It is about somebody else.'

'Who else is there? They are all dead now.'

The waiter returned, smeared the table with a greasy cloth, rasped, 'So you are happy now?' and spun away.

'Alice Hawkins,' I said.

Grace Dillinger lifted the menu but did not even glance at it.

'She was supposed to be their friend,' she said quietly, 'and I almost believed that she was mine but once all... this... happened, she disappeared. It is strange how many people never came by when they thought some scandal might attach to their name. What of her?'

'She has been found dead.'

She put the card down very carefully. 'How?'

'Murdered.'

Grace Dillinger paled and folded her hands into a prayer grip in front of her mouth.

'In the same way?'

I nodded and asked, 'Did you know her well?' And Grace Dillinger closed her eyes and put her fingertips to her forehead, and said, 'She used to come to the shop. You know what the Irish are like. Once they get talking there is no stopping them. She was a good girl, though. She was going to knit a shawl for my...' She fell silent and when the waiter came with unconcealed contempt to take our order, she said, 'I will have nothing.'

He wrote my order down resentfully and scooped her cutlery and napkin away.

'When did you last see her?' I asked.

'What? I do not remember. A few days before this all started. It did not seem significant at the time.'

'Did she seem all right?'

Grace Dillinger opened her eyes. 'My God. You are turning into your guardian.'

I said, 'We want to find out who killed her.' But she shook her head and said, 'The police and Mr Grice want the glory of solving cases. They do not care what the solution is. Find the Italian and you will have the man who murdered them both. God alone knows why he did it. He must have seen them at the shop. Perhaps he saw me too and I will be next. Not that I care any more.'

I took a breath. 'We *have* found him.'

Grace Dillinger stiffened.

'Where? Has he been arrested? What does he say?'

'He says nothing. He was found in a canal.'

Grace Dillinger blanched and clutched the tablecloth so hard that I thought she would overturn the glasses. She breathed in deeply and slowly and breathed out in a shuddering sigh, and gradually her grip loosened and she touched her hair and brought herself under control.

'Perhaps in a moment of sanity he was horrified by what he had done and committed suicide,' she said at last.

'The police surgeon said he was murdered.'

I needed a cigarette.

'I hope so. I hope he suffered first. I hope he was terrified and died in agony.' She lowered her hands to rest in her cleared place. 'Perhaps somebody discovered what he had done and decided to rid the world of a monster.'

'Perhaps,' I said, 'but is there nothing you can tell me about Alice Hawkins?'

'Nothing,' she said and straightened the tablecloth. Her eyes were deep and she was far away, and her voice was flat when she said, 'Let us hope these horrible murders will stop now.'

'But how could they continue if the murderer is dead?'

Grace Dillinger sat up.

'That is what your guardian said when poor William...' She turned her face away, unable to continue.

'I am sorry,' I said and she put her hand on mine and said, 'I know you are.' Her eyes flicked up to mine then down again, and mine went down with hers, and I could not help but notice a white envelope in her open handbag on the floor and the stamped address on it: *Geo. Woodminster, Shipping Agent, 14 Liver Lan...*

'What is that?'

Grace Dillinger followed my gaze and bent to scoop her bag up and snap it shut.

'He is training you well.' She held on to her bag. 'I worry about you living with that creature, March. But you will not have to worry about me for much longer. I am going to Australia. At least one knows who the criminals are there.'

'But why?'

Her face flared as it lifted towards mine again.

'How can I live in the land that murdered all my loved ones? How can I give birth to a child here, watch him walk the bridge where his grandfather was killed or the same streets as his sister and her husband, past the slaughterhouse that was their home, the prison walls... Imagine if my son or daughter were to come across Sidney Grice. If I were a man, I swear to God I would strike him down.'

'Kindly moderate your speech,' a corpulent man in a red jacket called from the opposite booth.

'Kindly be damned,' she retorted, and the man muttered something but returned to his kidneys.

'But what will you do there?' I asked.

'Start a new life.'

'When are you going?'

'In three weeks... if I can raise the rest of the money. I have paid the deposit on a ticket for the *Aphrodite*. She sails on the twenty-fourth. I shall sell my ruby ring and wedding band.'

'You cannot.'

'I cannot do otherwise.'

'But what will you live on?'

Grace Middleton opened her hands.

'I can still teach. They must have pianofortes down there, though I doubt they have much use for French.'

'Perhaps I can help.'

'You helped once before and we both know the result of that.' She wiped her eyes with a tissue. 'I am sorry. That was unfair. I should go.'

She stood up.

'But shall I see you again?'

'You know how to find me.' She turned and hurried away. I saw her through the side window as she went, tall with her head defiantly high, across the street.

The waiter brought lamb chops, clomping them in front of me with a half pint of porter. I had been looking forward to them all day but now I could not eat. I sat for a long time, looking into my drink, dark and deeper than the glass that held it.

48

—◆◆◆—

Return to Huntley Street

O N MY WAY home I went to Huntley Street.
　　　　Harriet Fitzpatrick was sitting by herself, in a
light blue dress.

'March, how lovely to see you.' She jumped up to kiss me
hello the moment I entered the room. 'It has been very quiet
here today. I was just about to leave. I was half afraid you had
forgotten all about me. I must seem very provincial now that
you are moving in the smart set.'

She poured me a large gin and topped up her own.

'There is nothing smart about the set I move in,' I told her,
'and of course I have not forgotten you, but I have been very
busy.'

'Helping Mr Grice catch more murderers, I hope. How
thrilling your life must be now. Come and sit by me and tell
me everything in grisly detail. I...' She stopped. 'Why, March,
my dear, whatever is the matter?'

'I am sorry.' I gulped half my gin down. 'I did not come
here to make a fuss. But it has been so horrible. Oh, Harriet,
those poor murdered girls and that man in the canal and
the little match girl. I am sorry. You cannot even know who
I mean.'

Harriet took my hand in hers. 'I have been insensitive,' she said. 'But when one reads trashy novels it all seems exciting and rather fun.'

'I need a friend,' I said, and Harriet squeezed my hand and said, 'I will always be that.'

We drank in silence for a while.

'I hear that your guardian had a narrow escape from the mob,' she said, 'but he got his conviction.'

I said very quietly, 'We killed an innocent man, Harriet.'

'We?'

'Mr Grice would not have taken the case on if it were not for my interference.'

'It was the judge and jury that condemned him.' Harriet stood up to pour us both another drink.

'I saw William Ashby's mother-in-law today,' I said.

'Grace Dillinger? She's a funny one.'

'You know her?'

Harriet took another sip.

'I should say. Quite a regular here.' She gave me a handkerchief.

'But why did you not say before?'

She put her glass down and rummaged in her handbag for her cigarette case, lighting one and giving it to me before lighting her own.

'I did not realize who she was,' she said, 'until I saw her photograph in *The Chandler Street Stabbings*. We call her Buttercup here. It gave us quite a thrill when we found out who she really was, but then, of course, she has not set foot in here since.'

I drew the smoke in deep and held it before asking, 'Why did you say she was funny?'

'Well,' Harriet drained her glass and I got up to pour her another. 'After her husband died she went into mourning, which was right and proper, of course, but she still came here. Created a bit of a scandal really – socializing so soon after she was widowed. Then after a month she turned up out of mourning in the buttercup dress she always wore, which is how she got her name, saying that life was too short to spend it as a memorial for the dead and she was going to start living hers again – not that she had shown much sign of holding back before then. This created even more scandal, of course, but she was never a one to be frightened of that. Then about a month after that she went back into mourning, saying that perhaps she had been a little hasty in casting it aside. If you want my opinion – and I know you do, March – she rather enjoyed being in widow's weed. It got her sympathy and attention from the men, if you know what I mean. Her daughter's death was a different thing altogether, though. She cannot have been in any mood for socializing after that.'

I blew my nose and asked, 'Did she not love her husband then?'

'As much as any woman loves her owner.' Harriet stubbed her cigarette into an onyx bowl.

'Is marriage really so bad?'

'Worse.' She looked into her glass. 'William Wilberforce should have campaigned against it.'

'Then I should be glad that I shall never be able to find out for myself.'

'Poor little March.'

I finished my drink and kissed Harriet goodbye. I had no right to be weak when there was still work to do. My father taught me that.

It was a minor skirmish with bandits but they caught our men off-guard in a deep gulley. One man was killed instantly and four were injured before their company managed to fight their way into the open plain. My father and I were having supper when they dashed back into camp.

The wounded were carried in and laid on camp beds in a row – a subaltern, a corporal and three privates. In most field hospitals the officer would be treated first regardless of medical considerations, but my father believed in helping those most in need of him first. The corporal was bleeding heavily from a neck wound and my father set to work on him immediately, applying a pressure pad to the wound. It was left to me to carry out a triage on the others.

The subaltern had been shot at close range, his sergeant told me. His head was bandaged clumsily with torn shirts. He was unconscious and his breathing was almost undetectable.

Two of the privates had light wounds and could wait, but the third had a sabre slash to his stomach and was bleeding heavily through the rolled-up blanket he was clutching against it.

My father came over to me. 'I lost the corporal,' he said.

'The officer is beyond our help,' I said. 'I think you should look at that private next.'

Two men lifted the private on to our table. He was clearly in a great deal of pain and we had some difficulty prising his hands away from the blanket. The men held his arms for my father to lift the blanket away. The wound went right across his stomach. The private screamed and it opened wide and his intestines burst out over him and on to the tabletop. He screamed again. They were spilling over the edge and I tried to catch them. The man lifted his head up to watch. I have never seen such a look of horror, but I was busy trying to stop his guts ripping out under their own weight. They were hot and slippery. My father tried to help me but when I glanced again the man looked puzzled, then disinterested, and his head fell back.

I sent the sergeant for a padre and took another look at the subaltern. He must have been about the same age as Edward, I thought, and I felt a shadow of guilt for thanking God that he was twenty miles away and safe.

That shadow hung over me. It follows me still. Sometimes I think I will never see the sun shine again.

49

—◆◆◆—

Back to School

THE FLAG WAS already up when I returned to 125
Gower Street.

'March.' My guardian had sent his eye to be re-
ground and was wearing a patch. 'You are just in time.'

I turned to see a cabby coming up the steps behind me.

'For what?' I said as we clambered into the hansom.

'A visit.'

If he was trying to be mysterious, I was not in the mood.

'Do you not want to know about my lunch?' I asked.

He shrugged. 'Did Mrs Dillinger know Miss Hawkins?'

'A little, from seeing her at the Ashbys' shop.'

'Did she know anything else about her?'

'Not really.'

Sidney Grice adjusted the buckle on his satchel. 'Then
there is nothing else to discuss.'

'She was very upset.'

'No doubt she was and no doubt either that she still
believes me, rather than her murderous son-in-law, to be the
architect of her misfortunes.'

We travelled on in silence, but I knew enough of London
by now to see that we were heading for the East End. The
traffic was even slower than usual that afternoon, but at last

my guardian tapped on the roof and we pulled up outside a pawnbroker's shop.

We walked down a side street and then another. Then Sidney Grice ducked suddenly under a low doorway and I followed into a large dark room.

'Looks like class has finished,' he said, indicating to the rows of small desks and benches.

'You are a little old for lessons, I should say,' said a voice from the shadows, and we turned to see an elderly woman wiping the chalk from a slate on a tripod.

'Surely your pupils should do that,' my guardian said. 'Though perhaps you do not want to risk them breaking another board, Miss Brickett.'

She stepped forward. 'How do you know they broke the last one?'

'I can see the fresh slate scratches on the wall and floor and that the board is unscathed.'

She hung her duster on a nail. 'You are a quick one, Mr Grice, but how do you know my name?'

'It is over the door. How do you know mine?'

'It is over the newspapers.'

Sidney Grice perched on a desk. 'Then you should know who I want to talk to you about.'

'No sitting on the desks,' Miss Brickett said and he stood up promptly. 'The only person I am aware of that we had a common interest in is the late and controversially executed William Ashby.'

'Quite so. Do you remember him as a pupil?'

'I remember him well.' Her voice was sharp and strong, though I would estimate that she was into her eighth decade. 'His mother was a friend of mine.'

'And when did he leave your school?'

'He would have been twelve. I am sure you can do the mathematics for that, Mr Grice.'

'Did you see anything of him afterwards?'

Miss Brickett straightened a pile of red textbooks. 'A little. He worked in the old blacking factory on Straight Street before he joined the army.'

'Did you know his wife?' I asked, and my guardian looked at me sharply.

'Only by reputation,' she said, 'and a shrewish one at that, I gathered.'

'Were you surprised that he murdered her?' I asked.

'Why is this relevant?' Sidney Grice asked.

'Yes.' Miss Brickett ignored him. 'I always thought him a gentle boy. A great many of my former pupils have gone on to felonious careers. One boy, Owen Richards, was hanged before he had even left my charge.'

'I have that name on my files,' Sidney Grice said. 'He set fire to a doctor's house.'

'The doctor had refused to come out and treat Owen's mother when she was dying,' Miss Brickett said, straightening the pile that she had already straightened. 'The scullery was slightly damaged but nobody was hurt.'

Sidney Grice shrugged and said, 'Incompetence is not an extenuating factor, and if you let all the vengeful arsonists back into society the whole country would be ablaze in no time.'

Miss Brickett took a breath and drew herself up. Even then she was little more than four and a half feet tall.

'Why have you come here?'

'To find out what kind of a pupil William Ashby was.' He dusted his sleeves, though I could see nothing on them.

'He was a good boy.' Miss Brickett screwed the cap on a bottle of ink. 'A hard worker and a regular attender.'

'Bright or stupid?'

'One of the best. If he had had the opportunity he could have followed any profession that he chose.'

'A street boy is a street boy,' Sidney Grice said. 'Spare me your socialist fantasies.'

Miss Brickett took a yardstick from her desk.

'I do not know what educational establishment you attended,' she waved the stick in my guardian's direction, 'but you obviously missed the lessons on humanity and courtesy.'

'Ouch,' Sidney Grice said as Miss Brickett rapped him smartly on the head.

50

The Man in the Cave

'WHAT WAS THE point of that?' I asked my guardian as we made our way back up the street.

'I am merely collecting more evidence – not that any is needed – to prove what I have already proved.' He jerkily sidestepped two boys riding an old perambulator towards him.

'But all we have found out is that William Ashby was a model pupil.' I skipped over a puddle.

'Precisely.' Sidney Grice stopped. 'Tiger Street. I think we can cut through here... Do you know, March, what I find most terrifying about this area? There is not a tea shop within one hundred yards in any direction.'

'Where are we going?'

Sidney Grice pushed a little girl out of his way and marched on.

'To see an old army friend,' he called over his shoulder.

I caught up with him and said, 'I did not know you were ever in the army.'

'Nor was I,' he said, 'and, if I ever have a friend, it will not be somebody who lives in a cesspit like this.' He stopped again and peered down a narrow alleyway. 'No street signs. You there.' He grabbed a young boy's arm and said, 'Does this pile of ruins have a name?'

'Give me a tanner and I'll tell you.'

'I'll give you a sore ear if you do not.'

The boy kicked my guardian's shin and wriggled away, and I asked a woman with a basket of laundry on her head.

'Chipper Street,' she told me. 'Spare a copper, darlin'.' I gave her thruppence.

'I knew it was,' Sidney Grice said, and I followed him down it.

We came to what looked like a disused drain and, after a moment's hesitation from my guardian, scrambled in to find ourselves in a sort of cave crudely hacked into the foundations of one of the old buildings which lined the alley.

At the back was a man, and it took me a while in the grey light to realize that he had no legs and was sitting on a low trolley with iron-rimmed wheels.

'Corporal Lambeth?' my guardian asked and the man looked up.

'At your service, sir.' He was busily whittling a short stick from a pile at his side.

'My name is Sidney Grice.'

'The famous detective,' Corporal Lambeth said and chuckled. 'What brings you to my stately 'ome then? 'Ave you found my legs?'

My guardian smiled and said, 'Where did you last see them?'

'We was in Nova Scotia repelling the Yankee Fenians from Canadian soil,' the corporal said. 'I 'ad 'em one minute. Next thing there was a flash and a bang and I sailed into the air. Came down with a bump and the blighters had vanished – gone to meet their maker before me. I'll be joining them soon enough, though, I expect.'

'Nonsense,' Sidney Grice said softly. 'You have many a year in you yet.'

Corporal Lambeth coughed. 'I 'ope you're a better detective than you're a medic, Mr Grice, but you're not just passing by. What can I do for you?'

'You were in the Loyal North Lancashire Regiment, I believe,' Sidney Grice said.

'Man and boy.' The old man nodded. 'It was the 47th Regiment of Foot before we joined with the 81st. Went through the siege of Sevastopol I did without so much as a scratch, and I got the medals to prove it until I 'ad to pawn 'em. Sitting in some rich man's glass cabinet now and I 'ope 'e's proud of 'em. I was a month off retirement when this 'appened.' He shifted on his trolley. 'When the rains come, the wheels sink in and I can't get out of 'ere unless some kind soul carries me, and there ain't many kind souls this side of Old Father Thames, I can tell you.' He blew down one end of his stick.

'Do you remember a Private William Ashby?' my guardian asked.

'Young Bill Ashby? The one you 'anged?'

Sidney Grice nodded. 'The very same. He was in your platoon, I believe.'

The corporal tugged his tangled beard. 'Company cook and a damned good one, as I recall. Knew 'ow to boil an ox a treat, but I never 'ad 'im down as a wife-killer.'

'Did he see much action?'

Corporal Lambeth sniffed. 'Action? Not 'im. 'E stayed back and baked the bread while we was scrapping.'

'Some cooks fight,' I said, and the old man looked up at me.

'And 'ow would you know?'

'My father was a surgeon. We saw a bit of the world. India mainly.'

'Calcutta,' the corporal said almost wistfully.

'I was there,' I said, 'when the *Empress of Persia* derailed. My father and I worked through the night binding wounds.'

'Now that's something young Bill could never 'ave done,' Corporal Lambeth said. 'Couldn't stand the sight of blood, 'e couldn't. I remember 'e cut the side of 'is 'and carving a roast pig once. Fainted clean away 'e did. You can imagine the ragging 'e got for that.'

'But—'

'Thank you, March,' my guardian said. 'I think we have troubled this gentleman enough for one day.' He brought his hand out of his pocket and said, 'I wonder, sir, if I could shake your hand.'

Corporal Lambeth held his up and said, 'Excuse me not standing.'

Back on the street I said, 'You gave that man a five pound note.'

My guardian looked indignant. 'What are you raving about now?'

'I saw it – when you shook his hand.'

Sidney Grice looked more abashed than I would have thought him capable of, and said, 'I owed him the money.'

'How did you get in his debt?'

'We are all in his debt,' he said. 'He and his comrades have carved out an empire that will bring civilization to the savages for the next thousand years. And the man is reduced to making penny whistles.'

We walked on a little.

'Might I make an observation?' I asked as we got back to the main street.

Sidney Grice flicked a pigeon into flight off the pavement with his cane and said, 'If it amuses you.'

252

'I cannot see how anything we have heard today does anything other than support William Ashby's case.'

Sidney Grice stopped and stared at me. He put his hand to his patch and said, 'How can you not understand? In the course of one afternoon we have proved conclusively that Ashby was a model pupil at school and that he was terrified of blood. On those grounds alone I could have secured a conviction.'

51

The Confessional Box

I WAITED UNTIL the last woman had come out of the box before I went in, closing the curtain behind me. In the half-light I saw a metal grille in the partition and I kneeled before it.

The priest was whispering in Latin. I waited.

'How long is it since your last confession?' he asked.

'Is that Father Brewster?'

'It is.'

'I am March Middleton.'

A wooden hatch slid open behind the grill and I saw him sitting side on to me, in black vestments with a white stole around his neck.

'Miss Middleton. How are you?'

'I am well, Father.'

'But troubled.'

'How can I not be?'

The priest's head dropped as if he were praying, but then he looked up at me and said, 'William Ashby is beyond the cares of this world.'

'But Mrs Dillinger is not,' I said. 'I should like to help her.'

'In what way?'

'I have a little money and she has none. Can you tell me where she is?'

Father Brewster clicked his tongue.

'I can but I will not,' he said. 'I will ask her if she wants to meet you again, though. Can you come back here at eight o'clock?'

'I will be here.'

'Come to the vestry door at the side. You will have more privacy. How is your guardian?'

I swallowed. 'I think he is going mad.'

'In what way?'

'He is still looking into the Ashbys' case because he feels that his judgement has been brought into question.'

'That is a very charitable way of putting it,' Father Brewster said. 'Many of my parishioners say that he is the one who should have stood on that scaffold. But there is nothing mad about wanting to be right.'

I said, 'But he seems to see everything, however good a light it casts on William, as further proof of guilt when it is exactly the opposite.'

'I should not imagine he is a man who would admit when he is wrong,' Father Brewster said. 'That would take a great deal of humility and, from what I have seen of Mr Grice, he is far from burdened by that.'

I laughed and said, 'You have judged him well there.'

Father Brewster took off his stole and kissed it and folded it on his lap.

'Why do you stay with him?'

'I need him.'

Father Brewster shook his head.

'No, March, it is he who needs you.'

I peered through the fretwork.

'He shows no sign of it.'

Father Brewster nodded. 'That is because he does not know it yet.'

'I am sorry but this makes no sense to me.'

I picked my handbag from the dusty stone floor and he said quietly, 'You are in a great deal of pain, my child.'

I looked at the stuffing creeping out of the leather kneeler and said, 'I am quite well, thank you.'

Father Brewster put down his missal.

'Does the drink help to ease it?'

'I do not know what you mean.' I half stood to go but Father Brewster raised his hand.

'Will you let me bless you?'

I kneeled again and his hand made the sign of the cross as he said, '*In nomine patris et filii et spiritus sancti...*'

I closed my eyes and listened to the words and waited to feel something, but there was nothing other than the agony.

52

Rugs and Pictures

'THIS,' MY GUARDIAN declared as we went through an open doorway, 'is where Sarah Ashby was brought up.'

We entered a series of low rooms, which to judge from the bars and rusted mangers must have been a stable once. The first was empty apart from a few fat rats wandering lazily between piles of human excrement. Two families squatted in opposite corners of the next room. It was ten feet square and there were about a dozen of them.

There was moaning in the darkness of the room beyond.

'I have a florin,' Sidney Grice declared, 'for whoever knew Sarah Ashby as a child or can take me to any person who did.'

A girl called out, 'I knew 'er, mister. Gimme the tin.'

'You are too young.'

'I knew 'er,' a sunken-chested woman said from where she lay propped wheezing against a wet wall. 'When she was a Dillinger. I used to do for them, I did.' Her clothes were so scant that I could see the outline of her thighs, caved in and twitching like a dreaming dog.

'*Do?*'

The woman shifted uncomfortably and I saw that under her makeshift cloth shawl was a yellow-faced baby.

'Clean and cook and the like.'

'They had servants in this place?' I asked.

'They 'ad me.' She coughed wearily. 'And this place used to be a likkle palace when they 'ad it. Crystal Court Mansions they called it. Chairs and tables and beds raised off the floor, candles, rugs. There was even pictures on the walls – art, like.'

If ever a square was misnamed it was Crystal Court. We had stumbled over refuse and around dung hills to enter the building.

'How did they make their money?' Sidney Grice jabbed a fat spider, squashing it on to the wall with his cane.

'Mrs Dillinger.' She wiped her mouth with the back of her hand. 'Came from money or so she 'ad us believe, 'er wiv all 'er airs. Still 'ad to go learning toffs' brats foreign gabble to make ends meet, though. Most of their money came from Mr Dillinger, I reckon. 'E was a lot older than what 'is missus was and scrawny as a bat. Funny bloke 'e was, Jeremiah. All smiles and good fellow but I never trusted 'im.'

'Why not?' I asked.

She scratched her armpit, making it bleed. 'Ran a gambling den – poker and the like. Many a geezer come 'ere of a night but I never saw none leave wiv anyfink in their pockets.'

'Sharp, was he?' Sidney Grice stamped on something that scuttled towards him.

'Sharp as cheese.' The woman broke off to clear her chest.

'Did anyone ever complain?' I asked.

'A few but the missus kept a pacifier under 'er seat and she was a dab 'and at using it.'

'What was Sarah like?' I asked, and my guardian grunted impatiently.

'Stuck-up little cow.' The woman scratched her stomach

through a rip in her dress. 'Gawd, 'er father spoilt 'er stinkin' 'e did. Nuffink too good or too much trouble for 'is likkle princess and Gawd, she be'aved like one. She—'

'Why are these tiles cracked?' Sidney Grice broke in and I looked at the floor.

'There are lots of tiles broken.'

'Yes.' He traced an arc in the grime. 'But why these ones?'

'I neither know nor care.' I turned back. 'Did you know William?' I asked and she spat down herself.

'Only when 'e came courtin', Gawd 'elp him. She 'ad a pretty face, I'll grant, but it 'id an ugly 'eart. We was all s'prised she went for a man wiv so likkle prospects. Her father had 'er set up for a duchess at least. Spittin' teeth 'e was but would she listen? I fink she only went off to spite 'im.'

'Did she not love her father?'

Sidney Grice started humming tunelessly.

'Nobody loved 'im. You couldn't if you was paid to.'

My guardian examined his fingernails.

'Did William play poker?' I asked.

'Not 'im.' The woman found something under her dress and slapped herself a few times to kill it. 'A proper gent 'e was.'

'Do you think he murdered Sarah?' I asked.

'I did not realize she was an expert witness,' Sidney Grice grumbled.

''Ope so.' The baby started crying and his mother licked her thumb and stuck it in his mouth. 'Or they strung 'im up for nuffink.'

'Were you surprised?' I asked.

'Not s'prised that somebody did away wiv 'er. S'prised at Willy, though – gentle as a snail 'e was. 'Aven't I earned my florin yet?'

Sidney Grice tossed her a coin and she tested it between her gums, wheezing helplessly.

'For another of those you can 'ave your way wiv my body, mister. Whatever you want so long as I don't 'ave to stand up. I can't do that but I ain't got no diseases.'

My guardian regarded her with disgust. 'For God's sake, woman, you have a child.'

'Baby don't care, but the girl can 'old it if you're shy.'

'Animals,' he said.

'Your baby has jaundice,' I told her. 'You could take him to the London Hospital for free treatment.'

The woman looked up at me.

'One less mouth to feed,' she said, her face blank with pain.

53

The Vestry

GRACE DILLINGER'S FACE WAS ghostly when she ushered me in, peering out before she closed the door.

'You have not told your guardian you were coming here?'

'No, but I cannot see what harm—'

'Who knows what harm that man can do me or my baby yet.' She slid an iron bolt across and we sat between two racks of altar boys' vestments.

'Has there been any progress on Alice Hawkins' murder?' she asked.

'Not much,' I said. 'My guardian still seems intent on finding more evidence against William.'

'He will find none because there is none.' Grace swept her head back. 'Oh, why can he not let poor William rest in peace? Even Mr Grice cannot kill him twice.'

'Are you still intent on emigrating?' I asked and she bit her lower lip.

'My desire is as strong as ever, but my means have never been weaker. I stood surety for William's legal fees so I am obliged to settle before I can leave. I have had to sell my rings.' She held up her bare hands.

'I am not a wealthy woman either' – I handed her an envelope – 'but would this be enough?'

'Good heavens.' She flicked through the notes. 'There must be nearly two hundred pounds here.'

'Two hundred and twenty,' I said. 'I think that should pay for your voyage and support you for a while until you find your feet.'

'But I cannot take this.' She tidied her hair in agitation.

'You must. My money got you into this... situation. I know there is nothing I can do to rectify that, but at least my money may do some good this time.'

Grace Dillinger took my hand.

'You are so good.' She kissed me. 'Too good... I shall go to the shipping office first thing in the morning. There is only a week to spare.' She looked into my eyes and hers narrowed a little. 'You will not tell your guardian anything of this – meeting me or your kind gift?'

'Of course not.'

Grace Dillinger smiled, but then said, 'What is the matter?'

'I am sorry it is ending this way. Can I see you off?'

'It is better to say goodbye now.'

We stood up.

'Shall I never see you again?'

Grace Dillinger hugged me.

'God bless you, March Middleton,' she whispered.

She opened the door into the church and was gone.

54

Cats and the Marriage Detective

T HE MAN WHO sat hunched in my guardian's study was
milk-faced with scattered tussocks of hair on his jowls.
'March,' my guardian called from his armchair by
the fire, 'I should like you to meet someone. Miss Middleton,
this is Mr Froume.'

'Delighted,' the little man said, but made no attempt to rise
or take my hand or even look at me.

'Mr Froume is a marriage detective,' my guardian
continued.

'Such is my calling.' Mr Froume's voice was nasal and
unclear.

'What exactly *is* a *marriage detective*?' I asked, and his
lips curled like worms on a hook.

'Your ignorance is quite excusable' – he crossed his legs –
'for there are only four or five of us in the land – three in
London, one in Edinburgh and one in Cambridge who is
missing, presumed dead.'

He twined his legs around each other.

'Yes, but that does not tell me what you do.' I sat in the
armchair opposite my guardian.

'Why,' he said, as if I were a slow child, 'I investigate
marriages.'

His legs tangled into a knot.

'So you are one of those people who sneaks around checking if people are having assignations?' I asked.

'Oh, the very idea.' Mr Froume wiggled his bony fingers. 'No, Miss Middleton, I am more of a modern historian. I look into the documentation of marriages to find out if they are valid. You would be surprised how many people's certificates are invalidated by clerical errors. You would be appalled also to discover how many marriages are in fact bigamous whether by design, deceit or oversight. I hope I have not shocked you, young lady, with such rough conversation but such is the world in which I move.'

'You will have to try harder than that to make Miss Middleton blush,' Sidney Grice said and turned to me. 'Mr Froume has some news which might be of interest to you, March.'

'Indeed?'

'Indeed.' Mr Froume uncurled his legs. 'I have been looking into the marital status of one William Ashby and his deceased wife, Sarah née Dillinger.'

'And what have you found?'

Mr Froume simpered. 'Absolutely nothing.'

Sidney Grice clapped his hands in satisfaction. 'Capital. Excellent. This man has done in six weeks what the entire police force would have wasted six months over.'

'I have been in countries where I knew not a single word of the language,' I said, 'but I could understand the natives more easily than I can make any sense at all from your remarks. What is remarkable about finding nothing out in six weeks? I could have found nothing out in six minutes and not expect to get applauded or paid for my pains.'

'Ah no, miss.' Mr Froume tapped his nose infuriatingly.

'You devalue the sweep of my achievement. I and the men I sent out across the land have managed to show in six weeks that there is nothing *to* be found.'

I could not bring myself to look at this man who could not bring himself to look at me.

'The last time I screamed was when a Bengal tiger jumped on to my bed,' I said. 'It was such a loud, long and piercing scream that the tiger took fright and leaped out of the window. If you do not stop playing silly parlour games I shall demonstrate it now.'

My guardian touched his eye. 'Mr Froume has managed to establish by a detailed trawling of all the records held in this country that William Ashby and Sarah Dillinger were not and never had been married.'

'And what of it?'

'Are you not horrified?' my guardian asked.

'Not in the least,' I said. 'I have known many people who have lived as man and wife without going through a wedding ceremony. It is usually because they cannot afford it. They are not necessarily immoral.'

Sidney Grice threw his hands up as if tossing a large balloon.

'Poverty is a vice in itself,' he said, 'but I hope I have never given you the impression that I am interested in morality. Do you not see, March? This is one of the most damning pieces of evidence we have uncovered yet.'

Mr Froume looked up. His eyes flicked over to me as if I were that tiger and then away again. I looked at both of them and said nothing. Life was simpler when I was dealing with cats.

It was only after we had treated the privates that we turned our attention back to the subaltern. The bandage was soaked in blood which had caked hard, gluing it to the man's skin. He cried out in agony as I tried to peel it off. I poured some water from a jug and that made it a little easier, but he still whimpered as I cut through the cloth.

I pitied him, of course, but all I could think was, thank God he was not you.

Oh, Edward, if you had only seen what I saw... I know you would understand. I tell myself a thousand times a day.

55

Shoe Laces

'T HESE SHOE LACES are absolutely delicious,' my
guardian observed over lunch.

'Lovely,' I said.

Sidney Grice grunted. 'So how is the book?'

'Lovely,' I said.

My guardian put down his knife. 'You have been staring
at the index for over twenty minutes now.'

'Not that long, surely?'

He drew out his watch and flipped open the lid.

'Twenty-four minutes without turning a page or uttering a
word.'

'I am just a little tired and, anyway, you often do not speak
to me.'

'That is when I am studying a book or considering a case,
or I am angry with you,' he said. 'You are not studying a book
and you do not look angry. Your eyebrows form a hedgerow
across the bridge of your nose when you are. So what are you
engrossed in?'

'I saw Mrs Dillinger again a few days ago.'

Sidney Grice clipped the lid of his watch shut. 'Why did
you not tell me this sooner?'

'I did not think it important.'

He slipped the watch back into his waistcoat pocket and said carefully, 'You had a meeting with the mother-in-law of a man that I helped convict of her daughter's murder, a woman who has sworn publicly to destroy me and who, with the aid of her clerical lackey, stirred up riots resulting in the destruction of property and very nearly the loss of my life. I have been pilloried in the press and abused in public because of her. My reputation has been tarnished, my integrity brought into question and my professional expertise ridiculed at her instigation. And you did not think it worth a mention that you were socializing with her?'

'I saw no—'

'I am surprised you did not invite her round for dinner or offer her lodgings. It is just as well you had already spent all your money on her.' He touched his eye. 'You *had* spent all your money, hadn't you?'

I hesitated before I said, 'Almost.'

'And how much did you have left?'

'Two hundred and twenty pounds but—'

'And how much did you give her? Let me guess. Two hundred and twenty—'

'Pounds,' I broke in, 'but I would have given her a thousand if I had it.'

'It is just as well you did not then.' He picked up his pencil and pointed it at me. 'Explain.'

'Do you want to know why I met her or kept it a secret or gave her the money?' I asked.

'All three.'

'One, because I felt sorry for her; two, because I knew you would try to stop me before I went and berate me afterwards; and three, because I felt sorry for her,' I said, and pushed my plate away.

Sidney Grice took his pince-nez off and polished the lenses with his napkin.

'I want you to promise me something, March,' he said at last. 'That you will never meet with or have any communication with Mrs Dillinger again.'

'I have no plans to see her again.'

'Promise me.' His face was deadly serious.

'But why?'

'Because,' he said quietly, 'she is by far the most dangerous woman I have ever known.'

56

Gulph's Grief

I SAT AND stared at my guardian for a long time. Was this his macabre idea of humour? He did not look like he was joking but returned my gaze steadily.

'How can you say that?' I asked and his gaze fell away.

'I am reluctantly forced to that conclusion.'

He took out his watch again but did not glance at it, only twiddling the chain around distractedly.

'But why? How?'

He wrapped the chain around the little finger of his left hand. 'I have been looking through my archives.' He unwrapped the chain and put the watch down.

'You are not going to tell me that because you found a similar case—'

Sidney Grice raised his hands. 'Bear with me, March. There was a case in Birmingham some twenty-three years ago, which is why I was unfamiliar with it. A man by the name of Brian Gulph had an argument with his wife about an expensive cutlery set she had bought. He tried to take it away from her and in the struggle she was fatally stabbed in the throat. His sister came into the room and suggested that they make the death look like the work of an interrupted burglar, which they proceeded to do, ransacking the cupboards and hiding a few small pieces of jewellery. Gulph's grief was clearly genuine and their story might well have been believed had his sister not been greedy and kept some of the jewellery, appearing in public in her sister-in-law's pearls and pawning a brooch. Gulph was arrested and found guilty of murder. His sister was sweet-faced enough to convince the jury that she believed that jewellery to be innocent gifts, and he was sentenced to death. At the last minute he told the truth – that the death had been an accident but that he had panicked. He was not believed as his sister stoutly denied it. She was frightened that she might be charged with being an accessory after the fact and hanged alongside him. So Gulph walked to the gallows alone, protesting his innocence until the moment he dropped.'

He looked down at his watch again. 'Does any of that sound familiar?'

'Are you suggesting that William Ashby killed Sarah by accident, as he claimed?' I asked, but my guardian shook his head. He looked up. His hair had fallen into a curl on his forehead and his face was pale.

'No, March,' he said. 'I am suggesting that William Ashby did not kill his wife at all.'

57

Plum Duff

'YOU ARE STARING again,' my guardian said. 'It is neither polite nor ladylike.'

'I cannot believe you said that,' I said.

'Good manners may be going out of fashion,' he told me, 'but they are still important if one hopes to be accepted in polite society.'

'I am talking about your calm declaration that William did not kill Sarah.'

He twined the chain around his thumb.

'Why should I not be calm? The house is not collapsing and there is not a pride of lions in the room.'

'But William Ashby is dead.'

Sidney Grice raised his left eyebrow and untwined his thumb. 'Then panic will not help him.'

'But he was hanged because of you.'

He reached across to the wall and tugged the bell pull.

'I like to think so,' he said with an unconcealed smile. 'Oh, I do hope we are having Spotted Dick today for it is the very king of puddings in my estimation. I cannot—'

I stood up and threw my book on to the floor.

'Shut up,' I said and my guardian blinked.

'I beg your pardon?'

I picked up a fork and pointed it at him. 'You are worrying about pudding in the same breath as you have admitted to me that you helped to hang an innocent man.'

Sidney Grice shook his head. 'You excel yourself, March. Three factual errors in one sentence. Firstly, I am not remotely *worried* about pudding. I was merely making what I make so little of that you did not recognize it – polite conversation. Secondly, I believe I took two breaths in my last series of remarks to you. And, thirdly, William Ashby was a number of things – a schoolboy, a factory hand, an army cook, a shopkeeper and a husband, to name but five of them – but one thing he most certainly was not was innocent.'

The dumb waiter thudded into place and Molly came into the room to clear our plates, slide open the doors and serve us with two large bowls. Sidney Grice's face fell.

'Oh no,' he said. 'Plum Duff.'

58

The Angle of the Spoon

THE PUDDING WAS stodgy, but almost anything would have been preferable to the soggy mess of reheated vegetables that Molly had cleared away. I looked at it. 'Tuck in, March,' my guardian said.

'How can you sit there and eat after what you have just told me?'

'I merely said that it was Plum Duff.' He opened his hands innocently.

'You too have excelled yourself,' I said. 'You have told me three things of which I can make neither head nor tail. Firstly, that Grace Dillinger is the most dangerous woman you know; secondly, that William Ashby did not kill Sarah; and thirdly, that he is not an innocent man.'

Sidney Grice swallowed and took a drink of water. 'They are quite simple statements.'

'Then perhaps you would be so kind as to explain them.'

'Very well.' My guardian dug his spoon into his pudding, but let it stay sticking out at forty-five degrees. He had a crumb on his chin. 'Let us start with Mrs Dillinger. To have a husband stabbed to death may be regarded as unfortunate; to have a daughter stabbed to death looks like carelessness; to have a family friend stabbed to death is extremely negligent;

add to that tally the killing of the alleged murderer of the two women and things are looking downright suspicious.'

He took his spoon out, and wiped it clean and rotated it slowly.

'Is that it? The fact that this poor woman has had so many people close to her murdered makes her a suspect? Are you saying that Grace Dillinger killed all these people herself?'

'Of course not.'

'So what *are* you saying?'

'Three recent discoveries changed my point of view,' my guardian said. 'That Ashby was a good boy at school, that he was a poor soldier and that he was not married. All of those things should have counted in his favour – his good character, his fear of blood and the fact that Sarah, who was presumed to be a living angel, was, in the eyes of society, a woman of no morals at all.'

'So why were none of these things mentioned in his defence at his trial?' I asked, and Sidney Grice nodded vigorously.

'Precisely my point.' He wiggled his spoon. 'It is because he knew that those facts would only damn him more... What on earth is Molly up to now?'

In answer to his question Molly came clattering up the stairs and into the room.

'Inspector Pound wishes to speak with you, sir,' she announced breathlessly. 'Lord, those stairs get steeper.'

Inspector Pound stood in the hall, holding his hat. 'I shall not delay. I have to interview a man who claims that all his family have been killed by a phantom hound.'

'It sounds more like a job for the supervisor of a madhouse,' Sidney Grice said.

'Or an exorcist,' I said, and the inspector blinked slowly.

'My superiors think otherwise,' he said. 'But I thought I

would call in on the way and give you the news – not that it matters much now – I had a message this morning that Sir Randolph Cosmo Napier has been found.'

'Where?' my guardian asked.

'At his ancestral home,' the inspector said. 'It is outside my area so the local police are dealing with him, but I thought you might like to take a look.'

'Does he still claim—' I began, but Inspector Pound raised his hand.

'He does not claim anything,' he said. 'Sir Randolph Cosmo Napier is dead.'

59

The Mausoleum

THE CHAPEL STOOD in a clearing on the edge of the grounds, the great house only just visible through the mass of sycamores around us. A cheerful man introduced himself as Sergeant Crabbe and led the way.

The head gardener, he explained, had found the body. He had worked for the family since he was a boy and kept the area clear out of respect.

Sidney Grice paused to examine a rhododendron bush.

'Spotted a clue?' the sergeant asked.

'Not unless you are the murderer.' My guardian let the branch spring back. 'From the way the sap is oozing, this twig was snapped less than five minutes ago and there is a smear of it on your right shoulder.'

We followed Sergeant Crabbe into a small chapel. The floor was dotted with moss and lichen. The two long sides were lined with raised marble tombs. Most of them had statues of knights and ladies resting on them. One had a dog curled at her feet. Some were bare. On one in the far corner with his arms crossed over his chest was the body of Sir Randolph. His face was grey and he had a deep wound in his neck.

Sidney Grice glanced at the body.

'This is our man,' he said.

'We don't get many murders out here,' the sergeant said. 'What do you make of it all, Mr Grice?'

My guardian puffed his cheeks and blew out.

'Very little,' he said. 'Since this is not my case.'

'Surely you could make some observations,' I said and my guardian snorted.

'The only thing that interests me is that Sir Randolph is dead, and therefore anything he may or may not have said to that troublesome priest is hearsay and inadmissible in court. So I can proceed with a writ for criminal slander, knowing that my reputation remains unsullied. Come, Miss Middleton. We shall be late for afternoon tea.'

Sergeant Crabbe opened his mouth, but Sidney Grice waved him away and went to the door.

'Might I take a look?' I asked and my guardian grunted.

Sir Randolph was still in the suit he had worn for his court appearance. It was soaked in blood but seemed otherwise undamaged.

'The cut goes straight through his windpipe.' I steeled myself to tip Sir Randolph's head back, and the wound gaped wider. 'And almost through to the spine. There is no blood on the ledge or the floor. So he was not killed in here.'

'Obviously,' Sidney Grice muttered. 'Now, if you have quite finished playing...'

'It is difficult to judge how long ago he died by the state of decomposition because the cold in here would have preserved the body.'

'My mum could have told me that.' The sergeant sniggered. 'Except she would not be so unladylike.'

Sidney Grice put his hand to his eye.

'There are no other obvious wounds or bruises... There is

something greasy on his forehead,' I said, but it was obvious to us all that I was floundering.

Then something occurred to me. I went back to the door and crouched to look behind it.

'He was brought here six weeks ago,' I said.

'How can you possibly tell that?' Sergeant Crabbe laughed, but Sidney Grice said, 'Go on.'

I pointed to the floor. 'Look at that.'

'Moss,' the sergeant said.

'Middleton's Liverwort,' I said. 'It was named after my late uncle, who was a botanist at Kew Gardens. It takes at least six weeks to grow to its full two inches. When the door is opened it grates against the floor and scrapes the moss off. There are two piles of moss behind it. The first is still alive and would have been disturbed when the gardener came in yesterday. The second is old and dead from when the door was opened to place the body here.'

'You said *at least six weeks*,' Sergeant Crabbe reminded me. 'So it could have been growing for longer than that.'

'We know that Sir Randolph was alive six and a half weeks ago when he saw Father Brewster, his parish priest,' I said, and the sergeant clapped his hands.

'Well, Mr Grice, you appear to have a rival. The good Lord may not have given you looks, miss, but he certainly gave you brains.'

I had managed to control my horror at the deeds of men many times, but I was sick of listening meekly to their insults.

'What a shame he gave you neither,' I said. 'If Edward were here he would...'

Sidney Grice filled the sudden silence. 'Miss Middleton is quite welcome to take over this case, considering that it is unpaid.'

I looked at them both and at the remains of the man. He had been a child once and now he was a pathological specimen.

'Good day, Sergeant,' I said.

On the way back I said, 'Why would anybody go to the trouble of taking Sir Randolph there and laying out his body like that?'

'Somebody is trying to play cat and mouse with me, March.' My guardian sucked in and blew out through closed teeth. 'He will find out soon enough, though, which of us is the cat.'

We fell back into our own thoughts.

When we had returned to more familiar streets my guardian said, 'I was looking through some old *Army Gazettes* last night.'

'Oh yes?'

'I remembered reading something about your father a few years ago.'

'He was often mentioned.'

'I came across your name in the announcements. It—'

'Please,' I said.

Sidney Grice nodded and reached out and, for a moment, I thought he was going to pat me, but he put his hand lightly on mine and let it lie there all the way home.

Some people dream of having a cottage with roses. Every Sergeant Major I met was going to run a little public house by the sea when they took their pensions. Most officers were oldest sons and would retire to their family estates. Some would go on to run rubber or sugar plantations.

We were going to stay. We would have opened a school for the local children with a small dispensary for simple medical treatments. People laughed when we told them that. I remember Colonel Rees-James asking what the point was of teaching ignorant savages, and you said that they were not savages and, by the time we had finished, they would not be ignorant.

You controlled yourself so well but I could see how you felt. You were never angry but I was proud to see you angry about that.

60

Soot

MY GUARDIAN SAT and watched me pour our teas. 'Why were you so uninterested in Sir Randolph's death?' I asked. 'Surely it might have given us more clues about the murderer.'

'Four reasons.' Sidney Grice slid his eye outwards with one finger. 'First, I have no financial inducement to investigate his death. Second, we do not even know he was murdered by the same man. Third, I would have to list myself as a suspect since I had everything to gain by his death. Indeed, I expressed the hope that his throat would be cut and—'

'Yes, but you did not mean it.'

'I never say anything that I do not mean.' He swivelled his signet ring with his thumb. 'And, fourth, the whole matter is distracting me from my true purpose – to prove yet again that William Ashby was a murderer.'

'But you—' I began.

Sidney Grice raised a hand to silence me. 'I must have quiet while I think.'

He got up and paced across his study from the desk to the bay window, paused briefly to look out, spun round and paced back again. For the best part of an hour he marched to and fro and, having little else to do on that wet Monday evening, I sat in an armchair by the fire, warming my feet, flicking through an account in *The Times* of a series of gar-rottings on Waterloo Bridge.

'I am still missing something,' he said at last.

'Your tea?' I said, for it would be undrinkable by now, but he scowled at me and said, 'There is something not right about this letter.'

'Why is it so important?' I asked. 'And what is wrong with it? Inspector Pound vouched that William Ashby wrote it in his presence.'

'I knew there was something wrong before I even looked at it.' He reached the desk and picked the letter up. 'But what?' He took the letter out of its envelope.

'Remember I said it held the key to the mystery? Well, I am still convinced of that.' He unfolded the letter and read it out, though we could both have recited it by now.

DEAR MR GRISE
PLEASE HELP ME I AM AN INNASENT MAN
YOURS TRUELY
WILLIAM ASHBY.

'Ashby was, for his class, an educated man,' my guardian said. 'His old teacher remembered what an exemplary student he was, and yet he produces an illiterate meaningless scrawl in an attempt to save his life. How would this letter help him?' He reached the window and waved the paper in the air. 'Cheap paper provided by the police. No heading or water-mark. No...' He stopped and held the letter closer. He clipped on his pince-nez. 'Soot,' he cried out.

'You have found soot on the letter?'

'No. We need some.' He hurried to the fire and, oblivious to the heat, reached inside the chimney, his hand coming out black with a fistful of soot and his cuff quite ruined. 'Hold the letter flat on the rug, March.'

I pressed it down by the corners, and my guardian kneeled beside me and sprinkled the soot all over it and the sleeve of my dress.

'Molly will not be happy with the state of this rug,' I said.

'Molly can go and practise her curtsies on the bottom of the Thames. Let go of the letter.' Sidney Grice picked it up carefully, tipped the soot from it on to the hearth, and blew, a black cloud billowing into his face and over his starched shirt. He sprang up, almost knocking the table over, and ran back to the window. 'Turn up the gas light,' he said and I twisted the valve, seeing the flame swell and the mantle glow orange then red then white on the wall. He hurried to it and held the letter up again. 'See.' His voice rose with excitement. 'See the imprint of the other letter.'

I stood close by him and looked up. The effect was smudged and unclear but the words were unmistakeable.

FORTY TIMES IN ALL. I COUNTED EVERY CUT. SHE NEVER DID ME ANY WRONG EXCEPT FOR ONE THING. I SAW HER WALKING DOWN THE STREET. SHE

I did not need to read any more to recognize the letter.

'It was the envelope that was wrong,' my guardian said. 'I should have spotted it straight away. It was slightly too big for the letter. It had been stretched by another.'

'Which was taken out before it was given to you,' I said.

'Exactly,' he said. 'Look, March, at the well-formed letters and the punctuation. It is an educated hand. It is the hand of a murderer, the man who called himself Caligula but whose real name was William Ashby.'

61

The Windows of the Soul

I THOUGHT ABOUT my guardian's words and said, 'I thought you told me William Ashby was innocent.'

'Then you thought wrongly. I said he did not kill his wife.'

'But—'

'The truth was there all the time.' Sidney Grice sat back in his armchair. 'If only you had looked into his eyes.'

'But I—'

'Forget all that windows-of-the-soul silliness.' He flapped his hand. 'The eye is a sensory organ. You might as well say somebody has innocent ears or a guilty nose as to say it of their eyes. What about my glass eye? Is it any more or less innocent than the other?'

'No, but it is greener.'

'No, it is not.' He looked at himself in the mantle mirror.

'In the daylight it is.'

'It is not. Anyway, for you and the inspector to tell me that William Ashby had innocent eyes is childish drivel.'

'I can see the logic in that,' I said, 'but—'

'We will deal with all these *buts* another time,' my guardian broke in, 'when we are bored and have nothing useful to say to each other. We can, however, deduce something from

watching a man's eyes just as we can from observing his lips
– whether he smiles or frowns, for example – what he does
with his hands, feet, general bodily demeanour, et cetera.'

'I cannot see the relevance of your point.'

'I watched Ashby's eyes' – my guardian jabbed his finger
at nothing – 'when I interviewed him and at every point of his
trial. I saw who he looked at and how he looked at them. He
regarded you cordially, for example, and me with a degree of
loathing.'

'Do you blame him?'

'I would have been puzzled if he had not.' My guardian
produced his pencil with the flourish of a magician. 'I also
observed Mrs Dillinger's eyes when we met and during the
trial. I noticed that she and Ashby spent a great deal of time
looking at each other, but I mistook their meaning.'

'Surely he looked to her for support and she did her best to
give it.'

'There was that, of course,' my guardian said, 'but there
was more and, once I had realized that, almost everything
else fell into place. It is obvious now and I am annoyed with
myself that I did not see it at once, but William Ashby and
Grace Dillinger were in love.'

Tiny wisps of smoke fluttered from the embers.

'She was his mother-in-law.'

'As Mr Froume ascertained, she was not, but, even if she
were, she was closer to Ashby's age than his wife was. Despite
all the jokes about mothers-in-law it is not uncommon for them
to form a platonic affection for their sons-in-law. Sometimes
this is based on a mutual affection for the wife. In this case it
was based on a shared resentment of her. We have already heard
how Mr Dillinger doted on Sarah. In my experience, if a daughter is the apple of her father's eye it is because his wife is not.'

I took a while to consider this opinion. 'But how can you prove it?'

Sidney Grice tapped his teeth with his pencil and said, 'I cannot yet but, once we take the idea as a premise, almost everything else falls neatly into place.'

Molly came in and set some fresh tea on the tray before us, and her employer touched the pot.

'You have finally delivered a beverage of the requisite temperature,' he said.

'Sorry, sir.'

Sidney Grice shook his head in exaggerated despair as she left.

'Pour it, March. I am getting thirsty and I have quite a problem to unravel yet.'

——◆◈◆——

62

The Nail

'IMAGINE THE SITUATION.' My guardian shuddered as I poured a little milk into my cup. 'William Ashby meets Sarah. She is a pretty girl, as we have seen, and he is, no doubt, besotted. Sarah has a father who adores her and grants her every wish, but for whom she has no affection. She sees William, who is fifteen years older than her, as the man to take her father's place. The relationship is a disaster. William needs a frugal, hard-working partner and gets an idle spendthrift. They quarrel. Sarah's mother sides with William. She too has had enough of her daughter's behaviour.'

Sidney Grice paused to sip his tea. 'William becomes very fond of Grace. She is, if anything, more beautiful than her daughter. She is only five years older than William and looks young for her age. Her husband is old and unsavoury. William is sturdy and kind-hearted. They have what I believe modern novels describe as *an affair*. The trouble is that William is a decent man. He knows it is not right to have congress with someone he regards as his wife's mother. Perhaps Sarah suspects. Either—'

'But if William was so decent, why did he not marry Sarah?' I asked.

'Her father would not allow it,' my guardian said. 'He had

better things planned for his daughter than a tuppence-half-penny shopkeeper and, until Sarah reached the age of majority at twenty-one, he could withhold his permission and they could do nothing about it.'

'So she must have loved William once.'

'What is love?' Sidney Grice sniffed. 'It is nothing more than a feeling.' He sniffed again. 'But to continue – William tries to put an end to his relationship with Grace but she refuses to be cast aside. Why should Sarah have everything her own way?'

'And, as there is no legal relationship between Grace and William, there is nothing in law to stop them from marrying.' I put two sugars in my tea. 'Except for William's decency.'

My guardian nodded. 'He wants to do the right thing, but suddenly what the right thing is changes dramatically. Grace Dillinger tells William that she is with child and, since she has not lain with her own husband for many years, William must be the father.'

My guardian flicked a speck of soot, smudging it over his shirt. 'Her husband has died recently – the removal of the only impediment to William marrying Sarah also left him free to marry Grace, who is about to be delivered of their baby. William must do the right thing by her but he is torn.'

Sidney Grice fished two halfpennies out of his waistcoat pocket. 'Perhaps he agrees to do it – more likely he dithers and fudges – but then events take another turn. Alice Hawkins sees or overhears William and Grace together. I expect Grace wanted her to, for Grace is not a careless woman.'

'And Alice is Sarah's best friend.' The mantle clock struck the half-hour as I spoke. 'She would tell her everything.'

His left heel drummed the floor arrhythmically. 'On the Sunday night Sarah confronts her mother in William's presence. The women have a bitter and violent argument. William, ever the weak one, says he cannot desert Sarah and goes off into the kitchen. He cannot bear it.'

'For all Sarah's faults he still loved her too.' I stirred my tea. 'I could see it in his eyes.'

'Absurd as your ocular observations are, yes, he did.' He flipped the coins over each other in his left hand. 'The row gets worse. Sarah takes off her meaningless wedding ring and flings it in the fire, or possibly Grace rips it from her finger. In the tussle Sarah kicks her mother, bruising her toe – and rips her dress – hence the yellow thread caught in her finger-nail, though I have yet to prove that Mrs Dillinger ever had a yellow dress.'

'Buttercup,' I said. 'Her dress was buttercup before she dyed it black.'

My guardian looked at me.

'How long have you known that?'

'A few weeks. A lady I met on the train told me. I did not think anything of it.'

'You did not think anything.' His face flushed. 'If I had been in possession of that fact...' He passed a hand over his forehead. 'We shall come back to that later.'

'I am sorry.'

'I do not care if you feel remorseful or not.' He shook his head in despair. 'Let us continue. Mrs Dillinger sees that she is in danger of losing William, especially if he finds out she has been lying to him.'

'What lie?'

'Why, she is no more carrying than I am.' He clicked his fingers. 'I was never completely happy with her swelling so, when I was pretending to help that fat common woman in the coffee shop with her hat, I took a pin. I penetrated Mrs

Dillinger's bump with it when I goaded her to attack me, the whole length of a four-inch shaft, and she did not even blink.'

'But William would have realized sooner or later.'

My guardian topped up his cup.

'How can I put this delicately?' He put the pot down. 'I cannot. Grace Dillinger would not have let William near her whilst she was supposed to be with child – no doubt claiming it was doctor's orders, and she could pretend to miscarry once they were married. There was no legal impediment to their union, just an inconvenient daughter, and I have checked the records using Mr Hartington, the famous birth detective from Bath. Grace Dillinger was definitely Sarah's mother.'

'But why does she still pretend to be with child?'

'In all likelihood she is blackmailing other men with whom she has had relations, and think how much more willing they would be to pay once they knew they could be connected through her to such a major scandal.' He started to flip the coins again. 'Where was I?'

'She was in danger of losing William.'

'Ah, yes, and Mrs Dillinger is not a woman who likes to lose. She goes into the shop, selects a knife from the cabinet – one short enough to hide up her sleeve but long enough to do the deed – and goes back into the living room.' The half-pennies were clicking furiously now. 'Sarah turns her back on her mother, which suits Grace perfectly. If you stab somebody from behind they cannot see the blow coming, but she is too experienced to stab Sarah in the back where all the problems with hitting the ribs and the spine arise—'

'Experienced?'

'Obviously she had already killed her husband. It is too much of a coincidence that he had been stabbed to death by a third party. Perhaps she had killed others before that, most likely Matilda Tassel and her two daughters. I do not know yet but I shall.' He rotated his teacup to make the handle parallel with the spoon. 'So she slipped the knife into her daughter up and under the ribs. Death would be instantaneous and she would not get splattered with blood, and there would be, as we discovered on the floor and walls, a great deal of blood in the last spasm of that burst heart.'

I twisted a lock of hair around my first finger. 'So Grace Dillinger deliberately and calculatingly killed her own daughter?'

'In her mind she was killing the girl who had stolen Mr Dillinger's affection and looked likely to keep William Ashby.'

I picked up my tea, but my hand was shaking and I put it back on the tray, slopping it into the saucer.

'This is not natural.'

The unlit coals shifted in the grate.

'It is uncommon but by no means unknown.' He slipped the coins back in his pocket. 'In Greek mythology Medea murdered her own children to punish Jason, and I could give you half a dozen similar modern examples from my files.'

'But surely when William sees what has happened he is horrified.'

'Of course.' He raised his hands in a gesture of innocence. 'But this is where Mrs Dillinger shows her true metal. She screams. William rushes in. He has a horror of blood and probably never even touched his wife's dead body. Mrs Dillinger is in an apparent frenzy of grief. Her daughter threatened her with the knife, she tells William, and in her mother's attempts to take it off her Sarah was accidentally stabbed.'

'*You know it was an accident*,' I quoted.

'Precisely.' His hands rose further apart. 'Hence William's

seemingly bizarre insistence on sticking to that claim to the very end. He genuinely believed that this was the case. His mother-in-law knows that the police will not be so gullible, however, especially when they find out about her relationship with William, as she knows they will. So she tells William that they must make it look like the frenzied attack of a maniac. They must copy the Slurry Street murders as best they can, thus the multiple stabbings.'

'And the smearing of *Rivincita* on the wall.'

'Quite so.' My guardian touched the scar on his ear. 'Remember I asked Parker if the body had been washed, and he promised me that it had not. The small amounts of blood around the other wounds and the lack of sprayed droplets around them showed that the cuts were made shortly after and not before she died.'

I struggled with my thoughts. 'But when you inserted the probe into the wound you told us that the killer was left-handed, and Grace Dillinger is right-handed.'

'I had not considered the possibility of an initial attack from behind,' Sidney Grice said, 'as all the other wounds were clearly inflicted from the front.'

'So then she leaves and William cries out *Murder*,' I said, but Sidney Grice shook his head.

'If only it were that simple. Grace Dillinger is all too aware that Alice Hawkins knows enough to hang one or both of them, and she cannot be sure that William will not tell the truth and be believed. You met him and he was such a patently genuine man that it was difficult to imagine he might be lying. She kills two birds with one stone. Alice has to go and William has to do it. He is in a state of shock and a man in shock becomes as a sleepwalker.'

'I have seen it after battle,' I said. 'Men wandering about

in a daze. Some of them did not even notice they had been severely injured.'

'I have heard it was so after Waterloo.' My guardian got to his feet. 'Everything is unreal and William knows that, whatever he does, he will awaken and find that it was just a dream. Grace Dillinger is a very persuasive woman. He does not want to see her hanged for a dreadful mishap.'

'Especially as she is carrying his child,' I said, 'and he knew that he could be convicted as an accessory. So he would go to the gallows first because they would wait until she gave birth before they executed her.' I found myself winding my hair so tight that it hurt. 'Then their baby would be imprisoned in an orphanage and treated as the child of monsters and therefore a monster itself.'

'Exactly.' He paced the room again. 'It is all or nothing now and Ashby has to continue the deception to its nightmarish conclusion. Grace is but a weak woman and cannot do the job. William must do it for them both and their baby. He cannot bring himself to touch the knife that killed his wife, so he takes the other knife of the same design and goes out of the house through the yard and along the alleyway on to Chandler Street, slipping in through the back entrance and down into Alice Hawkins' room. But where to hide?'

'In the old meat safe that she used to hang her things,' I said. 'Dear God, I cannot imagine what went through his mind while he waited. Every creak of the house must have terrified him.'

'But nonetheless there he stands.' Sidney Grice picked the ebony rule from his desk. 'For an hour, or maybe more, until at last he hears the door open and Alice return to her room after having taken her dog for a walk. It is dark by then. She goes to the shelf to light a candle and Ashby springs out.' My guardian clutched his rule like a dagger, hacking the air wildly as he spoke. 'It is a botched job. He swings the knife around in a blind panic, hardly bearing to look at what he is doing to this innocent girl who had befriended them, only wanting to silence her screams.'

'She fought back.' I closed my eyes. 'Poor Alice tried to defend herself... all those wounds to her arms and hands...'

'And that is why the wounds bleed so much. She is still alive until she finally succumbs to that one last desperate lunge that snapped the blade off inside her lacerated body.'

'Her little dog,' I remembered. 'It must have tried to protect her.'

'A stout kick would be enough to finish that off.' I had never seen Sidney Grice so animated. He threw himself into miming every movement. 'Ashby staggers out of the room, fighting for air. He runs off and is nearly out of the gate when he realizes he has forgotten something, but what? He leaves the weapon anyway.'

'*Rivincita*,' I said, and he snapped his fingers.

'Of course. Ashby remembers and walks back. The devil alone knows what demons he summons to help him re-enter that room and be confronted by what he has done, and to dip his finger into the freshly flowing blood that so horrifies him and daub on the wall before he runs away. The alley is always flooding and has flooded again whilst Ashby is out. He hurries through the sewage and into his own back yard.'

'Which was how the blood got on to the gate handle.'

My guardian placed the rule carefully on the mantle shelf and took a breath. 'Ashby takes off his shoes, rinses the mud down the sink and goes back in to the house. Meanwhile Grace has thought of a refinement to the plan. The Slurry

Street Murders were supposed to have been committed by an Italian. So why not provide such a suspect?'

'James Hoggart.'

'The very man.' He pointed his forefinger at me. 'Grace is familiar with him through her husband's gambling den and knows he is an actor who plays the part of an Italian and that he is down on his luck. For a hundred pounds he can be persuaded to put on his costume, go to the police station making himself as conspicuous as possible, give in a letter addressed to Inspector Pound, confessing to the murders and giving proof of a knowledge that only the murderer could have known. Then all he has to do is walk away, collect his payment from Mrs Dillinger, and disappear.'

'But Hoggart was illiterate,' I said. 'That was why he insisted on having his scripts read to him.'

'And could not write so much as an IOU at Mr Dillinger's poker school.' Out came the halfpennies, clicking rapidly in his hand. 'Grace cannot write the letter because her hand is obviously feminine, but William can. He can then write a note to me, the only object of which is to convince me that he has an ill-educated hand.'

'The fire,' I remembered. 'They burnt every scrap of paper they could find with William's handwriting on it. So it was not *what* was written but *how* it was written that they were hiding.'

My guardian pinched the bridge of his nose while he collected his thoughts.

'Mrs Dillinger leaves, and on the way out she takes a box of matches from Tilly's tray. Perhaps it is from mischievousness. More likely she has the foresight to give William that extra detail to write in his letter. Either way she goes to church as usual, and William is no doubt about to write the Caligula letter when the shop door goes.'

'Little Tilly putting her cup back.'

'*We* know that, but Ashby panics and runs into the shop shouting *Murder* before he has had a chance to write the letter. All is not lost, however. He writes it in his cell on paper thoughtfully provided by the police, with the letter to me on top of it, slipping both letters into the same envelope when Grace Dillinger creates a diversion by pretending to faint.'

'That would explain why Caligula was misspelled,' I said. 'William had probably never even heard of him.'

'Precisely, and he misspelled his own name as a red herring.'

The image of Grace Dillinger sprang up in my mind and her unfeigned despair as dawn rose after the vigil. 'But how could she make him commit a murder if she loved him?'

'Whatever made you think she did?'

'But you said that they were in love.'

'And so they were.' My guardian clicked his tongue. 'He with her and she with his money. Grace Dillinger never loved anyone except perhaps herself and that is what makes her such a dangerous woman.'

'But to do all that for a rundown shop and a hundred pounds insurance...'

'Which doubtless she suggested he took out.' Sidney Grice shook his finger at me. 'But Mrs Dillinger had her sights set on bigger game than that. You remember William Ashby told us he was to inherit the rest of his uncle's estate after five years. That time would have elapsed in little over a year from now. Well, I have done a little research into Edwin Silas Ashby's affairs and the shop was by no means his largest asset. He had properties in Bristol and Birmingham to a conservative value of over eight thousand pounds – a tidy sum by any reckoning.'

I had a thought. 'But you said the murderer of Alice Hawkins had a defect in his boot which William Ashby did not.'

'A horseshoe nail,' Sidney Grice said. 'Ashby sold nails. There were some loose in his backyard. One must have become wedged in his sole; it left its mark in the bloody foot-print and, somewhere on his flight home, fell out again.'

'But why did Inspector Pound not receive the letter?' I asked.

'James Hoggart lost his nerve. He was frightened that he would be recognized or detained while the letter was read. Then what defence would he have had? So he met Grace Dillinger at the canal as pre-arranged and told her that he had delivered the letter, hoping to collect his reward and make his escape abroad before she found out that he had not done so.'

'But Grace Dillinger had no money to give him,' I said.

Sidney Grice closed his fist on the coins. 'Besides which, why leave a man alive who could testify against you when you could leave him dead and silent? Once she was convinced he had carried out his task, Grace Dillinger stabbed James Hoggart in the back of his neck and pushed him, letter and all, into the canal.'

'Where the rats would have fed on him until there was nothing left if his wig had not floated away and attracted the attention of young Albert, who tried to pawn it.'

My guardian opened his fist. 'Imagine, then, William Ashby's dilemma. No letter appears. He has no defence and cannot even tell the truth any more without condemning himself and the mother of his child to death. I do not suppose they thought I would even take the case. It is well known how unashamedly greedy and snobbish I am.'

'They could not have dreamed that I would pay your fees.'

He tossed the coins in the air and scooped them back as they fell. 'Once you did, all they could hope for was that I would fall for their charms and support his case. It was a forlorn hope but they were clutching at straws.'

'At least Grace Dillinger stuck by William throughout his trial,' I said. 'And she still tried to rouse support for him afterwards. Surely she would have been better to let him die with as little fuss as possible, knowing that he might break down and confess what really happened. She *must* have cared something for him.'

My guardian snorted. 'Now you are attributing human feelings to her. If Ashby thought for one moment that she was deserting him, he would be far more likely to implicate her. Also, there was still a chance that he would be acquitted and get his inheritance. No doubt he would have met an unfortunate end as soon as was convenient after their wedding, when he was of no further use to her. I am only surprised that she did not take the opportunity after the execution to leave the country. She was not a suspect but she knew that I was still poking about.' He stopped and looked at me. 'March? What is it?'

'Today is the twenty-seventh, is it not?'

'It is.'

'Grace Dillinger is booked to sail for Australia on the *Aphrodite* by the first tide in the morning and,' I took a deep breath, 'I have given her the fare.'

63

Parma Violets

IT WAS MY guardian's turn to stare.

'You knew she was fleeing the country and you helped her?'

'I thought she wanted a fresh start for herself and her baby.'

He wrenched at the air. 'She has no baby.'

'I did not know that,' I said. 'You knew but you did not tell me. You were too busy being clever.'

'If you were a man I would knock you down for that,' he said.

'And another thing,' I said. 'If Inspector Pound had answered my question about how she fell, I could have told you she was feigning her collapse on the first day. People pretending to faint float decorously into a safe space. Genuine cases topple over and hurt themselves. But you and your friend were so busy being superior men that you did not even—'

'Damn it all, girl,' said Sidney Grice. 'You have aided and abetted the escape of a monstrous mass-murderess and all you can do is twitter on about—'

'Do *not* call me *girl*,' I said. 'Perhaps if you had kept me better informed—'

'So now *I* am at fault?' He slammed his notebook on to the table. 'You sneak about behind my back, meeting up with all sorts of vile unnatural women. Do not imagine that I do not know what goes on in that house in Huntley Street.'

'Nothing *goes on*,' I said. 'It is a haven from men like you, and God alone knows how we need it.'

'And smoke and drink. Do you think I have no sense of smell whatsoever or that those parma violets can begin to mask the stench of your vices?'

I swept my hand and accidentally upset my teacup. It did not break but I let it lie leaking on to the linen tray cloth.

'We cannot all be pure like you.'

'Why not?' He pointed his pencil in my face. 'Why can everybody not be pure like me? Is it because you are all weak and self-indulgent and bone-headedly stupid?' He sprang out of his chair and tugged the bell pull. 'But all may not be lost yet... I hope that wretched creature remembers the code.' He went to the desk and scribbled something on his headed note-paper, folded it, and glued it into an envelope. 'Well, don't just sit there like a stuffed squirrel, woman. Get your cloak.'

I stood up and followed him into the hall.

'Where are we going?'

'*We* are not going anywhere. I am going to the docks to try to stop Grace Dillinger boarding, if she has not already done so. You are going to Marylebone Police Station to give this note in person to Inspector Pound. I hope I can trust you to get that small thing right.'

'But what if he is not there?'

'Then you must use all your severely limited charms to insist that he is fetched immediately. Tell them I said it is of the utmost urgency.' He rushed into the hall and ran up the flag. 'Open the door to light up the entrance. They may not see the flag at this time of night. Stand in the doorway and wave your silly little hand, and squawk out to every cab you see until two stop. You will take the first. I may have to wait a little while yet.'

'But why?' I went to the door.

A cab was already pulling up.

'Because Molly has not yet responded to my urgent instruction,' he said. 'Ah, here she is.'

At that Molly ran down the corridor, carrying his insulated flask.

64

The Power of the Name

'MARYLEBONE POLICE STATION, as quick as you can,' I called up to the cabby.

'Been a naughty girl, 'ave we?' he called back.

More naughty than you can possibly imagine, I thought as I clambered aboard.

There was not much traffic and we made good time. I paid the driver, gave a good tip and ran inside, pushing my way through the assembled rabble to reach the desk.

'Miss Middleton.' The desk sergeant looked up from a stack of paperwork. 'You haven't been arrested for drunk and disorderly have you?'

'Not yet,' I said. 'I have an urgent note here for Inspector Pound.'

The desk sergeant put out his hand. 'I shall make sure he gets it first thing in the morning.' But I held on to the letter.

'I have to give it to him in person,' I said. 'Now.'

The desk sergeant chuckled. 'More than my job's worth to disturb him at this time of night.'

'It will be more than your life is worth if you allow a multiple murderer to escape because of your failure to act.'

The sergeant looked dubious and then horrified.

'Oh, for the love of Moses,' he said, and I turned to see an old woman vomiting copiously over the end of his desk. 'Foster, get her out of here and get that mess cleaned up. She's done it all over the charge sheets.'

An old man toppled forwards and caught hold of the desk.

'If I puke can I go too?'

'Just get out.' The sergeant swept them away with a wave of his hand. 'All of you. I'm blasted to hell and back if I'm going to fill all those forms out again.'

'Fanks, Serg, you're a toff.' The old man weaved towards the door.

'What 'bout me?' a gaudily painted woman called from where she stood propped up in a corner. 'I 'saulted one of your lovely big boys. That's got to be worf a night in a warm cell.'

'Get out.'

'It's on your 'ead if I 'ave to 'sault anovver hofficer,' she said, gathering her things in a piece of cloth as she marched off.

'Right.' The sergeant turned back to me. 'You were saying.'

'This letter is from Mr Grice.'

'Frightened to show his face here, is he?'

I ignored the question. 'Listen to me, Sergeant. There is a dangerous murderer on the loose.'

He rolled his eyes. 'This is London, Miss Middleton. There are a million people within a square mile of this building and probably a hundred murderers out and about tonight, and not one of them as dangerous as Inspector Pound when he is dragged from his bed.'

A constable turned up with a bucket and mop, clutching a handkerchief over his mouth and nose as he swabbed the desktop.

'They have no stomach these days,' the sergeant said.

I remembered something my father had told me – to command the man you must know his name.

'You are Sergeant Horwich,' I said.

'I am.'

'Oh, thank goodness,' I said. 'Mr Grice told me that you are the only man in this station capable of judging the importance of this case and taking the initiative to deal with it.'

'He did?'

The sergeant preened his moustaches and expanded his chest.

'I believe his words were: *Sergeant Horwich is worth the rest of them put together. Trust him for he will know what to do.*'

The sergeant tidied his mutton-chop whiskers.

'Beacon.' He struck the desk bell and a constable came from the back room, buttoning his jacket collar. 'Run down to Inspector Pound's house, Beacon, and tell him there is an urgent message for him from Mr Sidney Grice about a mass-murderer on the rampage, and that he is to come to the station immediately.'

'What? Me?'

The sergeant waved a hand. 'Go. And if you are not back with him in five minutes, I will put you on puke-cleaning duties with Foster for the rest of your short career.'

There was a black and brown mongrel snoring on a bench. It snarled when the constable prodded it with his truncheon and went back to sleep when he stopped.

'Thank you, Sergeant Horwich,' I said. 'I shall wait in Inspector Pound's office.'

'But nobody is allowed in there, miss.'

'Good,' I said. 'Then I shall not be disturbed.'

65

A Matter of Conscience

I T WAS ALMOST a quarter of an hour later, and the clock was striking midnight, before Inspector Pound appeared, slightly dishevelled, his hair and moustaches hastily combed. He was more than a little annoyed to be dragged in from his home.

'Miss Middleton.' He straightened his cuffs. 'If I had known it was you I should have come a little quicker.'

I handed him the note and he read it carefully.

'I see.' He sat on the edge of his desk. 'And there is no doubt about it?'

'None,' I said.

The inspector folded the note and slipped it back into the envelope.

'But why does Mr Grice wish me to join him?'

'To catch Sarah Ashby's murderer.'

'But Mr Grice has repeatedly assured me that we have already caught and hanged him,' Inspector Pound said. 'There is nothing to be gained by casting further doubt on the justice of that. It upsets people's faith in the law. If, however, Mr Grice can prove that William Ashby murdered Alice Hawkins, I would be most grateful to have that case cleared. Sir Randolph died outside my patch and, as for James Hoggart, his death did not even make the evening papers. So, if Mrs Dillinger flees the country, so much the better. Her presence here can be nothing but an embarrassment and we will be well rid of her.'

'Embarrassment?' I echoed. 'Is that all she is to you? This woman murdered her husband and her own daughter, and James Hoggart, and incited the murder of Alice Hawkins. She is a monster. Who knows who she will kill in Australia?'

The inspector flushed a little but only said, 'Then that will be their problem. With any luck they will catch and execute her, and you will not have to worry about her any more.'

'So you are going to sit here and let her escape?'

Inspector Pound shook his head. 'No, of course not. I shall go back to bed and let her escape.'

'I thought you were supposed to be on the side of good.'

'That would be nice,' he smiled grimly, 'but my job is to maintain law and order in the metropolitan area, and it is my judgement that this is best achieved in this case by getting the criminal permanently out of the country and not by shaking the confidence of the people we are supposed to be protecting. Imagine what her defending lawyer would make of it – we were wrong about William Ashby, how can we be so sure about Grace Dillinger? Besides which, juries are always reluctant to break the necks of beautiful women.'

I picked up my handbag from the floor. 'Then there is nothing more to be said.'

'Let me get you a cab.' He stood up. 'In fact we can share one, for Gower Street is on my way home.'

I said, 'But I am not going to Gower Street.'

'Where then?'

'Why, to the docks, of course. If nothing else, Mr Grice needs to be apprised of your indifference.'

The inspector put the envelope into his inside pocket and said, 'You cannot go to the docks alone. It is not safe even in the day. I can send a message to Mr Grice.'

I stood up and said, 'I shall not let that woman sail away, not while I can breathe.'

'I cannot let you go to the docks.'

'What?' I said. 'Will you detain me, an innocent girl, when you will not detain the slaughterer of innocents?'

Inspector Pound crinkled his mouth and pinched the bridge of his nose. He stood up and opened the door and called down the corridor.

'Sergeant Horwich, get one of the men to bring a Black Maria. We are going to the docks. And find a blanket for Miss Middleton. She will freeze to death at this time of night.' He turned to me and said, 'And I would not want that on my conscience.'

66

The Aphrodite

THE HORSES NOSED cautiously, stumbling through the thick stinking air.

'We are lucky there was a police vehicle free,' Inspector Pound told me as we sat up in the front seat next to the driver. 'You would never get a cab to come here at this time of night.'

'Is it a dangerous area?' I asked.

'Very. You should not even be here.'

'Are there lots of foreigners?'

The street was so narrow that we scraped the walls as the van rocked from side to side.

'There is worse than foreigners here.'

'Is that possible?'

The inspector grunted. 'I think you mock me, Miss Middleton, but there is many a man gone missing in this area only to be washed up on the Isle of Dogs with his wallet missing and a smile in his throat.'

The sides of the street disappeared and, from the swirling of the fog, I judged that we had come into an open space. Our driver pulled the horses up and spoke for the first time since we had left Marylebone Station. 'Here we are, sir.'

The inspector peered about us. 'Are you sure?'

'Yes, sir. My brother works here. And all my uncles.'

Inspector Pound clambered off and I could hardly see the hand held up to help me down into a deep puddle.

'Good job you aren't wearing a nice dress,' he said as I slithered about.

The driver passed us a lantern but it produced no more than a weak halo, casting the inspector's face into a ghoulish yellow glow.

'It should be straight on, sir. If you find yourself swimming, you've gone too far to the left.'

'Mind your tongue and wait there,' Inspector Pound said. 'And you had better keep hold of me, Miss Middleton. At least that way we will go over the edge together.'

'It cannot be much wetter,' I said and slipped my arm through his.

'That should be the *Aphrodite*.' The inspector pointed. There was a faint red light and we inched our way towards it, me sliding my feet and my companion tapping ahead of us with his cane. The water was slapping against a wall and I could hear voices, some shouting, and the ships creaking and banging against the piers. I stepped into another slimy puddle and our light went out.

'Blast that man.' Inspector Pound shook the lantern. 'The oil has run out. I sometimes think I am working in an institution for the mentally defective, and don't you dare tell Mr Grice I said that.'

I laughed and said, 'I think we need to go more to the left.'

'How so?'

'Because I can see the green starboard light as well now, and those yellow lights must mark the end of the wharf.'

'If you say so.'

We changed direction and, as I began to make out the

outline of a ship before and above us, I heard a familiar voice raised close by.

'I do not care if you are Admiral of the Fleet with the King of Siam on board, you will not set sail until I say so.'

A lower gruffer voice said, 'You have no authority on land or at sea, Mr Grice, and as my first mate has already told you, if you put one foot on to my gangplank, I shall have you cast in irons for mutinous trespass.'

Sidney Grice stood under a lamp with a small group of men round him.

'Having a bit of trouble?' Inspector Pound called out as we approached.

My guardian peered out from under the wide brim of his soft felt hat.

'Why have you brought her?'

'Well, there is a nice welcome,' I said.

'She insisted,' Inspector Pound said.

'Well, do not get in the way,' my guardian told me. 'Inspector, kindly tell this maritime muttonhead that if he does not let us on his ship you will have Customs and Excise swarming over it for a week.'

'Ever the diplomat,' the inspector murmured, and held out his hand. 'Good evening – or should I say morning? – Captain. My name is Inspector Pound of the Metropolitan Police.'

The captain shook his hand suspiciously. 'Friend of yours, is he?'

'He has no friends.'

'You amaze me. This man thinks he has the right to step aboard my ship and poke about it when we have still half our stores to stow before we can set sail.'

'Then you will have to postpone your voyage,' my guardian said. He had soot on his cuffs and smudges on his face, but this did not seem a good time to tell him.

The captain raised his arms to the invisible stars. 'Have you any idea what it costs to run a ship this size? There is a crew of forty-eight men to pay for a start.'

Sidney Grice pointed at the captain's chest. 'You know better than I that not a man jack receives a brass farthing until you weigh anchor.'

'Yes, but there are forfeits to be paid on the moorings if we miss our sailing time.'

'Which are nothing to the forfeits incurred by harbouring a murderer on board,' Inspector Pound said.

'I cannot be held responsible if a criminal stows away on my ship.'

'This criminal is a passenger – a lady by herself,' I said.

'We have no single women on this voyage.'

'You are sure of that?' I asked.

'I know my manifest. We have very few women at all. A nun and—'

'The nun...' I said.

'Is your criminal seventy-nine and blind with both legs missing below the knee?' the captain asked. 'Because my nun is. I helped her on board myself this very afternoon. She's a sweet old girl but how does she kill people? Bless them to death?'

'Who are the other women?' my guardian asked.

'Two married couples. Tell a lie – one married couple, the Malmondsleys who are regular travellers with us – the other couple cancelled at the last moment.'

'And what was their name?' Inspector Pound asked.

'How would I know?' The captain buttoned up his coat. 'Their names have been scratched.'

Sidney Grice looked at me, then turned back to the captain.

'And you are absolutely certain that they are no longer booked on this ship?'

'They had better not be,' the captain said. 'Their cabin has been occupied by a Chinaman and his cats, and I do not think they want to share.'

'What time do you sail?' I asked.

The captain looked at his half-hunter and said, 'In about six hours, providing you keep out of my way and this fog lifts enough.'

'Eight o'clock?'

'Thereabouts.'

'Do you know what time the shipping office opens?' I asked.

'About the same time, I should think. How would I know?'

My guardian gave him a long hard look and said, 'It is still a capital offence to conceal a murderer. Even if you are doing it unwittingly, at the very least you will lose your master's licence. If I find out you are lying I can get a police launch to you long before you leave territorial waters.'

The captain looked coldly back at him and said, 'I would give up my pension to have you serving under my command.'

'I would rather sail off the edge of the earth,' my guardian said.

'I would rather he did too,' the inspector whispered and Sidney Grice turned sharply.

'Stand still,' I said, and brought out my handkerchief to wipe the soot off his face.

67

The Booking Office

THE BOOKING OFFICE was closed when we arrived at ten to eight. It stood on a cobbled alley which sloped down to the jetty. Sidney Grice paced outside the door for half a minute, then hammered with his fist.

'Open up.' But the room through the etched-glass window was in darkness.

The *Aphrodite* had sailed early at seven, but my guardian hardly glanced at it as it glided through the lifting fog down the river. It was of no more interest to him now than the little girl who begged a copper from me for the baby sister she carried in a canvas bag.

The voyage to India was awful. My father and I were not good sailors and the seas were rough from the start. We sailed with the troops. The Jenny Brown *was overcrowded and there was an outbreak of cholera. Forty men died before we reached Cape Town. We unloaded the sick and continued round the tip of Africa where nature rose in a fury against us, roaring winds and tumbling cliffs of foaming water. The sails were lowered and for four days and nights (though we could not tell the difference) our ship was thrown helpless as a stick in a weir. My father tied me to my bunk where I lay listening to the screams and crashes of the warring oceans – the Atlantic battling to throw us out and the Indian to throw us back. The boards of our ship squealed in the agony of being stretched apart, the frothing black water forcing in between them before they snapped back into place.*

Three crew members, we were told later, were washed overboard. 'Sailors never learn to swim,' my father told me. 'Why take hours to drown when you can do it in a minute? Death can be kind if you allow him to be – sometimes.'

'Open up.' Sidney Grice banged on the door again and the glass pane rattled, but the lights stayed down.

'In a hurry, are you?' Neither of us had noticed the small, smartly clad lady who came up behind us.

'Yes, I am,' my guardian said, 'but the fool of an agent will not open the door.'

'Perhaps you are stopping the fool of an agent getting to the door,' the woman suggested, and gently pushed between us to slip her key into the lock. 'We are not due to open for another five minutes, but you had better come in before you ruin the paintwork.'

It was a large room with several unoccupied desks, each with a green-chimneyed oil lamp. The lady lit one of them and offered us seats across a desk from her.

'What time does your employer get here?' Sidney Grice tapped his cane on the floor.

'My employer never gets here.' The lady swivelled in her chair. 'For I have none. It is my husband's name over the door because, being a mere woman, I cannot easily own a business, but he is no more than a sleeping partner and, believe me, my husband is very good at sleeping. They could exhibit him in the Crystal Palace and the crowds could gawp all day without disturbing him.'

I said, 'So you are…'

'Mrs Woodminster.' The lady nodded. 'What urgent business brings you here?'

'I am on the trail of a murderess,' my guardian said and Mrs Woodminster blinked. She had field-mouse eyes, tiny, bright and alert.

'I hope you do not suspect me.' She took her gloves off and dropped them on the desk.

'We are looking for a Mrs Grace Dillinger,' I said, and Mrs Woodminster shook her head and answered, 'The name means nothing to me.'

'But we have reason to believe that she booked a voyage through your office,' my guardian said. 'Perhaps one of the other people here dealt with her.'

The lady's eyes flicked about. 'As you can see there are no other people working here, nor have there been for a long while. The small independent booking agent is a rare breed in these days of commercial gigantism, Mr…'

'Grice.'

'Not Mr Sidney Grice?'

'Yes.'

'Then I am delighted to meet you. I cannot wait to tell my friends that I assisted you in a murder enquiry.'

'Well,' my guardian told her, 'you have failed to give me any assistance so far.'

Mrs Woodminster's face stiffened. 'You asked me if a Mrs Dillinger had booked a voyage through my office and I informed you that she had not. I would remember if a single lady had made her own booking. I have never known a lady to do so, and in the case of married couples the husband usually attends to such matters on his own.'

'Do couples ever come to your office together?' I asked and my guardian shot a glance at me.

'We are not looking for a couple.'

'There was a couple recently.' Mrs Woodminster opened a drawer and brought out some crochet work. 'And they were highly unusual.'

'I dare say they were,' Sidney Grice said.

'In what way?' I asked, and my guardian shifted restlessly.

'In many ways.' Mrs Woodminster picked up a short broad needle. 'Firstly, the fact that they came together. Secondly, the wife did almost all the talking.'

'Sounds like any other wife to me,' my guardian said.

'Not in matters of business.' She selected a bobbin of thread. It was yellow. 'Thirdly...'

'Never mind all that,' Sidney Grice broke in. 'This is not a women's tea party and we are in a hurry.'

'Do you remember their names?' I asked.

'Mr and Mrs Brewster,' the lady said, 'and coincidentally they were booked on the ship you were enquiring about, the *Aphrodite*, but thirdly—'

'Brewster,' I said, 'but that is the name of—'

'That pestilential priest.' Sidney Grice spat the words out. 'Obviously his interest in Mrs Dillinger was not purely pastoral. Well, we are on to them now sure enough and they have not escaped us yet. A river police launch can overhaul them before they reach open waters. Come on, March. We have not a moment to lose.'

Sidney Grice made as if to rise but I stayed seated.

'What was the *thirdly*?' I asked.

'For heaven's sake.' He snatched his hat off the desk.

'They came in and cancelled their trip last week,' Mrs Woodminster said.

'What?' Sidney Grice spun back to her.

'That was what really stuck in my mind,' she said. 'The *Aphrodite* is a little old-fashioned perhaps, but a very comfortable ship, and they had booked a nice cabin with two portholes, but then they came in last week and asked to change their booking. I explained that they would lose their money at such short notice but they would not be persuaded. It was all very odd. The *Framlingham Castle* is a much older and – dare I say? – insalubrious ship, and not due to reach Sydney for four weeks after the *Aphrodite* is scheduled to arrive there.'

'When does she sail?' Sidney Grice asked, dropping back into his chair.

'Why, she sailed the next day, last Thursday,' Mrs Woodminster told him, choosing another needle.

My guardian's cheek ticked. 'And they were on board?'

'As far as I know.' Mrs Woodminster allowed herself a small smile. 'I do not wave my clients off, Mr Grice, but I have not seen them since.'

'Damn.' Sidney Grice stood up again, so violently that his chair crashed back on to the floor. 'Damn and blast.' He kicked the chair out of his way and threw his cane across the room. It bounced off the wall and clattered on to a cabinet. 'God damn that godforsaken bitch to hell eternal.'

His face was drained – white with fury.

'There must be something we can do,' I said.

'Nothing.' Mrs Woodminster put down her needlepoint. 'They will be well out of territorial waters by now.'

Sidney Grice clenched his fists and almost doubled up in a paroxysm of rage.

I heard a clink and saw that my guardian's eye had fallen on to the floor. He put a clawed hand to his face in unspeakable hate and frustration and, raising his right foot, brought it crunching down, grinding the glass with his heel into coloured shards and sharp crushed powder.

'Well, it looks like your murderer has outwitted you and escaped, Mr Grice.' Mrs Woodminster clapped her hands together. 'Oh, I cannot wait to tell my friends in the Sewing Society.' And in the lamplight her eyes positively sparkled.

On the way out I fell over. The pavement was slippery and I missed my footing.

68

The Doctor

'IT IS A nasty sprain.' The doctor's voice was soothing with a soft Scottish accent. 'You are fortunate not to have broken it. Make yourself comfortable, Miss Middleton, and I will bind it for you.'

The doctor opened a drawer in his desk and brought out a roll of bandage and a pair of long straight-bladed scissors with flattened ends.

'It will feel a little tight,' he said, 'but we should be grateful it was not your right hand. I should not want your writing career to be hampered.'

'How did you know I write?'

He wound the bandage around my wrist in a series of figures of eight.

'I read your biography of your father,' he said, 'and thought it excellent, especially the battle scene. It almost made me believe I was there.'

'Thank you,' I said, 'but it sold very few copies.'

The doctor wound the bandage over the webbing of my thumb and back up my wrist.

'The trouble is that the book market is swamped with so much romantic rubbish these days that quality literature like ours tends to get overlooked.'

'You write too?' I asked.

He shrugged modestly. 'I try, and I have to say that your work made me think that a retired army doctor might make a good character in a story I am writing.'

'What sort of a story?' I asked as he cut the bandage and ripped a tear from the free end.

'I am not sure,' he said, tying the ends neatly together, 'but your guardian is an interesting subject.'

'I think he has probably been written about enough by now,' I said, and he shrugged again and said, 'You are probably right.'

I stood and paid him.

'You are my first patient of the day,' he told me, 'and I would not be surprised if you are the last. It is so difficult to establish a medical practice from scratch.'

'Well, I shall certainly be recommending you,' I said. 'Thank you for your help, Dr Conan Doyle.'

You were a hopeless dancer. You never trod on my feet but that is all I could say in your defence. You had no sense of rhythm and were the only man I ever met who would try to waltz in 4/4 time. You could not sing either. Your voice was a pleasant baritone but you could no more hold a tune than consommé between your fingers.

Once, after a few drinks and no doubt encouraged by your comrades, you tried to serenade me from the garden by my window – a romantic ballad, I think, but I could not stop myself giggling. You were hurt at first but then you started chuckling and we were both bent double, trying to catch our breaths, when father came out to see what was going on and you tried to run away but fell into a mulberry bush.

Sing to me now, my darling. I won't laugh, I promise.

69

News

FOR A WHOLE week Sidney Grice did not appear. He locked himself in his room and though Molly left pots of tea outside his door he rarely touched them or the bowls of stewed vegetables she replaced every few hours.

'I don't know what he's living on,' she told me, and I did not know when he slept either, for I could hear his footfalls in his bedroom throughout the day and whenever I awoke in the night he was still pacing.

'I have not seen him this way since...' Molly said, but could not finish her sentence. 'Oh, I do hope he is not indulging in his secret vice.'

The idea of my guardian having a vice was rather appealing.

'But what is this vice?' I asked.

'I can't say I know, miss.' Molly screwed up her pinafore. 'For it is a secret.' Her eyes filled and she scurried off.

A few callers came and Molly sent them all away.

On the eighth day, when I went down to breakfast, I was surprised to see my guardian already seated at the table and crunching on a pile of charcoaled toast in the shelter of his copy of *The Times*. He greeted me with a cheery grunt but did not lower his paper, contentedly humming behind it as he rustled the pages.

'Excellent, excellent,' he said, happily sipping his tea. 'One hundred and twenty-four dead.'

'Why? What has happened?'

My boiled egg was cold and I resolved to skip breakfast and go out to a tea house.

'Wonderful news in the Thunderer,' he said, lowering the paper, and I saw his face happier than I would have believed possible. 'A storm in the Bay of Biscay. Most ships managed to ride it but one rotting hulk sank with the loss of all hands and passengers. Guess the name of that ship, March.'

'The *Framlingham Castle*.'

'None other.'

'Oh,' I said, 'but all those poor souls...'

I remembered Grace Dillinger, so elegant and beautiful and a little flushed when I opened the front door to her on my first day. I remembered Father Brewster, his clear honest face and the intensity of his prayers for the man she was sacrificing. How much did he know? Did he try to save her as the ship broke up? Did they cling to each other as the raging sea choked and tossed and sucked them down?

'Well, March,' Sidney Grice said. 'I think this calls for a celebration.' And reaching out, he pulled the bell twice for a fresh pot of tea.

70

The Last Letter

I OPENED THE secret compartment, took out the bundle and undid the bow. The paper was dry, a little yellowed, and brittle as I unfolded it.

The last letter ended with the same words as the rest but this time I read them.

Always remember...

I told you a lie once. I thought it was a small lie and harmless and just for that once, but some lies grow malignant and live for ever. Would you forgive me if you knew? I like to think you would.

I touched the gold and untied the black ribbon knotted through it.

Always remember... you wrote.

I watched a man in torment and, in my heart, I actually said a little prayer of thanks. Could you forgive me that? I am not so sure.

I saw the chip that made it less real at first but more real now.

Always remember, you wrote, and I could hardly read the words, *that you are beautiful.*

I slipped the ring on to my finger and my hands trembled just as yours did those few years so very long ago.

71

Grasping the Nettle

'I STILL DO not understand,' I said, the afternoon after the news of the shipwreck, 'why Grace Dillinger killed Sir Randolph. Surely he was the one man who could help William?'

We were having hot buttered muffins by the fire.

My guardian shook his head. 'On the contrary, he would do nothing of the sort. Sir Randolph never said he had perjured himself and indeed it was his refusal to do so that sealed his fate. If he would not be her witness, at least she could claim that he was and sow more seeds of doubt.'

'But why was his body taken to the family tomb?'

'Whatever his sins,' Sidney Grice licked his fingers, 'Father Brewster was still a priest and Sir Randolph was one of his parishioners, albeit an irregular attender. He laid out the body and performed last rites.'

'The oil on his forehead,' I said.

'Precisely.' My guardian helped himself to another muffin.

I had never seen him in such good spirits and it seemed unlikely that I would ever find him in such a forgiving mood again. So I decided to grasp the nettle and confess.

'I think I owe you an apology.' I hoped my voice did not betray my nervousness.

My guardian put down his knife and looked at me.

'For doubting my judgement?'

He wiped his chin.

'No,' I said. 'I still doubt your judgement but I have to apologize for defrauding you.'

My guardian took off his pince-nez and peered at me as though I were a clue.

'How so?'

'Those shares in the Blue Lake Mining Company of British Columbia which I gave you to take on William Ashby's case...' I swallowed. 'I believe I told you they were worth a considerable sum of money.'

'One hundred and twenty-five pounds,' he said. 'Enough to pay Molly's wages for five years.'

'Well,' I took a breath. 'I feel I ought to inform you that one of the reasons my father became financially embarrassed was that he invested heavily in the Blue Lake Mining Company only for their excavations to fail to find any gold at all.'

My guardian put his pince-nez back on the bridge of his slim nose and looked at me through the sparkling lens.

'My dear girl,' he said, 'you really should spend less time on the shockers and more on the financial journals. Why, the Blue Lake Mining Company hit a seam of gold which sent their shares soaring through the ceiling of the stock exchange into the outer firmament. If you thought you were being clever to pretend they were worth half a crown each, you were very strangely deluded indeed. They were worth over four shillings at the time and have more than tripled in value since. Those thousand shares which you so kindly gave me are now worth at least six hundred pounds on the open market.'

'And when was this strike?' I asked.

'As I recall, it was late February.'

'Would this be just before you wrote to me?'

My guardian stretched lazily and selected another muffin from the tiered plate between us.

'Do you know? I believe it was.' The butter trickled down his fingers.

I put my teacup down carefully.

'Is that why you offered to take me in?'

Sidney Grice's mouth opened and shut. His hands rose and fell.

'March,' he said, 'I am wounded.'

'You will be,' I said, and I thought, *Thank heavens I still have forty thousand shares left.*

'Have another muffin.' Sidney Grice held out the plate.

'Why not?' I said, and the fire crackled and a long flame shot up and disappeared, and in our dull distorted reflections on the silver teapot I could almost believe that we were smiling.

Postscript

LESS THAN A month after the *Framlingham Castle* went down there was another twist in the sad story of Sarah Ashby. Jeremiah Dillinger's sister Gertrude, eaten by consumption, made a deathbed confession. She had been present – though she swore she had not assisted – when Sarah's real mother was stabbed to death by the woman we knew as Grace Dillinger. Sarah was three years old at the time and grew up believing that woman to be her mother. The impostor's real name was Eleanor Quarrel.

Eleanor Quarrel was four years older than the woman she impersonated for the rest of her life and she had good reason to change her identity. She told Gertrude that she had killed her own father after he forced himself upon her when she was thirteen, but some sympathy for her might evaporate when it becomes known that she had already killed her younger sister for being their father's favourite. At the age of fifteen she served a prison sentence for stabbing a policeman in the face, her account of his advances to her being dismissed by the court out of hand.

Upon release Eleanor left her native Birmingham and moved around the country. Her journey was uncharted but may well have been marked by a number of unsolved murders, always of men for money and always with a knife. In 1862, when Eleanor Quarrel was twenty-two, she was caught in the act of murdering a wealthy widower in Portsmouth but, the day before she was to be brought to trial, escaped through a privy window, possibly with a warder's help.

It was then that she went to London, struck up a relationship with Jeremiah, and disposed of the unfortunate Grace on the very day that the Dillingers moved into Crystal Court. Matilda Tassel and her two daughters, who lived on Mangle Street, had also lived near the Dillingers at a previous address and would have known Grace, and so they were slaughtered too.

In response to this confession, the floor of the old stables was lifted and the skeleton of a young woman discovered, with the rusty blade of a knife still embedded in the neck. When Sidney Grice was told this, his only comment was, 'I said the floor tiles were broken.'

And so it was apparent that Grace Dillinger was no more than an innocent victim of a multiple murderer and that it was Eleanor Quarrel who was responsible for the chain of deaths which became notorious as the Mangle Street Murders.